Day of the Dead

Day of the Dead

XXX,
Mercedez

THUNDER'S MOUTH PRESS
NEW YORK

DAY OF THE DEAD
A Vivid Girls Book

Published by
Thunder's Mouth Press
An Imprint of Avalon Publishing Group Inc.
245 West 17th St., 11th Floor
New York, NY 10011

AVALON
publishing group incorporated

Library of Congress Cataloging-in-Publication Data is available.

ISBN 1-56025-781-4

9 8 7 6 5 4 3 2 1

Book design by Maria Elias
Printed in the United States of America
Distributed by Publishers Group West

To all my fans.
May they enjoy reading my story
as much as I enjoyed living it . . .

CHAPTER *1.*

" *M* ercedez, it's so good to have you home!" Consuelo cried, hugging her sister.

"I know! I can't believe that it's been a year since we've seen each other," Mercedez said, hugging back. She pushed Connie an arm's length away from her, still holding onto her shoulders, and said, "You're a mother now. It's as if we were just in high school together yesterday."

"It wasn't yesterday, but it wasn't *that* long ago!"

"Well, longer for you!" Mercedez joked, poking fun at her sister, older by one year.

Connie slipped the car keys into her small shoulder bag and abandoned the red SUV in the beach parking lot. This end of the sand was crowded with sunbathers and saltwater swim-mers, and people just resting under umbrellas. Everywhere around them were tanned muscle men and beautiful women, handsome and voluptuous, wearing the skimpiest bikinis. It had been a while since Mercedez had been to a beach, and the sultry flesh surrounding her made her a bit horny.

The sisters glanced at one another and grinned. They both knew they had bodies that could rival any of the women on this beach, and from the looks they were getting, others knew this, too. Mercedez felt herself almost glowing under the Corpus Christi, Texas, sun as they strolled, arms around each other's waists, along the white sand of the Bay, Mercedez' feet bare, Connie's in huaraches, the skirts of their sundresses swaying as the two attractive sisters took in the day and enjoyed one another's company.

Mercedez was so happy to be home. Corpus Christi, the "Sparkling City by the Sea" as it was known, was filled with pleasant and comforting memories. Her life had been exciting since she'd moved—so much had happened—but there was no place like home, that was for sure. She'd visited with her par-ents and now had a few days with her sister and her family before they headed off on their first vacation since the new baby was born. And then Mercedez would go back to her own home in Southern California. Back to the routine of work and classes in the evening. And too many dateless Saturday nights.

As they strolled the beach of Corpus Christi Bay, Mercedez looked out over the blue water, feeling the warm sand rubbing the feet of her skin smooth, the soft breeze caressing her body through the thin summery material of the yellow sundress she wore. She closed her eyes, letting the sensations weave through her body. Naturally, the feelings led to sexual thoughts and she wondered just how long it had been since her last lover. Too long, that was for sure. The fact that she couldn't remember off the top of her head said as much.

"So we've had a lot of red tides lately," Connie was saying, and Mercedez suddenly tuned into her sister. "Hot weather, no rain, and no wind. Today's not too bad, though. The algae count is low, so people can swim."

"Say," Mercedez purred in Connie's ear, "what's it like being married?"

Connie stopped suddenly and turned to her sister, her face quizzical.

"You know, the sex part. I mean, you've had a kid, you've been getting it regularly—"

"Jeez, you're nosy!" Connie laughed. Then said, "You were married. You must know what it's like."

Mercedez stiffened. "I'd rather not talk about Joe." Of all the experiences she'd had since leaving home, most had been wonderful. Her short and traumatic marriage was not one of them.

A volleyball rolled into her feet and Mercedez' mood shifted as if a light had been turned on. She bent to pick up the ball, the low-cut dress revealing just enough cleavage for the guy who came to retrieve the ball to notice. Mercedez caught him looking as she stood up.

"Must be yours," she said, holding out the ball.

He was tall, at least six foot, skin tanned a darker color than hers, hair to his shoulders, a touch more red to his than her chestnut locks. His handsome face was streaked with sweat that rolled down his chiseled cheeks and dripped onto his bare chest. Mercedez could feel the sweat between her breasts.

He took the ball from her, his brown eyes roving her body quickly, but she noticed. Those eyes felt like lasers, hotter than the sun, burning a path along her flesh. "You two from around here?" he asked.

"Connie is. I used to be. I'm just visiting."

"Yeah? You should come by Entrophe tonight. It's down the beach, at the curve. We're all going there to party."

Mercedez glanced at the people gathered on each side of the volleyball net, five on one side, four on the other. Of the four, one was a curvaceous blond sending daggers Mercedez' way. Must be the girlfriend, or the wannabe, Mercedez thought. "Come on Larry! We're waiting," the blond yelled.

"Thanks. Maybe we'll stop by later," Mercedez said as Larry turned away, but not before giving her a wink. She watched his tight butt in the cutoff jeans as he ran to join his friends.

"I think he's either taken, or taken enough that there would be trouble," Connie said.

"No kidding," Mercedez laughed. "So, you never answered. What's the sex like now?"

Connie poked her in the ribs gently. "Oh, you! It's good. I mean, we haven't had much sleep since Sarah was born—wow, six months of no sleep! No wonder I'm tired!"

"Stop avoiding!" Mercedez shrieked.

"Oh, the nitty gritty. Sex is great. Was before, is now, just not as frequent as it once was. And you, missy?"

"Me, what?"

"Getting any? From the way you looked at that guy, I'd guess not."

"Well, it's been a while . . . I'm pretty busy, and—"

"Oh, come on Miss Hottie! I can't believe you can't meet guys."

"Sure I meet guys. There are plenty of them, just not the right ones."

"Well, what about the almost-right ones? Something to tide you over until you get to Mr. Right Around the Corner?"

Mercedez pulled her long hair back off her neck and lifted it, letting the bit of breeze cool her. "I tell you, Connie, be grateful that you met Len. I mean, it's a rat race out here. Trust me. The world is full of jerks that treat you like crap."

"You sound pretty cynical."

"I guess I am a bit. Not so much though."

"Well, no woman wants to be treated like crap," Connie said in a consoling voice.

"Nope. We want to be treated like the goddesses we are!"

They both threw back their heads and laughed, at the almost-joke, at the beauty of the day, at just being alive.

Once they'd walked another half mile, Connie said, "Hey, want to go to the Mexican market?"

"It's been ages since I was there. Not since we were kids. Sure, let's do it! Race you to the car!"

The sisters turned and ran back the way they had come, this time close to the waves in the wet sand as water broke onto the shore. Mercedez could feel her braless breasts bouncing inside the sundress and the muscles of her bottom cheeks stretch as her long legs reached out in front of one another like a colt using all its strength just for the pleasure of movement.

As they passed the volleyballers, Larry turned to watch the sisters. Mercedez tossed back her long hair and gave him a brilliant smile and a wave. Larry lifted his hand to wave and the blond, who had the ball, used her fist to punch it right at him, hitting him on the back of the head. He looked stunned for a moment, and turned angrily. "Sorry!" the blond said, showing him all thirty-two pearly whites while Larry rubbed the back of his noggin.

Mercedez and Connie ran for another few seconds then stopped simultaneously and at the same moment burst into laughter, synchronized, just as they had always been growing up together. They laughed so hard they were bent over. Finally Mercedez got enough control of herself to grab her big sister by the arm and pull her along.

Connie gasped, wiping tears from her the corners of her eyes. "Girl, you're going to kill me! I haven't laughed this hard in years!"

"Me neither," Mercedez said, slipping her arm around Connie's waist again, thinking, *it is so good to be home!*

The sisters drove off Staples Street into the parking lot of the Mercado, a single-story market that was bustling on this Saturday noon. Mainly families were descending on the entrances, or emerging with boxes or shopping bags full of goods. Mercedez and Connie sat looking through the windshield for a few minutes. Connie still lived in the city, and this market wasn't that exotic for her. Mercedez used to come here with her parents. She had secretly met one of her first boyfriends here, behind the market, where they had necked in the hot summer sun.

"You know, it's funny," Mercedez said, watching a young girl who reminded her of herself at the age of fifteen, full of vital energy and excitement about life, just discovering her body, her sexuality, "our parents are from Mexico, we speak Spanish, but we have always lived here. We know so little about our Mexican roots."

"Well, we know the state they each came from—"

"I don't mean the statistics. I mean we don't have a cultural feel for our roots, or at least I don't."

"I kind of know what you mean. Now that I have a daughter, it seems more important to me to be able to pass along some of our ancestry to her."

Mercedez looked at Connie. "How come Mom and Dad never talk about Mexico?"

"They do sometimes."

"I know they talk about the landscape and all that, and what it was like when they were kids. But they never talk about what it means to them to come from there. Our ancestors must go back centuries."

"To the Mayans."

"You're kidding?"

"No. Mom told me that once. Well, she didn't really talk about it. I was doing some world history project in school and I said something like 'Did you know the Spanish came over to Mexico?' I mean, this was news to me. Mom laughed and said of course she knew that. The conquistadors were in our blood.

DAY OF THE DEAD

'What do you mean?' I asked her. 'How?' 'Through the Mayans,' she said."

"That's it?"

"Yep."

"How come you didn't ask her more about that?"

"Because I was, like, twelve years old and I didn't really care! I just wanted to finish my homework and watch TV."

"Wow. We're descended from the Mayans. And the conquistadors. I mean, how amazing is that?"

Connie opened the car door. "I'm not sure it will change my life."

Mercedez got out and joined her sister on the flagstones to the main entrance. "Well, it might change mine."

"Yeah, right!"

"Hey, chiquitas!" Two Mexicans in ten-gallon hats grinned at the sisters. Connie held up her wedding ring hand and pointed at the gold band.

"What about you?" the copper-skinned cowboy grinned at Mercedez. "You got a ring, too?"

"Only one for your nose, Toro!"

The two guys laughed, and the sisters high-fived each other as they entered the market.

Noise and lights and colors and chatter and the push and shove of people crowding around stalls selling furniture, clothing, food of all sorts, appliances. . . . There was nothing upscale about the Mercado. This was a down-to-earth, of-the-people shopping mall, old-school, where older people came to buy the type of products that were familiar to them, but younger parents could also find some of the latest electronic gadgets that their offspring demanded. Children ran through the aisles eating cotton candy and hard taffy. Young people flirted, oldsters sat watching the action, and vendors hurled sales pitches at anyone who came within earshot.

"Oh, wouldn't Sarah love that!" Connie exclaimed, pointing to a small silver mini–train engine that chugged along on its own circular track. The engine emitted "steam" that the vendor explained was a pellet dropped inside the chimney.

"She'll love it in five years," Mercedez laughed.

"Well, I'll buy it for her now. It's good to have something to look forward to."

"Maybe you should buy a bigger house. From all the toys she already has, you'll need space for the future gifts!"

"Oh, you!" Connie laughed.

"Let me buy it for my niece." Mercedez paid for the little engine and a package of spare pellets and the vendor wrapped both in brown paper. As Mercedez slipped the parcel into her shoulder bag, she saw something else silver glint in the bright lights.

A girl, maybe eighteen, with lush features, high cheek-bones, and soulful brown eyes was busy working with aluminum foil, bending and folding it into smaller and smaller corners, the whole resulting in a very well-done rose, with a stem and leaves. "That's amazing!" Mercedez exclaimed.

The girl looked up, her full lips parting into a smile, her liquidy eyes locking onto Mercedez'. She thrust out the aluminum flower. "For you, señorita. For love."

Mercedez took the rose and as she did so the fingers of the two women brushed. Mercedez kept staring into those eyes the color of the earth. She felt her heart beat faster and a tingling in her nipples as they pressed against the fabric of her dress. The girl looked down at Mercedez' breasts and saw the hardness there. She smiled and without a word, she edged past Mercedez, making sure to brush one of those nipples with her upper arm as she passed. She turned briefly with a look that clearly said, "Come with me!"

Mercedez felt heat rush up through her body. The room seemed too quiet, and a space parted as the flower girl moved, hips swaying, down the aisle. She turned left at the end and headed for the door marked "Ladies."

"Okay, I've got it. Is there anything else you want to see here, or should we head out?" Connie was asking as she stuffed the toy into her bag.

"I'm just going to hit the ladies' room first."

"Want me to come with you?"

"Uh, no, I'll be fine. Why don't you wait in the car? You look like you could use some air-conditioning."

"Good point."

The minute Connie turned toward the exit, Mercedez headed the other way. She entered the room marked "Mujeres." The place appeared to be empty at first. She listened for a moment: nothing.

There were three stalls and she bent to see if there were feet on the floor of one, but there were not. Gingerly she pushed open one door, then the next and finally the third. All the stalls were empty. "Okay," she said, "I saw you come in here . . ."

"I'm here!"

Mercedez spun on her heels. "Where were you?" she asked,

looking around the small room, which had no other doors, no place to hide.

"I was here. Waiting for you."

The flower girl moved, undulated really, toward Mercedez until they were very close. Mercedez could feel the hot breath on her cheek, and the hot body pressed against her own.

The girl reached up and pushed the strap of Mercedez' sundress down her arm, farther, farther, until her left breast was exposed. "What if someone comes in—?"

But the girl's lips had found her beadlike nipple, those full, fleshy lips sucking and pulling, sending shivers through Mercedez' body. A small moan came from Mercedez' lips and she began to fall back. Amazingly strong hands grabbed hold of her behind, clutching on, pulling her hips closer. Their crotches ground together as the girl guided Mercedez.

Not to be outdone, Mercedez ran her hands down the flower girl's body, up and down, feeling the delicious curves, the softness, the firm breasts, tight buttocks, and soon slipped a hand up and under the miniskirt. She wasn't wearing panties!

That set Mercedez' heart pounding faster, and moisture began to form on her own panties soon making them sopping wet in the crotch as the two kept grinding together.

Her fingers found the flower girl's hot spot and slipped inside her hot pussy. The thick lips of her mouth sucked harder at Mercedez' tit and one of her hands found Mercedez' clit. The girl rubbed the wet nub, making it burn with heat and passion, her lips never leaving Mercedez' breast.

As the girl rubbed Mercedez, Mercedez used two fingers like a penis to enter the shaved mound deeper and find the spot inside along the front of the girl's fleshy folds. When she did, she began rubbing fast and hard, while the girl kept pace with her lips and her own fingers.

Steamy heat rippled through their sweat-soaked bodies as the climaxes built. Mercedez felt herself driven crazy, and knew she was doing the same to the flower girl. The heat escalated. Both of their pussies burst into flames at the same moment. Both cried out their pleasure and it was the first time the lips had left the nipple.

They kissed then, lips sliding wetly together. The girl took her finger slowly away from Mercedez and stuck it into her mouth. Mercedez did the same, tasting the sweet-tart fruit of this exotic flower girl.

Her legs were weak, and she had to pee, so she entered a stall. Releasing the urine felt so good that she closed her eyes and savored this sensation, too. Her sundress was still down on one side, the breast exposed, and she opened her eyes to look at the hard red nipple and the swollen areola surrounding it, so nicely tormented by those luscious lips.

As she came out of the stall she was saying, "You know, this was such a nice surprise—" but stopped short. The room was empty. "Hello?" She looked under the stalls. No legs. She opened each one. The only face she saw was her own in the mirror, her hair damp against her face, her eyes shining, her nipple pert and exposed. . . .

The door to the washroom opened and a middle-aged woman came in. Mercedez quickly pulled up her sundress. She didn't know what the woman saw, but she gave Mercedez a funny look.

After she washed her face and hands, Mercedez headed out

into the Mercado. She returned to the booth where she had met the flower girl. Instead of the vivacious girl, a short and stocky old woman dressed in black from head to toe stood behind the table, folding aluminum foil, making roses.

"Excuse me, señora. Where's the girl that was here?"

"There is no girl here. Just me."

"But . . . there was a girl here a few minutes ago, about nineteen. Making the flowers you're making."

"You must be mistaken. I've been here all day."

"But . . . but you weren't here when I was here about ten minutes ago."

"I went outside for a smoke," the old woman said. "I'm gonna quit soon."

Mercedez felt stunned. Someone had been here, making flowers, leading her to the washroom. Sucking her nipple until she swooned, clutching her bottom cheeks, fondling her cunt until she went over the cliff of passion.

The old woman suddenly stopped what she was doing and stood up. She couldn't have been more than five feet tall. Her dark dress reached the floor, and the shawl she wore around her shoulders hid most of her body. From beneath that shawl she pulled out one hand and opened it. "Take it, señorita."

Mercedez reached out for the object, a stone tied with yarn. On the stone—which was a deep green, so dark it looked almost black—she saw a streak of red that seemed to make a triangle. She held it up by the green yarn, dangling it before her eyes. "That's an odd marking for a stone," she said. "I don't think I've ever seen a stone like it before."

"You have but you do not remember."

Mercedez tried to hand it back to the old woman but she shook her head. "Keep it. You will need it with you for luck."

"I—I couldn't . . ."

"I said, keep it!" The voice commanded.

"Thank you."

"Keep it with you. Always."

Obediently, Mercedez closed her hand over the stone.

"You must keep it with you or bad luck will befall you. Do you understand me?"

Mercedez looked into eyes dark as black olives. "I—I understand. Thank you."

"Do not thank me," she said. "You are chosen."

"Chosen for what?"

"There you are! I thought you fell in!"

Mercedez turned toward the voice of her sister.

"Sorry. I didn't know I was taking so long."

"Hey, no problemo. It's kind of nice to have a break from changing diapers and feeding Sarah, not that I don't adore her. Where'd you get that?"

Connie pointed to the stone nestled in the palm of Mercedez' hand. Mercedez looked up at her sister. "From this woman—" she said, half turning, but the old lady was no longer behind the counter. A quick glance in all four directions of this crossroads aisle told Mercedez that she was nowhere in sight. Just like the flower girl.

"From who?" Connie asked.

"Never mind. She's gone."

Connie picked up the stone and studied the symbol. "It's

kind of cool. A bloodstone, I think—I had one once. This design looks Mayan to me."

"You think so?"

"Maybe. Not that I know much about Mayan symbols. What did you pay for it?"

"I didn't. This old lady gave it to me."

"No way!"

"Way!"

"Boy you're lucky! Nobody ever gives me anything."

"Hey, Len gave you a baby."

"Oh you!" Connie said, shoving her sister playfully.

Mercedez reached into her shoulder bag and pulled out the aluminum rose. "Here. For you."

"It's beautiful! Thank you!"

Connie looked genuinely touched. She kissed Mercedez on the cheek. "You're the best little sister in the world."

"Not the galaxy?"

Connie laughed. "So, have we done this Mercado?"

"Been there, done that, ate the T-shirt!" Mercedez said.

"Oh, gosh, it's almost four. We'd better get moving. Len's bringing home a work buddy for dinner and—"

"Hey, you guys aren't trying to set me up, are you?"

"Of course we are! What's family for if not to meddle in each other's lives."

"Just so we've got that clear!"

While baby Sarah slept in the nursery, Mercedez, Connie, Len, and Bill, the international trade relations manager of Len's company enjoyed perfectly barbequed steaks, green peppers, and onions, and a salad of vegetables Connie grew in her small garden. They also enjoyed good conversation. The four found a number of topics they could all relate to, and also jokes they could all laugh at.

"Not a peep!" Connie said at one point, nodding at the nursery walkie-talkie that had recorded the odd giggle and gurgle from Sarah. "I think this is the first meal I've eaten without interruptions since—"

"Since Sarah was born!" Len laughed. "You've gone above and beyond the call, little mother." He reached out and picked up her hand and kissed it.

Romance, Mercedez thought. If only it could happen to me. She glanced sideways at William R. Templar III, as he had introduced himself—finally admitting that everyone called him Bill, so Mercedez did. He, too, noticed the intimacy of the moment and turned to smile at Mercedez.

He was a lean, forty-something guy, handsome in a kind of rugged Midwestern way. "Were you born in Chicago?" she asked him, knowing that's the city he worked out of.

"I was and I wasn't."

"Well, that sounds intriguing."

"He's full of intrigue," Len said, winking. He stood, and Connie joined him. "Tell her the one about the rodeo you put on in Berlin that scored you the biggest account the company has ever had!"

"We're just taking the dishes in," Connie said, motioning for Mercedez and Bill to stay seated. "We'll check on Sarah, then bring out dessert."

"Not sure I can pack more in here," Bill said, patting his

stomach, a bit paunchy but not bad at all for a middle-aged corporate guy.

"It's just fruit cocktail. Help yourselves to more wine."

As they disappeared through the patio doors, Bill reached for another bottle of Merlot and began driving a corkscrew into the cork with a well-practiced motion. *You gotta love a guy who knows how to open a wine bottle!* Mercedez thought, laughing a little, enough that Bill turned to her with a raised eyebrow.

"So, how is it you were and were not born in Chicago?" she asked.

He grinned and focused his attention on getting the cork out of the bottle. Hazel eyes, sandy hair that had recently been trimmed pretty short, he wore a beige button-down shirt, jeans, and Dockers, about as ordinary a look as you could get, and without that smile he was the kind of man who went unnoticed on the street. But when his thin lips lifted at the corners, he suddenly looked younger, lighter of heart, and Mercedez found herself attracted.

"Well, my mother was on a plane, just entering air space between Canada and the US."

"And you were born at that precise moment?"

"Right on the forty-ninth parallel. We landed where my parents live, or lived I should say, in Chicago, about half an hour later. But I'm told that I can also get dual citizenship if I want it."

"That's a pretty amazing birth."

"Probably the only amazing thing that's ever happened to me." He paused and turned to look at her. "Maybe until now."

Mercedez grinned and met his eye. "Why now?"

"You're a very attractive woman."

"Thank you, sir. You're not bad yourself."

They kept eye contact for a moment, and then he poured half a glass of wine for each of them.

He picked up his glass and with his other hand took her arm, indicating she should stand up, which she did. "Let's walk down by the water."

The beach was two short blocks from Connie and Len's place, but a public walkway ran past their house.

"That's a fine muscle you've got there," he said, meaning her bicep.

"I work out. And I dance. Keeps me in shape."

"I can see that," he said, letting his eyes do the walking over her body.

The night was warm but pleasantly so. The wine and the good food had satisfied her, and Bill was pretty nice. It had been a while since she'd let herself be charmed by a man.

They walked along the sandy cement, the water straight ahead, Bill still holding her arm, until they reached the beach, the dark ocean lit only with the waxing moon that hung over it and illuminated the horizon far and wide.

Once they were at the edge of the waves that broke gently onto the shore, Bill slipped an arm around Mercedez' shoulder. His hot hand on the flesh of her bare shoulder left her wanting more of this touch. She turned her face up to his. "Want to kiss me?"

He looked pleasantly surprised, and there was that enticing grin again. "I'd like nothing more."

Soon his lips met hers, the firmness of them insistent

against her mouth. The kiss was brief and romantic, but the minute he broke away she pulled his head back to her. Now his tongue became aggressive, exploring the hotness inside her mouth. Soon they were kissing more passionately, both panting, the hunger bearing down on them like a tidal wave.

"Wait!" Mercedez said, breaking away. She held up her wine glass. Bill shook his head and laughed, holding up his, too.

They both took another sip then Bill took the glass from her hand and placed both glasses securely in the sand. And when he turned back to Mercedez, she was untying the knot at the back of her halter, letting the satiny fabric slide down her breasts to her slim waist. She held onto the material there and lowered it slowly, exposing her belly button in a teasing way, and the little tattoo close to it. She swayed from side to side while he watched her in the moonlight, the fabric slipping down and down. All at once she let it drop, exposing her pubis, shaved in a straight path.

Bill stood and stared at her. "You are amazing! Gorgeous!"

Mercedez smiled at him and turned slowly, letting the moonlight highlight her ass. Then she fell down onto the sand onto all fours.

"I think I've died and gone to heaven," Bill said.

She turned her head, pulling the long strands of her dark hair to one side to watch him undo his belt and drop the jeans—that he didn't wear underwear was a plus in her books. He pulled off the shirt almost ripping the buttons.

He went down on all fours himself and crawled to her, sniffing her behind, licking her pussy as he went, making her laugh, and sending shivers along her skin. Once they were face-to-face they nuzzled one another. While they did so, he reached under and tweaked one of her nipples, and shock waves ran through her.

She felt like a bitch in heat, one that had not been fucked in far too long. Her cunt burned and she could feel the moisture seeping out and along the insides of her thighs.

Her head felt light, her nipple hard and tortured in a delicious way. She wanted to suck his cock so badly, but when she reached under him, he backed off, teasing her.

Before she could figure out how he did it, he was on top of her, doggie-style, his long, hard cock at her opening. He straddled her, arms close to hers, legs inside hers, and then he nipped at her neck like a stud and a moan escaped her lips. Her body trembled, anticipating being filled.

Bill did not disappoint her. He slid in deep, his cock pressing the walls of her cunt wide, reaching far into her until she took him all. And then he fucked her with long even strokes, making her moan, out of her mind with longing, her burning walls so happy to be given the attention they had been missing.

It was sweet but short. They came together, crying out in the moonlight like the animals they felt themselves to be. Then they lay in the sand on their backs staring at the sky, shoulders and hips touching, pointing out the constellations that they both knew, laughing like kids with a new toy.

Suddenly Bill turned toward her. "I know this is crazy. We just met. But I'm heading to Mexico tomorrow on business. Come with me. I'm on the expense account, so it won't cost you a dime. Ten days."

Mercedez looked at him for a long time. Connie and Len and Sarah were taking off tomorrow. She'd already seen her parents. She'd planned to stay at Connie's alone for a week then return to LA, but she had nothing waiting for her there. Len had worked with Bill for years, so he must be safe. Suddenly, for no reason she could identify, she remembered the charm that the old woman had given her. "You know, I've done wacky things in my life, but this might be the wackiest. Okay, I'll come. Why not?"

"This will be fun," Bill said. "And interesting. For both of us."

"That's for sure," she said.

"And hey, no commitments. We're fuck friends. That's it. Both free to do anything we want to do, with anyone else. No ties. Sound alright to you?"

The idea was a little startling to her, but she said, "Sure, okay." It probably would be best that way. They'd just met, she wasn't sure how they'd get along in the long term, and this way there wasn't any pressure. Of course, there wasn't much mystery either, since it all sounded so preordained, a kind of dead end before they even got started on trying out a relationship. But, sometimes, like John Lennon sang, life is what happens when you're busy making other plans. She reached for his cock that was already hard again.

CHAPTER *2.*

Mercedez and Bill caught a flight to Cancun around 9 A.M. Bill didn't need to be at any meetings for two full days, which gave them a couple of afternoons and evenings to spend together before he would be tied up with business, leaving Mercedez to her own devices.

As they flew over the lush and magical landscape, the plane descending, Mercedez snuggled closer to Bill. "It's so beautiful!" she sighed.

"You're beautiful," he said, kissing her cheek.

She nuzzled against him, her breast softly pressed to his chest. He slipped a hand around her shoulder and caressed the side of her other breast while she placed a hand on his blue-jeaned thigh in a strategic but discrete spot, given that they were on a plane.

The typically Mexican town of Cancun was overshadowed by the many hotels and resorts that had sprouted out from it along the pristine beaches of this peninsula. Bill had selected a hotel along the strip of white and pastel stucco high-rises that gleamed in the brilliant sun. Their penthouse room at the Ritz-Carlton faced the Caribbean Ocean and Mercedez stood outside the lobby for a moment, entranced by the white waves of the green waters washing up on the clean pale sand.

Their room—a suite really—was sumptuous. A living room with an adjacent bedroom, and a huge round bed in the center! It had all the appointments, including chocolates on the pillows and a basket of fruit and wine on the table. Bill opened the minibar and took out a cooler for himself, holding it up to ask Mercedez if she wanted one. She nodded, and turned toward the balcony.

"Bill, this place, this suite, it's all breathtaking!" Mercedez cried. "Your company must be paying a fortune!"

"Not really. We have a lot of deals with large corporations, exchanges of services, that sort of thing."

She threw open the balcony doors and stepped out of the air-conditioning and into the warmth of the tropical sun, letting it bathe her exposed arms and legs with the heat of those luscious rays. She'd worn a bolero jacket on the plane and stripped that off, giving over even more skin to the god of sunlight. The sound of waves, the gleaming white beach, the fragrance of the red and yellow bougainvillea flowers mixed with the delicious spicy food scents as chicken grilled poolside. . . .

All of it lulled her into a dreamy state. And under everything the faint but consistent sound of lively Mexican music tinkled in the distance, snatches of lyrics drifting along the air.

A slight breeze from the ocean caused her hair to fly around her face and Bill, who had come up behind her, pulled her long dark locks behind her head and kissed her deep on the neck, sucking the skin between his teeth. The heat and moisture from his lips sent a tingle through her body, all the way to her groin, warming her further. The spaghetti straps of her dress slid down her arms, exposing her breasts to the sun, and her nipples perked under the heat like little mouths being fed nourishment.

Mercedez reached up and behind Bill's neck, pulling him closer, lifting her breasts higher in the process. As he pressed against her back, she could feel his penis through the fabric of his pants and the back of her thin dress. He rubbed back and forth against her, the hardness of him brushing her taut bottom, stimulating her.

Bill's hands had come up and suddenly she felt the icy coldness touch the tips of each nipple. She sucked in air quickly and a quick glance down showed the frosty coolers that he held rubbing her hot nubs. The chill felt delicious and her nipples hardened even more. She could smell the pussy juice from her body as wetness formed between her legs and soaked through the crotch of her panties. All of it made her squirm.

Bill bent down to place the bottles on the small table, and then he wrapped his arms around her waist, locking her against him. She closed her eyes and leaned back into him. The rhythmic lapping of waves along the shore, the heat of the sun, his hot fingers sliding down her naked body, shoving her moist panties down, exposing her further to the sun, rubbing over and around her shaved mound, then down further, and up inside her . . .

Mercedez moaned, her body smoldering.

Slowly he pulled her backward and both of them down onto the chaise longue. He lifted her at the waist a few inches, just enough so that her hot wet opening met the tip of his hard cock. She felt burning liquid oozing from her body and the heat of his flesh against her pulsing opening; she was ready to be impaled!

Her hands gripped his thighs as she used her strong dancer's legs to hold herself up. She eased down and onto him. As the flesh of her ass touched his belly and his cock flesh met her deep inside, heat roared through her body, colliding with the heat of the sun. Bill's hands guided her moves, up and down, sliding with her slickness along the hard fleshy rod, and Mercedez moaned with sensual pleasure as she burned and burned, a delicious heat. Time stood still but not their bodies. Her orgasm built as his hot flesh teased her, tensing even more inside her, and Mercedez broke his rhythm to move faster, wanting him deeper still, wanting him to stroke her flesh until it felt scorched with fiery passion, ready to ignite.

Soon the heat outside gave way to the heat inside her and she burst into flame, crying out her pleasure as Bill groaned out his, filling the air with the sounds of their shared ecstasy.

Afterward, bodies covered with sweat that cooled them under the hot sun, they lay back and napped, his still-firm cock remaining inside her, Mercedez resting against him as the solar rays beat down on her taut body, encasing it with a heat that spoke of life and passion. She opened her eyes a slit and saw nothing but gold, like the metal the conquistadors wore, glinting in the sun in triumph.

They showered, headed down to the beach, and lay on beach chairs drinking piña coladas under the afternoon sun, listening to the surf, and chatting about what they would do the next two days, Bill's only free days in Cancun.

"I'm sorry, honey. I've got those damned meetings."

"Don't worry about it. I didn't expect you to be with me every minute. And if you didn't have business, we wouldn't be here together, would we?"

"You're very understanding," he said, reaching over to stroke her stomach, exposed, as was much of her golden flesh, by the red microbikini, strings over her hips that held a small swatch of fabric over her genitals, and more strings that barely held in place the matching tiny bra that lay over not much more than her areolas. Mercedez knew she looked good. Sexy. And she reveled in Bill's attention.

She loved the feel of his fingers touching her. It had been so long she'd wondered if she'd ever meet a nice man again. There were so many losers out there, but Bill was one of the good guys, and she thanked her lucky stars for him already.

"Listen, I thought we'd go to the ruins tomorrow," he said. "It's not far. We can rent a Jeep and drive into the jungle."

"Oh, that sounds exciting! I can't wait."

"What part of Mexico is your family from?"

"Well, Connie and I were born in Texas. My mother comes from Oaxaca, and my dad from around Mexico City."

"We'll be going to Mexico City."

"Great! I've never been. Once I was in Tijuana, when Connie and I were in high school and the school did a trip to Hollywood. We met a couple of guys and they drove us just across the border."

"That was brave of you, going with strangers."

"They weren't strangers. Connie had dated the brother of one of them. We drove down and back in a couple of hours. It was fun. But you know Tijuana isn't a place I want to visit again. I'm kind of amazed that this is also Mexico," she said, gesturing to the gorgeous environment surrounding her—so different from the tight streets and dusty shops in the hectic border town where you could buy anything or anyone, what had until now been her only experience of Mexico.

"So, what's your life like, Bill?"

He shrugged. "Normal. Middle class."

"'Burbs, 2.5 of everything? How come there's no missus?"

He laughed. "Hey look! A wind surfer!"

She scanned the water where he pointed and saw a guy on something that resembled a surfboard with a sail, weaving through the air. "That looks so cool," she said.

"Want to try it?"

"Sure!"

He glanced at his watch. "Uh, sorry. Maybe another day. Look, I have to make a call. Then, let's get dressed and find a nice restaurant. Hungry?"

"I am a bit. You?"

"Always!" he growled and leaned over to nuzzle her neck, making her laugh and cry out.

"Oh! Stop! You're tickling me!"

"That was the plan!"

When he finished tormenting her for a few minutes and she was doubled over in laughter, he stood up and began gathering his towel, slipping his feet into the thongs provided by the hotel. Mercedez sat up to join him.

"No," he said, waving her back. "I'll be a while, and you might as well get the benefit of the sun. Take your time. You have a watch?"

She reached into her beach bag and pulled out her cell phone, holding up the face with the time—it wasn't international so it was useless here except for the time.

"Okay, good. Come back to the room in about an hour. I should be finished by then."

"Will do."

She watched him walk away, his tight butt cheeks inside the black swimsuit turning her on. She liked everything about his body. He was slim but muscular, and the way he moved seemed to reek of masculinity.

Mercedez sighed and turned back to the ocean. "Down girl," she told herself. It was all hot and heavy right now but she didn't want to expose herself to hurt. After all, they'd just met. This might not work into anything long-term. Just enjoy the moment, she told herself. Have some fun. This was a great opportunity to see parts of Mexico she'd always wanted to see with a guy that got her hot and bothered pretty easily, and was nice, too. She'd just see what, if anything, followed.

Out on the water at some distance a brown boat loomed. She watched it, growing drowsy, thinking she should take the magazine out of her purse, or her paperback, but instead found her eyes closing as the lapping of the waves lulled her into a relaxation she hadn't felt in a long time.

Through the slits of vision the boat grew closer. It seemed to be an old boat, ancient, like one of the Spanish galleons that resembled in her dreamy state nothing less than towers floating in the sea.

"Señorita, usted querría comprar un sombrero?"

Mercedez opened her eyes to see a bright-eyed dark-skinned child holding a short pole onto which a dozen straw hats were stacked at the top.

"A sombrero, to protect you from the sun," the girl said. "Only ten American dollars."

"Ten dollars?"

"Five dollars."

The girl smiled sweetly and Mercedez said, "Let me see them."

The girl lifted the stack of hats from the pole and Mercedez looked at one after another. All were identical but for the colorful fabric band around the brim. They varied also in size, smallest at the top, and she chose one near the top of the stack that fit her best, the band a red that came close to matching her bikini.

"You are beautiful!" the girl, who seemed about ten years old, cried.

Mercedez gave her a smile and a "Thank you," and reached into her purse for her wallet. As she did so, she saw the cell phone and picked it up. Five o'clock! She was supposed to be back at the hotel half an hour ago.

She hurriedly gave the girl five dollars and a one dollar tip, which made the sweet face glow even more and several "Gracias tanto señorita!" tumble from her upturned lips.

Mercedez grabbed her bag and the towel and started up the sand at a fast clip, feeling well rested, but a bit rushed. She hoped she hadn't kept Bill waiting.

When she reached the hotel room she entered calling, "Bill?" No answer. She went to the bathroom and peeled off her skimpy suit, then hopped in the shower. Before doing that, she returned to the bedroom to get her overnight case.

Bill stood on the balcony with the door closed behind him, which is why he hadn't heard her. He was still talking on his cell phone, but he was dressed for dinner in beige slacks, a loose-fitting blue shirt, and Dockers with no socks. She took her cue from this informal attire and laid out a bright yellow halter dress and espadrilles that laced halfway up her calves, and then she returned to the bathroom and hopped under the spray.

The water cascading down her body felt delicious. She lathered the shower mitt with body scrub and sweet-smelling bubbles soon coated her honey-colored skin. She shampooed her long hair, letting the water cascade over her and run in rivulets down her flesh, savoring the sensual delight of warmth and cleanliness and the lovely fragrance of rose.

She took her time drying and styling her hair, ensuring she looked her best for Bill. She wanted him to show her off, to be proud of her beauty and her sensuality, just as she was proud to be with such a handsome, sexy man.

Once she had styled her hair and sprayed on some floral eau

de cologne, she applied makeup, enough to enhance her natural beauty, a bit of eyeliner and mascara, and color to her cheeks and lips. The moist air precluded any type of face powder—it would be gone in an hour—and really she was lucky to have good skin and could get away without it.

She left the steamy bathroom naked, feeling very good indeed. In the bedroom she slipped into the dress, tied the shoes, placed around her neck a rope of pale puca shells and gold hoop earrings at her ears and with a last glance in the glass, she was ready.

She noticed the little charm the old woman had given her sitting on the table where she'd left it, and slipped it into her purse.

Bill was still on the balcony but no longer on the phone. He sat in a lounge chair and from his profile she could see that his face was set in a worried line. She hoped business wouldn't put him in a bad mood, but she knew that sometimes people had problems, with life, with work, and maybe she could help. At least she could make him feel better for a few hours.

She slid the glass door open and Bill turned to look at her. His eyes lit as they roved up and down her body appreciatively and he stood, opening his arms. "Honey, you look gorgeous!" he said, kissing her mouth.

Mercedez smiled up at him. "You, too."

She thought she saw a faint darkness in his eyes and said, "Everything okay? With your phone call?"

He pulled his arms away and took her upper arm, leading her back through the doors. "Nothing I can't fix. Hungry?"

"Famished!"

"So am I. I know a great little spot up the road that serves barracuda."

"Barracuda? Isn't that shark?"

"It is."

"Can you eat that?"

"Absolutely! They serve it with a lovely spicy sauce. Do you like fish?"

"Yes, but I've never had shark before."

"There's a first time for everything, missy," he said, allowing her to step off the elevator first.

They walked hand in hand along the main road lined with hotels, the ocean on one side, the sky fading from blue to a darker blue as the sun descended and the moon rose, the bay on the other side of the road dotted with small boats docked here and there. They passed a lighted statue that Bill identified as Mayan, a "Choc Mool, but it's a re-creation. You'll see real ones tomorrow."

Finally they came to a little restaurant at the end of a short pier raised up on stilts, and entered. The style was pure Mexican, with colored lights draped everywhere and tinny fiesta-type music playing. The maitre d' seemed to know Bill and greeted him warmly. Finally they were seated at the best table in the narrow restaurant, overlooking the ocean on one side and the bay on the other, and Bill asked Mercedez what she would like to drink. "A cosmopolitan," she said, and soon had one sitting before her, as well as a bowl of tortilla chips and some salsa. He ordered the barracuda for both of them, and while they waited, they sat back to watch the sea rolling in, the sky darkening, and from time to time gazed into each other's eyes.

"So, you never did answer me on the beach. What about your life? Where do you live? What's your world like?" Mercedez asked. She didn't want to be pushy, but somehow felt that he had conveniently avoided her question earlier.

"Not much to say," Bill said, taking a sip of his rye and ginger. "Married, divorced, two kids living with my ex. She got the house, I got the Lexus."

"Anybody since her?"

He grinned. "Well, there's you."

She laughed.

"What about you?"

"You already know pretty well everything there is to know."

"Oh, I doubt that very much."

"Married, divorced. Born in Corpus Christi, lived in New York briefly, and mainly in California, first San Francisco, and now Southern California. Studied a variety of subjects, like photography. Did a year of university, but the divorce set me back. I'm on my feet again, though, so it's full speed ahead. Girl power!" She raised a fist into the air and laughed and Bill laughed, too.

"I like a spirited woman."

The barracuda came and they dug in. "God, this is good!" Mercedez said. "I like fish but I'm not an overwhelming fish fan, but this is great!"

"Told you!"

They ate in silence and Mercedez found that she was very hungry. They'd skipped lunch by mutual agreement, and just had a continental breakfast on the flight. The fish came with the requisite refritos and guacamole, and Mercedez was half finished with her plate when she sat upright and pushed it away from her. "Stop me! That is so good! But I'm totally full."

"Me, too," Bill said, scraping the last bits up with his fork.

Once they left the restaurant Bill asked if she was tired. "Not really."

"Feel like dancing?"

"Always!"

They walked for maybe a minute along the main road until a taxi came into sight and Bill hailed it.

"Daddy-O's," he said, and they drove a short distance to a multilevel nightclub.

Outside, the lineup was long and Mercedez said, "We'll never get in."

But Bill led her to the front of the line. Again, he seemed to know the bouncers—he must have been here before too—and with a few words and a handsome tip they entered.

"This place is huge!" she said. She could see the multilevels, and there were at least two bars in view and she suspected more. The dance floor was large and packed, as was the room in general. Green lasers stroked the air from all directions as a disco ball littered the walls with moving lights. The DJ played house music, hip-hop, and salsa, and she felt like dancing.

They headed to a bar and while Bill ordered drinks and her hips swayed to the music, he said, "Go ahead," nodding to the dance floor. "I'll join you for the next song."

Mercedez left her purse with him at the bar and headed to the dance floor. The '80s song that came on was one of her favorites and she managed to find a spot just inside the edge of the dance floor. She swayed to the music, her arms lifted above her head, singing along, getting into the rhythm of the song, feeling great, really great. Nearby she saw a couple of guys watching her, smiling, nodding approval, and she knew she looked as good as she felt, young, sexy, and full of life.

The DJ spun another one she liked and Mercedez kept dancing, one partner after another cutting in to join her as her hips swayed and her long, strong, shapely legs lifted and fell onto the dance floor. She danced and danced, song after song, suddenly realizing along the way that Bill hadn't joined her. She stopped suddenly to glance around the room. He was still at the bar, the cell phone held to his ear as he talked and stared off into the distance.

The music changed again, another favorite and Mercedez felt an arm snake her waist. One of the previous dance partners had returned, cutting in on the more recent of the string of guys wanting to dance with her, and he led her in a kind of salsa spin that left her twirling and laughing, feeling light and free.

She danced another two songs or so with him as he skillfully managed to move them out of the way of guys who wanted to cut in. Then decided she'd better rejoin Bill, just in case something was wrong. She found him at the bar where she'd left him, sitting on a barstool, into his second drink.

"This place is great, isn't it?" he said.

"It's wonderful. I could dance here all night if they keep playing 'em like this. How about you? Doing okay?"

His arm circled her waist and pulled her close so that his face nuzzled her breasts, so voluptuous in the yellow halter. He looked up at her with those baby blues. "What do you think?"

She ruffled his hair. "I think you're doing fine!"

At some point she managed to drag him to the dance floor and they got there just in time for the macarena. The entire bar joined in and everybody had their arms out, palms down, doing the arm movements, then the hip movements, and hundreds of people were laughing together. Mercedez hadn't had this much fun in a long time.

After this anomaly on the dance floor, the DJs began spinning hip-hop and the dance steps changed. They danced a bit then retreated to the bar to quench their thirst and catch their breath, Bill saying, "Wow, I think I'm too old for hip-hop!"

"Nobody's too old," she said. "Hey, what's that stuff they spray into the air?"

"CO_2. Just keeps everybody alert."

"You've been to Cancun a few times, haven't you? You seem to know everybody, and all the ins and outs of the place."

Bill just smiled and said, "Want another drink?"

"I'm good," she said, slowly sipping the cosmo.

The hip-hop lasted for a half hour until the announcement of the bikini contest, with its "First prize of 2,500 US dollars!"

"You should enter," Bill told her. "You could win hands down."

Mercedez laughed. "My bikini is back at the hotel."

As if reading her mind, the announcement came that bikinis could be purchased in the adjacent shop. "Come on," Bill said, "let's get you suited up."

At the shop she found a selection of microbikinis in a variety of colors. Knowing her skin tones worked best with the hot colors, she chose one that revealed a lot, with a riot of reds, yellows, and oranges that swirled in and out and seemed to crescendo at the nipples on the bra and at the bottom of the crotch on the bottoms.

Bill paid an exorbitant price for the designer bikini and they hurried back to the club. He led her to the door for the change rooms and she entered a large room with at least fifty girls in various stages of dress and undress.

Blonds, brunettes, and redheads filled the space, women who looked just past puberty, and some who were still shapely at fifty. Their skin tones ranged from Nordic pale to rich African dark chocolate. Mercedez took an empty spot by the mirror and slipped out of her dress and shoes and pulled the briefs up her long legs. She caught a redhead glancing at her in the mirror. "How do you stay so toned? Man, I work out six days a week and I don't have your abs."

"I work out seven," Mercedez said, making a face, and they both laughed.

"My name's Janice. I'm from Canada."

"I'm Mercedez. Lately from LA."

"Hey, good luck, eh?"

"You, too!"

Finally, an organizer entered the room and she told the girls to form two lines. "First, there's a walk-through," she said. "This is the first round, elimination. The judges will pick ten girls for the final round. Just walk to the middle of the stage, turn to the left, back to face the audience, and then turn to the right, then your back to the audience, then walk off the other side. Everybody confused?"

Some of the girls giggled, and Mercedez did hear one tiny

blond with a southern accent say, "Uh, was that left first, then right?"

The organizer demonstrated. "Okay, you're the audience." She did the left, center, right, back, and walk off. "Got it now?"

The confused girl nodded, but Mercedez and Janis glanced at each other, stifling a giggle, sharing the knowledge that the little blond still didn't quite get it.

One by one the fifty or so girls paraded across the stage, stopping in the middle for their viewing, then off. Within a half hour the results came that ten girls had been selected, and Mercedez was one of them. Janis hugged her. "Oh, you're so lucky! But you deserve it. Abs, thighs, beautiful face. You've got it all!"

"Oh, Janis, thank you!" Mercedez said. "But I'm soooooo nervous now!"

"Don't be, you'll do fine."

The organizer returned to tell them that this next phase required them to do a small dance to a piece of music they liked from the '70s or '80s, since that was the theme tonight. Mercedez picked "I Will Survive" sung by Gloria Gaynor.

The room emptied as the losers dressed and left. On her way out Janis stopped and said, "You know, that bikini is great on you, but you really looked terrific in that halter dress. What if you took the straps and tied them around your neck instead of over the shoulders?"

"You think?"

"I do. Here." Janis undid the straps at the back and pulled them up and tied them tight in a neat bow behind Mercedez' neck. A look in the mirror said Janis had been right. The halter effect lifted Mercedez breasts even higher and allowed their fullness to swell over the top of the bra.

"Break a leg, girlfriend!" the redhead said with a wink and a thumbs up.

When they were alone, the ten finalists stood around nervously chattering about this and that, mainly about how nervous they were, all but one, and that one was a Latina who seemed haughty to Mercedez. She stood apart on tall, shapely legs, with her long arms bent at the elbows so that fists rested on hips. Her body was lean but incredibly voluptuous. Her dark eyes glinted when she looked at the others, especially Mercedez.

Before much longer they were ushered out to stage left. Each girl in turn went onto the stage and danced to her song. Some of the girls were jerky with nervousness, and one even fell. A couple moved in such exquisitely graceful ways that Mercedez found her breath taken away for moments, especially the girl from Hawaii, who wore a flower in her hair.

Finally, only Mercedez and this girl named Juanita were left. Mercedez went first. She found she got into the music right away, letting Gloria's lyrics run through her as the instrumentals and her body aligned. She felt her ass muscles tighten as she spun and lifted her legs chorus-girl fashion, her breasts thrust out proudly, her hair flying about her head and bringing on catcalls.

When she finished, loud cheers rang through the room. She grinned from ear to ear and did a mock curtsy that gave the audience a great view of her cleavage. She spotted Bill in the front row and he blew her a kiss. She blew one right back. Then she saw Janice clapping, and waved.

After Mercedez had left the stage, Juanita came on. Her music was more hard-edged, a James Brown song, "I Got You (I Feel Good)," that rocked the room and allowed her to gyrate in all directions. The applause that followed was ear-shattering.

Well, that's that, Mercedez thought. But she was pleasantly surprised when the organizer called both her and Juanita back, saying the judges were tied. Both girls would dance together on the stage to the same song, one the judges picked, which turned out to be a Tina Turner hit, "Better Be Good to Me."

They took up positions, Mercedez on the right as the audience saw her, Juanita on the left. The music began, the low rumble that started the song, then the increasing beat as Tina started in on the intense lyrics that soon led to an escalation in sound, the audience screaming along. Mercedez moved slowly, sensually, increasing her pace as she went. Out of the corner of her eye she watched Juanita's jerky movements, full of fueled energy, a kind of angry syncopation with the song. Mercedez tried to not let herself get distracted or thrown off the beat. She had to stick to her own plan, but somehow felt that Juanita had the edge.

Mercedez knew she had good legs, strong legs, and she made every effort to use them to her advantage, raising and lowering them, dipping them, letting them hold her up as she spun and then bent low to straddle the ground and grind close to it. And by the time Tina began to belt out the core of the song, Mercedez was flying. Her body gyrated to the sounds, her hips flipped from side to side, her waist twisted and her hair flew in every direction while her legs parted and her breasts swelled even further above the bra. Finally she jumped high into the air and then slid down onto the floor into a full split for her finale!

The audience went nuts. The sound was deafening, drowning out the music completely. She got to her feet and only then dared to glance at Juanita, who had managed to remove her bra and her large well-shaped breasts with the hard nipples jutted out at the audience. She smiled broadly at the crowd, turned her head slightly in Mercedez' direction and shot visual venom at her through her eyes, then did a spontaneous back flip and ended up with her own split on the floor, arms above her head, bringing the crowd to an even higher pitch.

Finally it was over and the host came out onto the stage with the results. The judges were still tied. The two girls had both won, and would split the money and they would each get a trophy.

Mercedez felt pretty good about this. She knew if she could have been a bit more prepared, maybe even practiced dancing before this contest, she might have won it herself, but it was all so spontaneous. Still, she knew Juanita was a great dancer, and a real beauty, and she didn't mind sharing the prize with someone so talented, even if she was less than friendly.

"Congratulations!" she said to Juanita as they stood on the stage side by side, both receiving a crown and a trophy and an envelope of money while the crowd cheered. "You were great."

"And you, chiquita, sucked!" Juanita said, turning her back on Mercedez and bending on the pretense of waving at the crowd stage left, so Mercedez got an ass aimed at her.

What a bitch! Mercedez thought, but decided to not let Juanita's hostility get her down. She'd tied for first place, got some money, some accolades, and she had a great guy to go home with tonight who would, hopefully, fuck her brains out.

Back in the dressing room the two women changed in silence, Juanita's sullen, Mercedez' more from not wanting another hostile encounter. Mercedez was dressed first. She grabbed her bikini and headed to the door.

"Give my love to your boyfriend."

Mercedez turned and stared at Juanita, who had a nasty smile on her face.

Mercedez felt confused. Did Juanita know Bill, or was she just being even more of a bitch? She decided to not bother getting into it with this girl who was down on everybody and everything. Not tonight. Not when Mercedez was high on winning, or co-winning the contest. Not when she had had such a wonderful day and evening with more to come.

She reached the bar where Bill waited, holding her purse and drinking another rye and ginger. He'd ordered her a cosmopolitan and she sipped it gratefully, waving the envelope at him and saying, "I'm buying!"

"You did it!" he said, hugging her. "I knew you would."

"All thanks to you. I would never have entered if you hadn't encouraged me."

He looked deep into her eyes. "Do I need to encourage you again?"

"Not for what I think you're thinking," she said, staring back at him. Her body felt hot, on fire with excitement and the aftermath of all that activity. She wanted to play it out, let the release come to a natural conclusion. "Let's get out of here," she said.

"Yes, ma'am," he nodded.

They placed their glasses on the bar and Mercedez pulled out a couple of twenties, then they turned toward the door, making their way through the throbbing crowd of revelers. Somewhere along the way, Mercedez looked up to see Juanita in her path.

The woman looked at Mercedez, then at Bill, and smiled, raising her eyebrows in a familiar hello, with a "How you doing?"

Mercedez glanced up at Bill in time to see something— but what?—as he said, "Good. Really good." She couldn't guess what that response meant. Did he know Juanita, or not? Now it seemed he was looking elsewhere. Was this a trick of Juanita's, pretending that she knew Bill, that they shared a knowing look?

Mercedez grabbed his hand and pulled him toward the door, and heard Juanita laughing behind her back.

They caught a cab back to the hotel, Mercedez quiet in the back, Bill's arm around her, while she silently steamed.

She decided to take out her fury on him in a way that would satisfy them both. The second they reached the hotel room she ripped his clothes from his body, pushed him back onto the bed, and climbed up his torso. She slammed her cunt down onto his half-erect penis. Then she fucked his brains out!

CHAPTER 3.

T he morning broke clear and warm. Mercedez and Bill
ate a continental breakfast on their balcony overlooking the emerald ocean. As Bill poured a second cup of
coffee for both of them, Mercedez found her hand reaching
for his crotch. She ran her palm up and down the fabric of his
pajama bottoms and felt his penis hardening inside. Bill stood
and put the coffeepot down. Within seconds Mercedez had
slipped his pants down and took his long cock between her
warm hands.

She played with him, cupping her hands around the shaft,
running one up, and then the other down, in quick succession,

making him harder still. She slipped out of her satiny robe and placed his cock between her large breasts, bending her head so she could kiss the tip as he fucked her breasts. Then she opened her generous lips and took him into her hot mouth. Her tongue acted like a finger stroking him as she let his cock slide deep into her throat.

The warm sensual feel of the taut flesh, so filled with promise, got her hot and bothered, and she felt wetness seeping out of her onto the seat cushion of the chair. The satin robe beneath her was becoming soaked.

Bill stood there, not touching her yet, letting her work for it, and the anticipation made her even hotter.

Up and down her lips slid over the rock-hard cock. She held his balls in one hand and squeezed gently and, at the same time, used her index finger to rub that spot between the penis and testicles. She used her other hand on herself, sliding it down over her wet clit. Her mouth set the rhythm and her finger kept pace. She moaned, mouth full of cock, pussy wet and sparking, and she spread her legs open wide.

She felt the cum rush out of his throbbing cock just at the moment she touched her pussy bud the right number of times. She moaned and cried out as his cum shot into her orifice, filling her mouth, and greedily she swallowed it down as her pussy throbbed and convulsed.

Laughing, they headed to the shower and washed together. And then, while they were drying off and Bill was saying, "We'd better get an early start. There are a lot of ruins to see today," his cell phone rang.

He checked the number and said to her, "Better get dressed,

honey, while I take this," as he stepped back onto the balcony and closed the door behind him.

Mercedez chose a striped sundress, red, yellow, and blue, with green thread. She donned her espadrilles again, and the straw hat she had bought, with a small gold heart necklace and two thin gold bangles on her wrist. It wasn't until she was finishing applying the little makeup she'd wear in this sticky climate that Bill returned.

"Everything okay?" she asked. He seemed a little lost.

"Sure. Fine. Just give me a minute," he told her, and slipped into his clothes.

Bill rented a Jeep through the hotel concierge and it was waiting outside when they emerged into a day that had grown hot quickly. Soon they were cruising south down the main highway, the top down, Mercedez holding onto her hat for dear life, while a modern Mexican ballad played on the radio and the sun beat down on their bodies. Mercedez glanced at Bill, his profile strong and handsome, and all she knew was that she wanted him again. Maybe this time she'd met a man she could pour her heart into. If the gods are willing, she thought, something her grandmother might have said.

They stopped after an hour at a roadside cantina for Cokes. There, a flock of small women clearly of Mayan lineage descended on them, trying to sell everything from pottery to multicolored hammocks. While Mercedez laughed and told the women that she didn't know where she would string a hammock at home, Bill's cell rang again and he wandered down the road to take the call.

Mercedez knew these women worked hard, and their income was meager. She didn't want to insult them by giving them a few pesos but, on the other hand, she didn't want to cart around items she had no use for and that she would likely leave behind in the hotel room, which would be another insult. Ultimately, she bought them all Cokes and tacos, that being the only thing she could think of doing that made sense.

One of the women, who looked quite a bit like her grandmother, said something to her that Mercedez couldn't understand. She asked in Spanish for the woman to repeat what she'd said and when she did, Mercedez still couldn't understand her. Another, younger woman said "You are Mayan. She knows this. She is telling you to be careful. For Mayans, gold is the color of the conquistadors. It can blind you."

Mercedez had no idea what that meant, and was about to ask when she heard Bill say, "Ready, honey?"

"Sure." She waved good-bye to the women, who tried to offer her little tokens, flowers, a small bag of seeds, and she did take some things, not wanting to be rude. She stuck one of the pink blossoms behind her ear, and the Jeep pulled off the dusty shoulder and back onto the highway.

They reached Chichén Itzá about noon, the sun at its zenith. Bill pulled into a parking lot of sorts and handed the attendant a tip to keep an eye on the Jeep. Then they started across the green grass toward the enormous pyramid before them. Halfway there, a young, smiling, good-looking Mexican man with the broad features of the Mayans approached them, walking backward in front of them as they headed toward the ruins.

"I'm a good guide. You need a guide. There's a lot to know about these ruins. I'm from around here, my people are, too. Hire me. I'm cheap, and I can give you all the history you'll ever want or need. Just six hundred pesos for one hour!"

"That's, uh, what, fifty dollars?" Bill said, looking to Mercedez, who did a quick calculation in her head and nodded.

"Five hundred pesos," the sweet-natured young man said, grinning at them, all brilliant white teeth, shining black eyes, skin the color of dyed leather.

"Let's hire him," Mercedez said.

"Deal!" Bill laughed.

"Al-right!" the bright-eyed young man said, imitating the high-five he had obviously seen on TV and in the movies.

"You want us to pay you now?" Bill asked?

"Wait until the tour is finished. If you're satisfied, you pay. If not, you don't."

"Can't beat that," Bill said.

"My name is Pedro but you can call me Peter."

"Nice to meet you, Peter," Mercedez said, introducing herself and Bill, reaching out to shake the warm hand with the firm grip.

"You got Mayan blood, señorita," Peter said.

"Does it show?"

"Yep!"

They both laughed.

Bill had already started across the grass toward the giant pyramid, but Peter took Mercedez' arm and turned her left instead, toward an area that seemed to have no buildings.

"This way, Señor Bill!" Peter called.

But Bill said, "You guys go on ahead. I'm kind of a loner when it comes to things like this."

Mercedez felt a bit torn. She wanted to hear the tour but at the same time felt like she was deserting Bill. On the other hand, wasn't *he* deserting *her?* And on yet another hand, people couldn't do every single thing together. They'd get bored. This kept things fresh. And just as they turned away, Bill's cell rang. She glanced back to see him answer and figured he'd be tied up for a while anyway.

Peter led her along, giving her a short talk about the history of this place.

"Before the Spanish came here, Chichén Itzá was the New York of the Mayan world," Peter said, and Mercedez laughed.

"It's true! In the Yucatán, everything passed through this city. You couldn't buy anything, no decisions were made, nothing happened if it wasn't cleared here first."

"What's the name mean?" Mercedez asked. "Something about a well?"

Peter grinned. "You got it. 'Mouth of the Well.' They also used to call this place 'the city of the wizards of the water.' Cool, huh?"

"Very!"

"So, any idea what this place was used for?"

They had stopped before a bunch of large, heavy-looking stone pillars, which Mercedez stared at. "Uh, something about the military?"

"Bingo, Señorita Mercedez! This was the Templo de los Guerreros, the Temple of the Warriors. Only the pillars are left, what they called the Assembly of the Thousand Columns."

"Does the serpent have meaning?"

"Of course! The cult of Kukulcan, the God-serpent. Everything here has meaning."

"It looks amazingly symmetrical. Is it?"

"Very much so."

"And over there? Any ideas what those were used for?"

As they walked, Mercedez stared at several pillars with strange vertical appendages with holes going through them from side to side. "If you turned them around, I'd say they could work as basketball hoops."

"Señorita Mercedez, you know this intuitively! This is the Ballcourt, and they played an old game here. Only the best warriors, the best athletes and teams competed, and until only a few were left. Winning was everything. It was crucial to win."

Mercedez let her imagination run rampant, picturing golden-skinned men sweating under the hot sun as they chased the ancient Mayan version of a basketball around this stone court. She could imagine the highly developed pecs, the short skirts the men would have worn which likely had no other fabric underneath so that as they ran, their taut, muscular ass cheeks would come into view periodically. They must have had large hands that slid over the sweat-soaked skin of their muscular thighs. That she could imagine sliding over her skin . . .

She pulled herself out of the fantasy with a gasp. "Uh, what did they win?"

"First, you should come this way. After that, I will explain."

They walked a short distance, over new grass that was kept

well maintained for the tourists no doubt, and into a kind of field with a bit of shrubbery.

"Here we are!"

Mercedez looked around and saw a kind of rounded shaped pool of water.

"This is Cenote Sagrado. It's a natural well. Sacred."

She went to the edge of the water and looked down, unable to see anything. "How deep is it?"

"Maybe sixty-five feet deep. And it goes just over two hundred feet across."

"Why is it sacred?"

"The old Mayans, they thought that this is where the gods of rain lived. They used to sacrifice to those gods."

"Sacrifice. You mean like food and jewels?"

"Yes. Copper, gold, jade, carvings, arrow tips. And human beings."

"What?" Mercedez snapped her head around. "You're joking, right?"

"It was their religion, señorita. Not how we do things today, but back then, it is what they believed. Every year they selected the choicest virgin and sacrificed her."

"That's pretty grim."

"Well, to you and me. But back then, all the virgins competed to be chosen. A kind of beauty contest. To be chosen was a way of helping the community because when the gods were appeased, good things happened."

"And when they weren't?"

Peter shrugged. "They say the priests bound the girls up with gold ropes around their bodies, and tied onto them other offerings to weigh them down, but this was an honor. Then, into the well they went. They were drugged too, I think, at least that's what one man from El Museo Nacional de Antropología in Mexico City told me."

They had been under the sun for about forty-five minutes but already Mercedez was feeling its effects. A bit light-headed, her throat felt parched, and her vision was just a bit less clear than it should be. Even though the Yucatán wasn't so far from Corpus Christi, somehow the sun felt hotter here. She was wearing her hat but wished she'd thought to bring along the bottle of water from the Jeep.

"Is there water for sale here?" she asked Peter.

"I can get you some, señorita. Here, sit and rest."

She reached into her bag and pulled out a peso and handed it to him, then sat on the ground by the well. The grass beneath her wasn't exactly cool, but she knew the earth took away some of the humidity from her skin.

There had been only two tourists at the well when they arrived but they had gone and she was alone. She lay back against the earth, moving the straw hat so that it covered most of her face.

How had the people here survived the heat? She loved the sun, always had, yet here, perhaps because it was essentially a jungle, the density of the air and the pressure as the heat beating down left her wilted.

"You get used to it," a voice said.

Mercedez moved the hat a couple of inches to see a voluptuous girl with dark skin standing on the other side of the well. The girl, well, young woman actually, because she must be legal age, was dressed in some sort of period outfit that was composed mostly of ropes and ties wrapped around her body which left most of her exposed.

Mercedez sat up abruptly. The girl edged around the well, her movements exotic and catlike. Under the sun her coppery flesh glistened. Her breasts bobbed delicately, the nipples taut, the areolas a darker color and slightly swollen as if she were used to having them sucked.

As she raked her eyes over the sexy form that neared, Mercedez thought, well, she's old-fashioned. The bush between her legs was unshaved, as dense as the jungle they had traveled through. Those legs were thick and sturdy, shapely in a way, but not the reed thin that was so stylish elsewhere.

Mercedez started to stand but warm hands pressed against the flesh of her shoulder and kept her from rising. In fact, they pushed a bit harder and Mercedez found herself reclining again.

"Who . . . who are you?"

"I am Tula-Kuk, a devotee of both Tula the mild and Kukulcan the bloodthirsty."

"I'm—"

"I know who you are. You are the chosen."

"Chosen? For what?"

As the girl spoke she stepped over Mercedez' body until she was straddling her head. Then, slowly, she lowered herself into a squat.

Mercedez watched the pink slit hidden by the dark jungle between her legs drawing closer. It opened like a flower, and Mercedez caught the sharp scent of this exotic bloom.

The sight and smell and sense overtook her. Her body

trembled in the heat; her nipples tingled as if they were exposed and the sun burning them mildly through the fabric of her dress. She felt an electric energy at her pussy opening as the girl's nether lips met her lips and Mercedez used her tongue to taste the nectar. It was sweet and tart at the same time, and Mercedez found it so erotic she lowered her arm to reach down and touch herself. But the girl caught her wrist.

Mercedez licked and sucked the delicious cunt juices, her own pussy throbbing with an energy she wanted released. She twisted and writhed but the girl held both her wrists now, locked almost in her grasp, leaving Mercedez feeling helpless to the torment in her own body. But somehow the waiting to be pleasured only increased her arousal and she found herself panting, her pussy pulsing as she lapped at the pussy that had been thrust into her face.

Suddenly the girl leaped into the air a foot or so and spun around so that she faced the other direction. Before Mercedez knew it, the girl bent forward, her fleshy ass in the air. Her wrists released, Mercedez grabbed onto those luscious plump ass cheeks and pulled her hips down so that she could continue drinking this lovely juice of a natural fruit.

The girl used her hands to spread Mercedez' legs wide and lift the skirt of her sundress to her waist. Then she slipped her strong fingers underneath, walking them over Mercedez' ass cheeks until she was at the crack, then she gripped the behind firmly and pulled the cheeks apart. She lifted Mercedez' hips and then lowered her mouth, lapping and sucking, and they ate one another out under the broiling sun, a mirror image.

Mercedez, mouth full of cunt juice, nose filled with the scent of cunt juice, could only moan with the sensations that rode her body like powerful electric currents, like a fever, like a mounting spasm. Her lips felt the pussy she kissed and sucked contracting as more juices flowed and the powerful scent left her more light-headed and dazed. Her own pussy crackled like an electrified wire as it was lashed by a powerful and relentless tongue.

Then, all at once, the ass cheeks she gripped trembled violently, even as Mercedez felt her own ass trembling out of control. The great cry that came from her mouth entered the girl's cunt and sounded like an underwater echo. Mercedez felt both their bodies convulsing in delicious release.

As she lay resting, she became aware of the sweat from her body cooling her. She was also aware of a sound as someone seemed to be walking on the earth she lay against.

She opened her eyes and suddenly the sun was blocked. The young woman with the golden binding was gone. Mercedez realized that her skirt was up around her hips, her thong panties at her ankles, and Peter stood staring at her, a smile on his broad lips.

Quickly Mercedez pulled her skirt down, jumped to her feet and tried to discretely pull up her panties.

Peter only laughed as he handed her a bottle of water. "You've met Tula-Kuk."

Mercedez uncapped the water and drank long and deep, washing her parched throat. When she stopped drinking she said, "How do you know that?"

"She meets every virgin by the well."

"I'm not a virgin!" Mercedez blurted out, and then wondered why she was telling this to a stranger.

"One can be a virgin in many ways. But come, there is more to see. And your friend Bill is waiting by the great pyramid."

They took a roundabout route to the giant pyramid that had a place of prominence, not to mention height, in the plaza on the land that had once been the most prominent Mayan city. Mercedez felt something deep inside her, and wondered if this was a kind of connection to her remarkable ancestry. Maybe. It was hard to know. The Mayans certainly were an impressive people. They passed rounded buildings that Peter said were observatories, used by the astronomers of the day so they could watch the stars.

"They called this Caracol. It means 'spiral' because inside are spiral stairs that lead to the tower, where the observatories are located. The old Mayans reached the heights of their urban and cultural sophistication between the eleventh and thirteenth centuries, but the culture goes back before that time, to fifteen hundred B.C. at least."

"What's this wall about?" she asked, running her hands over images that looked a lot like skulls on the T-shaped structure.

"It's called the Platform of Skulls, the domain of Au Puch, the death god. These are depictions of the heads of enemies and also brave warriors."

As they neared the enormous pyramid, Peter said, "Here at Chichén Itzá, the old Mayans said that the gods engaged in a spear throwing match. Quetzalcoatl is said to have been born of two contestants, Mixcoatl, the cloud snake, and Chimalman, which means shield hand, who birthed the god. Quetzalcoatl, which means Plumed Serpent, is the main deity and we know he dates from around the ninth century, but most scholars acknowledge he is at the very roots of the Mayan religion; they believed he lies at the center of the world. You can see he's been canonized in the architecture. Most of the images surrounding you are representative of Quetzalcoatl. It is to him that this pyramid, the Castillo, was built as a temple."

"Peter, you're pretty good. You should have been an archeologist."

"I am," he smiled.

Mercedez didn't know if he was answering figuratively or literally but it didn't matter. Clearly he knew his stuff. She glanced up at the seemingly endless number of steps of the pyramid. They were made of stone, with a lot of height between each step, and she wondered how the shorter Mayans could climb up and down them. Ropes had been stretched from top to bottom to help tourists ascend and descend, but she watched most people crawl up on their knees and slide down on their butts.

Bill was just rounding a corner, still talking or once again talking on his cell. When he saw her, he waved that she should go up without him, and then turned away.

Mercedez felt annoyed. She knew that Bill had work to do, but today was supposed to be a free day. He seemed to be on the phone constantly.

She turned to Peter, but he was nowhere to be seen. "Great," she thought. Well, she didn't want to miss this opportunity. She hiked up her skirt and began climbing the high stone steps.

The sun beat down on her as she climbed, her strong legs

helping her as she stepped up to the next level and the next. Around her, the few tourists who were making the trek moaned and groaned, with a few curses tossed in. But for Mercedez, this was exciting, a quest of some sort. A small wind blew her skirt around her legs Marilyn Monroe–style and she knew the folks on the ground were getting a good show of her bare behind, the thong stretched between her ass cheeks, but she didn't care.

She stopped for a moment to watch the dark clouds in the distance of the brilliant sky, wondering if they would come this way. Her hair blew around her face and her skirt whipped up again, exposing more thigh and ass than was probably socially acceptable, but then she was three-quarters of the way up now, and few on the ground could see the details of what lay under her skirt.

It took her some time to reach the top, a flat platform with an enormous statue in the center, a kind of semihuman being with large ears and rings in them, reclining. He appeared to have a bowl on his stomach and his head was turned to the left. His eyes seemed to be staring straight at her.

Mercedez spent time with the handful of people who had made it to the top observing the area. Aside from this patch of cleared land which held the ruins, everywhere she looked was jungle, and she could see for miles. What must it have been like to be here in the past? The utter quiet of this place, even with a scattering of fellow climbers, made her wonder if only priests came up here, or if sometimes lovers snuck up at night to make love high above the world below, up in the clouds, closer to the stars.

"It's a Choc Mool," a familiar voice said. She spun around to see Peter behind her.

"Oh. What's that mean?"

"Remember the Ballcourt? The game you asked about?"

"Yes."

"This is where the winner was brought, the bravest warrior, the premier athlete. To win was all. To win was to be sacrificed to Quetzalcoatl."

Before Mercedez could open her mouth, Peter said, "His heart was cut out by the priest and placed in the bowl of the Choc Mool as an offering to the gods."

"Wow!" Mercedez said. "That was some victory. I think I might have tried to lose."

Peter laughed. "Their culture was different than our own. Their ways were based on nature, where something must die in order that something else could survive. They believed that a human sacrifice appeased the god who would then grant them a good harvest, good health, and many live births in a time when more died in the womb than were born. These are the things they needed to survive."

While Mercedez digested all this, the storm clouds approached fast. "It looks like rain," she said.

"Yes, here it rains almost daily in the afternoons. Come, we will go down."

Going down the steps was easier than going up, although they were just as steep. Mercedez prided herself on not using the "handrail," the rope, and not backing down as just about everyone else was doing. The narrow steps were made for feet that were likely half as long as an average foot today, and she found she needed to turn her feet slightly.

Finally they reached the bottom. The sky had darkened. Bill was nowhere in sight.

"Come. I will show you something special. And you can get out of the rain at the same time."

Mercedez followed him around to one side of the giant Castillo to an opening in the stone. A couple was coming out, their bodies covered with sweat, but they looked pretty happy, as if they'd just fucked.

"What's this place?" Mercedez asked.

"Here, you can go up inside the pyramid."

"To the top again?" she asked, wondering if she wanted to climb that height again, but knowing she did. If there was something to see, she wanted to see it. She wanted to experience everything.

Mercedez turned into the doorway. "This time you're coming, right?" she asked, looking back over her shoulder. No Peter. She sighed and held onto the doorway and leaned back, looking left then right, but he'd disappeared again. "Jeez, what are you, invisible?" she mumbled.

Suddenly the rain fell in earnest, hot rain, in tune with the climate. She turned back into the interior of the pyramid and started up the new set of stone steps. These were not quite a steep as those outside, but the stairwell was extremely narrow, so much so that she could easily touch both walls as she climbed. The walls were a bit slick, and reminded her of her vagina when she was stimulated. She giggled and the sound echoed around her.

She climbed and climbed but no one was coming down. The cavelike tunnel she ascended was lit every fifty or so feet with low-wattage light bulbs and she could not see more than a few yards ahead of her. Soon she reached a small landing and found a gay couple standing there. The landing was just a bit wider than the stairwell, but not by much. She stepped up onto the landing and the three of them crowded the space.

"Boy, this is pretty narrow," she said.

"No kidding!" one of the guys confirmed. He jerked a thumb up over his shoulder. "Wait till you get higher."

"We're outta here," his partner confirmed, and in single file they squeezed by her and descended. She realized that the landing would be the first of many and it was the only place where people could pass one another going up and down.

As Mercedez continued climbing, she began to perspire, sweat dripping down her body, wetting her dress under her breasts, under her arms, along her hips. This stairwell was hot and moist and the air thinned the higher she climbed. She passed another couple of stairwells and met only an old man on the way down. He nodded.

"Is it much farther to the top?" she asked him.

"Oh, you'll know when you get there," he said, laughing, then disappeared below her into the gloom.

The stairs seemed to narrow further and then, all of a sudden, she had reached the top. She stood for a moment, alone, looking around this cavelike room. Inside there were two statues. One was another Choc Mool, and Mercedez shivered as she examined it up close, the jutting nose, large boxy-round earrings, round childlike eyes carved into the stone, the irises painted blue, knees pulled up, the feet sandaled, the body supine. Behind, as if the Choc Mool were protecting it, was another statue, this one of an animal. She wondered which animal. The body was red in color, the eyes in the dim lighting seemed to be green, and it had four sharp looking white teeth protruding from the mouth.

For some reason, she wanted to touch it, and reached out to pet its head.

"I wouldn't do that if I were you."

This time she didn't turn around at Peter's voice. "Why not? Will he disappear the way you do?"

"I haven't disappeared. I'm right here."

Mercedez turned slowly, feeling her body heavy with heat and moisture, rooted to the stone beneath her feet.

Peter stood in a darkened corner, shrouded in shadows.

He stepped out into the murky light and now seemed to be wearing something quite different from the jeans and simple shirt he'd worn before. His body was girded in golden fabric, a skirt from the waist down, make of large metal pleats. His chest was naked and he had a large scar in the middle of his chest. Around his neck he wore a golden circular collar studded with jewels, and a feathered headpiece. He reminded Mercedez of many of the images she had seen here.

As he moved toward her, Mercedez felt her limbs grow weak. His chest glistened with sweat, the pectoral muscles prominent, and the nipples hard dark beads. His thighs were heavily muscled and his calves shapely, like those of an athlete. Part of her wanted to say, "we should go back down, Bill would be waiting," but she found herself unable to speak.

Yet, as if she had spoken, Peter said, "He is not your true love. You are a princess of the blood. You deserve a warrior."

Mercedez was about to defend Bill, even though he wasn't

exactly her boyfriend, just a "fuck friend," and that term sure annoyed her. Besides, there was no need to say anything to Peter, but she found herself distracted, her focus not on Bill, but on the scent of the masculine form that now stood before her and was so compelling.

Sweat dripped from her face, her hair, down between her breasts. The humidity in this cave was so high it was almost raining inside. She found herself taking deep breaths of air, as if it were in short supply.

One of Peter's hands reached out and took hold of the strap of her sundress. Mercedez moved her own hand up to block him, but the feel of his hot moist flesh sent a shiver through her body that reached her groin.

He slid the strap down and she found herself sliding the other one down and soon her dress and thong panties lay in a heap on the stone floor. Her body felt aflame with desire and when he touched her breast it was as if his skin burned hers, fanning the flames, making her breath deeper but the breaths closer together. She felt her nipples hard and aching as he bent down and took one into his mouth and pinched the other between his strong fingers. She moaned and fell backward but he caught her about the waist in his strong arm.

As he sucked and nipped at her nipple, and pinched and twisted the other, she swooned under the heat and passion. Then he had her turned, her knees on the ground, her body bent over the animal's body, her ass high in the air. As her hands reached out to brace herself on the floor, he spread her ass cheeks as the girl by the well had done, wide. As she straddled the back of this red beast, a beast of a different sort mounted her.

The penetration was scalding, refreshing, stimulating. She cried out, not in pain, but wanting him deeper. His penis slid far inside her cunt, burning its way through, and she could only moan and cry out, deliciously trapped in a position of submission to this man who reminded her of nothing less than an ancient warrior.

As his cock stroked her, long and steady, the rhythm picked up pace until she felt about ready to explode with the fire scorching her inside. Her breasts bounced against the side of the animal, her nipples scraping the stone floor, her long hair that had fallen over her head swept around her, blinding her, and she wanted nothing more than for this fucking to last forever.

Suddenly his cock left her, and the cry from her lips filled the hollow room. But it did not last long. Soon the hot wet penis nudged at her anus, knocking against it slightly, and Mercedez' body trembled in anticipation of this piercing, not knowing how it would be, what to expect, if it would hurt her. All she knew was that she wanted to feel him inside her there.

And then he entered her, slowly, the moisture from her cunt lubricating the tight passageway. She felt the bigness of his cock and wondered if she could take him without tearing, but he moved slowly, letting her walls expand to incorporate him as he went. She felt filled as never before, her entire body reduced to one area that cried out with desire for him to bury deeper within her, leaving her moaning.

She got her wish. He entered the full length of him and Mercedez felt her walls contract around him and her body spasm. She screamed, the sound echoing, her ass convulsing, as he shot sweet cum deep into her gut from the massive organ that impaled her rectum in a statement of ownership.

She lay limp. Wilted. A flower that needed refreshment but would revive. Small sighs and moans tumbled from her lips as he withdrew. Even this position as she lay so spread out over the back of the beast left her feeling sexy and vulnerable and knowing that her hunger would be back soon.

Finally she pulled her hair away from her sweaty face and managed to push herself up until she could stand.

When she turned and Peter was no longer there, she smiled, not surprised at all. She picked up her dress and slid it over her head, and brought the thong panties up her legs, dusting off the dirt from her knees as she did so. She smoothed her hair back with her fingers, holding it up in the back in a ponytail, and the relief of the hair off her neck cooled her by a degree or two.

One last look and she realized that this creature was a jaguar. Its eyes looked like jade. The teeth, maybe ivory, if that could be. As she passed the Choc Mool, she dragged her hand through his bowl. It felt moist, as if it held liquid. She lifted her finger expecting to see blood, but there was something darker. She brought her finger to her nose and sniffed. Chocolate! She tasted it. Yes, smooth, dark chocolate! Suddenly she was laughing.

Just as Mercedez began to descend, she ran into a small troop of tourists heading up and she backed up to allow them to enter the room. The two families with children changed the atmosphere. One of the teenagers said, "Hey, it smells funny in here. Punky! Like somebody's been doin' it!"

"That's enough!" a motherly figure told him, pointing a finger to indicate seriousness.

Mercedez smiled and headed down the slightly slippery stone steps. The lower she got, the cooler the air that slid along her arms, over her chest, and up under her skirt, until soon she was outside in the sunshine. The rain had come and gone, the grass and soil were wet but already drying, and the day more humid than before. The second she stepped out she saw Bill coming toward her.

"Honey, did you catch that storm? Lightning, thunder, the earth shook."

"Oh, I know. It was . . . special."

"Say, where's Peter? We need to pay him."

They looked around, walking the periphery of the base of the great pyramid, but Peter was nowhere to be found.

"His loss," Bill said.

Mercedez didn't feel right about leaving without paying him, but they had looked, and he didn't seem to be anywhere, and they couldn't spend the rest of the day searching for him.

They headed back to the Jeep. En route she asked one of the other tour guides if he knew Peter, Pedro, but he said he didn't, even when she described him. She kept looking, but did not see Peter anywhere, though at the top of el Castillo she saw something glint golden in the sun. Maybe Peter was as much a part of this place as the Mayan blood was part of her veins.

Inside the Jeep she drank nearly a full bottle of water.

"Hey, want to go swimming? There are some gorgeous fish not too far from here in a cove, and we can get there and snorkel for the afternoon."

"But we don't have suits."

Bill grinned. "Where we're heading, we won't need them!"

They took the highway and ended up at the Nizuc Reef where they rented snorkel equipment. Bill knew an isolated spot and they headed down the beach until they were free of people, changed into the flippers, life vests, masks, and nothing else. Air tubes in hand, they dived in. The instant they hit the water, Mercedez saw gorgeous fish of every color, shape, and size, swimming amid the red and black coral reefs. The water was warm enough but certainly cooler than the day, refreshing, the view underwater delightful, the liquid sea sensual as it caressed her naked body and filled her orifices. *This,* she thought, *is heaven. If only it could last.*

It lasted until she and Bill sat drinking margaritas at a small fish shack along the beach and Bill said, "Uh, sorry, honey, but I've got to work tomorrow. Big client coming in. Meetings all day and night."

Mercedez felt disappointed. "Oh, that's a drag. I thought we'd have another day together."

"No pressure, remember?" he said, holding up a hand in a "stop" gesture.

"Sorry. I just meant I'll miss you." She picked up her glass and had a sip of the fruity drink.

"Look," he said, reaching for her hand, "I'll get you a plane ticket and you go on ahead to Mexico City and wait for me there. I'll only be one day, and you'll have time to do some shopping. I'll call there and change the reservation at the hotel."

"I could wait here for you and—"

"Oh, there's nothing to do here but lie on the beach."

"Sounds good to me!"

He looked displeased. "If you'd prefer that, sure, but it would be nice for me to arrive in Mexico City and have somebody to welcome me who was all hot and naked in the Jacuzzi."

"Well, I guess I could do some shopping. I need a few things."

"Hell, I'll even contribute to the shopping trip." He reached into his pocket and pulled out a wad of pesos mixed with US dollars. He handed over several hundred dollars and several thousand pesos and still had plenty left."

"Bill, I have the money from the contest—"

"I know, but I want you to get some pretty things, and I don't want you worrying about money. This is on my dime, remember?"

"Are you sure you can afford this?"

"Of course," he said, placing the money in her hand. "Hey, it's the company's dime, remember? Buy yourself something pretty and sexy. And buy me a new shirt, okay? I could use something . . ." he flipped his button-down collar, ". . . less formal."

Mercedez laughed. She took the cash and put it into her purse. This was turning out to be one weird romantic holiday, that was for sure!

CHAPTER 4.

*I*t was a warm, sunny morning when Mercedez left Bill at the Cancun airport and headed, alone, to Mexico City. This wasn't her ideal way to spend her time, but she knew that Bill had to work, and there wasn't much he could do about it. He had been more than generous financially, and likely gave her as much time as he could spare. After all, they were not in a committed relationship, just hanging out together, "fuck friends" as he put it, having some fun. Nothing wrong with that. Besides, she could get used to this! Everything so far had been five-star!

She flew first-class, and the flight attendants treated her very well indeed. The meal was lavish, the seat had a massager that operated at three speeds, and she had a choice of movies. And best of all, she drank champagne and orange juice all the way! *What's not to like?* she thought. But she knew the answer to that. She was alone. Watching the couple across the aisle snuggle and kiss and surreptitiously fondle one another did nothing to lift her mood, although she did find them cute. She just wished she had someone. But Bill promised he would join her in another day or so. She just had to amuse herself for a little while. That wasn't a problem, so why did it bother her?

At the Mexico City airport, she pulled her luggage off the carrier and headed out the door. "Señorita! Señorita!" They all called at her from every direction. "Come this way! Come here! Use my taxi!"

She looked around in dismay. There were limos and endless numbers of green and white Volkswagen Beetles speeding by on the arrival blacktop road and she soon realized they were all cabs. The limo would be fun, but she'd been in a limo before, and would probably ride one of those with Bill when they left here. Right now, she wanted to get down and see the city by being immersed in it.

She stepped between the limos stopped at the curb and raised a hand. Four of the Beetles screeched to a halt before her. She chose the closest. The driver, a Pancho Villa look-alike, jumped out and took her bag, opening the trunk at the front and tossing it in. He held the door for her and right away she noticed that the front passenger seat was missing. The rear seat was large enough for two adults and possibly a small child as well, but no more.

"El destino?" he asked her once he was behind the wheel.

"My hotel is in the Reforma," she said. "Do you know where that is?"

The driver turned and looked at her as if she were from another planet. "Sí, señorita," his expression a wry grin. "All of the good hotels are in Reforma."

"I'd like to see the city on the way," she said. "Get to see the people, you know."

"Do not fear. You will see the city, and the people. Maybe not all ten million of the inhabitants, but there will be no shortage."

He took off like a bullet, the little Bug rattling and roaring with the noise of the rear engine and Mercedez suddenly regretted her decision. She would see things at the level of the people, that was guaranteed! She might even see things from the level of the insects! This car was so low to the ground she feared if the floor dropped away it would be propelled by foot power!

Noisy and crowded and busy. She had never seen anything like it. Maybe there were other cities on the planet as dense, but this was new to her. The streets were jammed with traffic, and the little Beetle wove in an out of it like all the other little Beetles, jerking to a halt here and there to avoid a collision, sliding into spaces where it should not fit but did.

Collisions seemed to be common here, at least she figured that was so because of the enormous number of cars and trucks and buses with dented fenders and bashed-in side doors.

Music blared from the cab's radio, as it did from the radios of most of the other vehicles, a mix of classic Mexican tunes and modern Mexican *rocnrol* plus a bit of Latino dance music from South America. It was as if the entire city was celebrating a fiesta!

Once she got over the shock of driving in this chaos called traffic, she turned her attention to the sidewalks, alive with people. Even in Manhattan there didn't seem to be so many people on the streets as here. And the shops! Every block was lined with them: pastel boxes that seemed to have no front wall or storefront, but were fully open to the sidewalks. The array of goods was mind boggling and every shop seemed to specialize. One sold a staggering array of mops and brooms, the next shiny hubcaps, the one after that liquor, the next bright plastic containers only, and then one with colorful scarves, and on and on. She even saw a show selling sex toys and X-rated videos!

They were high above the city it seemed and soon descended via this wide street, weaving in and out of traffic at a terrifying pace. She saw grand architecture of stone, ornate buildings with classical Spanish railings at the balconies and metalwork at the doors, tall structures possessing grace and charm that spoke of a highly romantic history. Here and there were parks that forced traffic to circle around them, green and lush with tropical vegetation, bushes alive with colorful flowers. She also noticed the sculpture, tall bronze and marble monuments to people who had done something important, and statues of animals, mainly birds. And everywhere domed churches and cathedrals with oxidized roves, giant crosses, and enormous bell towers, lavish in their facades, structures that seemed to be the heart and soul of the city.

Eventually the driver pulled up in front of the Meliá

Mexico Reforma, an enormous hotel that scraped the sky. The architect had designed it to resemble a pyramid, like the one she had just visited in Chichén Itzá. She paid the taxi driver and added a nice tip and he held out his card. "Señorita, if you need a taxi, call me. I will take you where you wish to go, safe and cheap. My name is Pedro."

"Another Pedro!" she laughed, but of course he did not get the joke.

Once she had registered, the bellhop led her up to her suite on the penthouse level. The rooms were enormous and elegant with an extravagant Spanish touch to the furniture and artwork. A welcome basket sat on the table, full of ripe fruits, high-end salsas and blue corn chips, chocolate, spreads and crackers, and several bottles of wine. Once she tipped the bellboy and the door had closed behind him, she sat on the bed and looked around. The place was spectacular. If only she wasn't alone.

She noticed a bouquet of lovely red, orange, and white flowers on the desk and a card, which read: "Enjoy the city, honey. I'll be with you soon. Love, Bill."

Mercedez looked at the card. He really was very sweet. She wondered, though, if "love" meant Love, or if this was just a general all-purpose gift-card signing. She picked up the phone and dialed her room number to see if there were messages on the answering service, but there were none.

"Well, girl, here you are, all by yourself in Mexico City. Are you going to sit around sulking, or are you going out there and do the town?"

She opened her suitcase and found a cute sundress that buttoned from the bosom to the hem and gathered at the waist. The tan color with streaks of pastels running through it suited her complexion, which is why she bought it. She would need some new clothes, though, and Bill was right, this was a good time to shop.

Mercedez had a quick shower, planning on a long bath later in that Jacuzzi where she could really indulge herself, shave her legs and her pussy, and generally do all the girly things she loved to do to take care of her body and keep it looking buff. Right now, though, she didn't want to lose the day.

Once her hair was dry and she had applied just a touch of makeup, she gathered her bag and headed out.

This hotel really was spectacular. As she walked around the corridor to the elevator, she looked over the railing to the reception and lounge below. It really did resemble the architecture of the pyramid. She was most impressed.

Outside, heat and noise surrounded her instantly. She probably should take a taxi. And definitely she should have asked at the desk about shopping. But surely in this area there would be some nice shops, and she needed to work her legs.

She strode down the street, happy to be stretching her long legs. Nearly every man she passed on the street turned to look at her. Even a few women gave her the eye. Well, it never hurt to look good. She smiled at everyone, happy to be here. She was very lucky.

Not two blocks from the hotel she found a stylish shop that sold designer clothing, several of the top names and one or two of the up-and-coming Mexican designers. She browsed the racks and the mannequins and finally found a couple of items she liked. A saleswoman showed her to a plush changing room with gold-framed mirrors and an antique settee. First she tried on the tight-fitting black dress that showed quite a bit of cleavage. She might need something like this when Bill arrived, and they went out for dinner. She decided to take it. The next was also tight-fitting, a two-piece outfit in red, with a peplum waist and extended shoulders. This one was created by a Mexican designer and she decided she'd take it, too. Three other dresses did not suit her, but she did purchase a pair of beige slacks, although she rarely wore slacks. They were nicely tailored and flattered her bottom, and if they went on any wild expeditions, she might need them.

The saleswoman rang up her purchases, which hardly made a dent in the money Bill had given her, and she picked up the shopping bags and continued on. Several shops later she had a new short leather jacket, and two new pairs of leather shoes, including red stilettos that matched the red dress. She had also bought a couple of shirts for Bill, which she hoped he would like. She also hoped they would fit him!

She wanted to unload the bags and caught a taxi back to the hotel. Once she had unwrapped everything and hung up the lovely new clothes, she sat on the bed and looked at the clock. It was not even two in the afternoon. She ate a peach from the basket, but wasn't really hungry for lunch. Maybe another area of the city would be worth checking out. In fact, she'd just take herself to the subway and ride it. That would give her a real sense of this city!

At the front desk, she inquired and was told that the nearest metro stop was a block away. As she neared it, the throngs grew. Everywhere, vendors sold entrada de lotería, and there seemed to be hundreds of different lotteries. Some of the sellers were fairly aggressive, waiving handfuls of tickets in her face with cries that she would regret it if she didn't buy a ticket and her numbers won!

The subway was fairly modern, but vast, with ten lines. But quickly she realized that it was based on the idea that each line was identified by the name of the last station, which made the maps easy to follow. She bought a strip of tickets and pushed through the turnstile.

Mercedez had no idea which direction to go in and just picked the line that had the most interesting name. The one she selected was pink on the map, the line known as Quatro Caminos. She decided to ride to the end, get out, walk around a bit, then get back on and return to the hotel. By then it would be time for dinner and she would ask the concierge for a good restaurant. Hopefully she'd have worked up an appetite by then.

The platform was crowded. On the other side a train pulled in that was painted front to back with graffiti, over-lapping revolutionary themes. The one that pulled in on her side was painted a Depression Era blue. She shuffled into the car with everyone else, and felt a hand pass over her ass. When she turned to look there were four men behind her, and none of them met her eye, but all had a smile on their lips. It could have been any of them. She inched further into the crowded train.

The stations came and went, with people entering and exiting, but eventually the people began to thin out. She fig-ured she had traveled far enough from the downtown core that the hustle and bustle of city life had dimmed for the more sedate life of the suburbs.

Suddenly the door between cars opened and three mariachis entered, strumming as they came, wearing full band costumes, black with gold pom-pom trim up the sides of the pants and around the sombreros. They played a lively tune as they strolled through the car collecting money from passengers and Mercedez gave them a few pesos and in exchange got a wide grin and a wink from the cute guitar player.

Finally there were just three people left on the train besides her: a teenage boy asleep at the far end; a housewife busily sorting through her shopping bags; and an old white-haired woman, with a thousand wrinkles on her face. She was dressed in black from head to toe, and held a huge bouquet of rust-colored flowers, the scent of which filled the car. She must have felt Mercedez staring at her because the woman's head snapped around and her dark eyes made contact.

Mercedez wanted to be friendly and nodded a greeting, but the woman just stared. Suddenly she stood, her frame bent, and hobbled toward Mercedez. She stopped right in front of her and plucked a flower from the bouquet. "For you, señorita," she said in Spanish. "Maravillas. They are the flowers of the dead."

The train pulled into a station named Panteones. The old woman exited the train and, on impulse, so did Mercedez.

She followed the woman up the stairs, smelling the orange-yellow flower she had been given as she went. When she came up to the street level she found herself standing before an enormous gate that she realized was the entrance to a cemetery.

She watched the old woman walk over the cobblestones and enter.

There were flower sellers to the right of the gate, and on the other side sat an old-fashioned black hearse with a running board from the 1930s, complete with white satin curtains in the windows, the shiny fabric folded to look like waves. Then she saw the sign: A company selling prepaid funeral arrangements! Clever!

She had come this far, and this station was only one from the end anyway. She might as well investigate. You could tell a lot about a people by how they treat their dead. At least her grandmother had always said that. And besides, this would be something fun and different. She couldn't wait to tell Connie about it!

She entered the cemetery holding the single marigold. A wide paved avenue lined with tall trees led straight ahead and she walked along it for a while, admiring the lovely and ornate crypts. Here, apparently, was where the well-to-do were buried in little stone and marble houses with ornate grillwork and stained glass in the windows.

The next cross path she turned right and walked for a while down this lane. Here, crypts were interspersed with cement-covered graves, some with niches that had small statues of the Madonna imbedded within.

It was very peaceful here, far from the noise and exhaust and crowds of the city proper. Here, she could smell the flowers, hear birds singing. There were few people wandering the grounds, but she felt very safe. She reached another crossroad and turned left onto an even narrower path. Ahead she saw a main road with a number of cars parked on it, many of them the green and white Volkswagen taxis. The lead car was a hearse and she knew an interment was taking place. It wasn't far to walk and she headed that way. When she arrived, the coffin was already above the grave waiting to be lowered. The funeral had drawn a large crowd, perhaps fifty people. Mourners in black crowded around the coffin. A trumpet player played music, very lively, happy music, given that this was a somber occasion.

Mercedez kept to the sidelines, not wanting to intrude. Suddenly, the entire crowd began to sing along as the trumpeter played, and the younger ones danced. Again, the song was excessively lively, and Mercedez thought that maybe the departed had liked this tune.

She turned away and headed back up the small dirt path, encountering only a gardener clearing away branches and undergrowth.

A few more twists and turns of roads and she was in an entirely new area. Here she found crypts as well, but every so often she spotted a kind of double cellar door. The double doors must open to a below-ground burial vault. At one of the cement crypts she peered in the glass door and was startled. Inside was a long table with skeletons sitting around it! A closer examination revealed that this was staged; small paper skeletons and the table were an optical illusion, which was, in fact, just inches wide.

She marveled at all the unusual approaches to death here. Her family had forsaken the old ways. They were very Americanized and seemingly had little connection to all this. Her grandmother had, though. Her mother's mother, who died when she was just eight years old, had told her many wonderful stories of Mexico and how she had lived. And some of the stories were about death.

As she walked, Mercedez saw that one of the cellar doors was wide open. She stopped before it and peered down. Wide steps led to a room below and the sunlight showed through enough of the gloom to say that there were no coffins in view here.

She looked left and right, but apparently she was alone. Mercedez had always been adventurous. She always had wanted to taste life to the fullest. She was a risk taker, and this was just another risk. She'd do it!

She hurried down the twenty steps. At the bottom she was in a kind of marble chamber, walls left and right. Ahead she saw a light and moved toward it. The light turned out to be a candle in an adjoining room, and Mercedez found herself in a kind of stone chapel, with four rows of pews, the space awash with candlelight.

"Amazing," she whispered. "And beautiful. Who would have thought this was down here?"

"You did."

She jumped at the sound of the woman's voice and spun around.

"Don't be afraid."

"I'm not," Mercedez said.

"I'm Jennifer." The delicately beautiful pale-skinned woman who introduced herself had long light-brown hair, as shiny as the sun, that fell well below her shoulders. "And this is Manuel, my husband."

The Latino with her was slightly taller. His build was

muscular to her willowy frame. He smiled and said, "Welcome. This is our family crypt, but we invite others to visit. That's why the door is always left open."

"It's lovely down here," Mercedez said, not feeling intimidated at all. "What a beautiful concept."

"Yes, we thought so," Jennifer said. "Manuel's parents built it ten years ago. It's very peaceful down here. Sometimes the world can be so . . . violent. It's nice to have a place that's private and apart from danger."

Mercedez didn't know what to think about all that. "I guess there's a lot of violence in the world. But there are some wonderful people, too. I like to think there are more of those than the bad eggs."

"No doubt you're right, señorita," Manuel said.

Jennifer sat on the bench at the front and patted the space next to her. "Come. Sit with me. You're from the States, aren't you? We rarely get visitors from the US here."

Mercedez sat next to her. "I guess not many tourists come to cemeteries."

Up close, the girl's skin was almost luminous. Clear and paler than pale, as if she rarely got any sun. Manuel, on the other hand, looked fairly healthy and robust.

"You're special," Jennifer said. "I could feel that right away. You're not afraid of life. You like to experience things. You're a lot like how I used to be."

Mercedez laughed. "You can't be that old. You're what, twenty? Twenty-two?"

"I was twenty-one on my last birthday." She looked up. "Manuel is twenty-nine."

As Mercedez looked at him, cool gentle fingers touched her cheek, pleasant after the heat above ground. Jennifer's fingers began to stroke her hair, and then they ran down through the long strands that Mercedez had pinned up with a Spanish comb she'd bought shopping. Jennifer removed the comb and Mercedez' silky tresses flowed down her back almost to her waist.

Within moments Manuel was seated on the other side of her, touching her arm, her back, her face. Jennifer's fingers moved down inside Mercedez' dress to fondle one nipple and Manuel imitated the action with the other nipple.

Mercedez found herself reaching out to both sides of her, stroking Manuel's cock through his jeans, and Jennifer's crotch through her long dress.

Buttons were undone, zippers unzipped, fabric slid down bodies, and soon the three were naked.

On the floor lay a small Oriental-type carpet and Jennifer knelt on it, her slim, pale body with the small but jutting breasts so inviting, as if calling to Mercedez, who knelt in front of her. The two women kissed, lips sliding over lips, tongues probing mouths, hands feeling buttocks and breasts and sliding between thighs.

Mercedez felt Manuel behind her, close up against her, his hot cock nudging her buttocks. Jennifer lay back on the floor and Mercedez bent down between the white thighs and her mouth found the nether lips. She sucked and licked the sweet juices and while she did this, Manuel slid his cock into her pussy from behind. He was big and long and Mercedez moaned into the folds of sweet, vulnerable skin.

Jennifer moaned, too, her hips riding the quick-moving tongue. Manuel thrust long and deep and hard, over and over, and Mercedez left all thoughts behind as she gave herself to sensation.

Delicious tension built and Mercedez could feel it building in Jennifer and Manuel as well. His fucking made her lick and tongue-fuck Jennifer harder. The three built to a climax and came together, with moans and groans and cries of pleasure reverberating around the stone room.

They lay on the carpet resting, touching one another, laughing, and talking softly. Mercedez felt connected to these two strangers. How could it be that she had just met them and was already intimate? And in such a place? It was as if she had entered a magical realm since being in Mexico, maybe even before she came here. So many unusual, intriguing experiences had burst upon her.

But these thoughts gave way as Manuel pulled her to him on one side and Jennifer on the other. He grasped a handful of hair of both women. Mercedez knew what he wanted. She bent down and took his cock in her mouth, licking the tip, then sliding her lips over him, then up and off as his hand directed her. Then Jennifer's head lowered and her lips slid over him. When she was off, Mercedez took him into her mouth again. Then Jennifer. Once they got the rhythm going, Mercedez and Jennifer both reached across and finger-nipped one another's breasts, pulling and twisting and pinching the nipples until they were hard and red and slightly burning. Manuel slid his hands down both women's backs and his fingers inside their cunts and their anuses at the same time. Mercedez felt heat inside her in both orifices. Every part of her was being stimulated.

While Manuel finger-fucked both her and Jennifer in both holes, the two women became innovative. Jennifer took his cock to herself and Mercedez bent lower, lifting her ass high into the air, and went underneath to suck on his balls. They were hot and sweaty and she sucked on one, then the other, back and forth, feeling them grow even tauter, feeling his cum building for release. All the while she pulled on Jennifer's nipples and Jennifer pulled hers, and the fingers slid in and out both of her holes.

The room reverberated with kinetic energy; the air became dense with the scent of sex. Moans filled the room. Heat built in and around them and the explosion of three orgasms happened, again, simultaneously, just as Mercedez devilishly inserted a finger into Manuel's ass.

They lay back on the carpet again to rest and Mercedez closed her eyes briefly. Her hand slid down her sweaty torso and over her cropped bush, leaving a finger touching her clit. What a delicious feeling! Her clit was wet and slippery and her pussy hot and wet and throbbing, just like her asshole. She played with her clit, eyes closed, while two mouths took in a nipple each, nipping, sucking, pulling, twisting, and Mercedez rubbed her button making it hotter than hot until her body arched and she spasmed in orgasm.

Cool air drifted over her that she realized must be coming from the doorway. She wondered how much time had passed. How long had she been down here? "Listen, guys, how about getting something to eat and—"

But when she opened her eyes, she was alone. The stone room was the same, the carpet, the pews. The dozens of candles had burned low. Her dress, panties and purse lay on the floor by the pew, and the golden marigold rested on the seat where she had left it. But Jennifer and Manuel were gone.

"Hello?"

No answer.

"Okay. Time to go, I guess."

She dressed quickly and headed up the steps, leaving the flower behind. The sun had gone down but the sky still held some light. She pulled her hair up with one hand and inserted the comb to hold it, looking around. Nobody in the cemetery. "Just us ghosts!" she laughed.

On impulse, she lifted one of the cellar doors and there was a marker. As she read it, a chill set in. "Jennifer Lawrence Ramirez and Manuel José Roberto Ramirez. Died December 31, 2000, victims of murder."

Mercedez just stared at the plaque, unable to comprehend what she was reading.

"Señorita, the cemetery is closed. You must leave." It was a guard in uniform, with a walkie-talkie, and a gun.

"Yes, I'm sorry. I was a wandering around and got a bit lost. Can you point me to the entrance?"

"Come, I will show you."

As they walked, Mercedez, still shaken, asked, "That crypt. Jennifer and Manuel Ramirez. Do you know anything about them?"

"Oh yes, they are famous, legends in the cemetery, although everyone here has a story. She was from the United States but

I do not know where exactly, and came here to teach school. He, too, was a school teacher, who had only recently arrived from Guadalajara. They met, fell in love and married. It is said they were both beautiful to look at, and very spiritual. Their love great and strong."

"They died at the turn of the millennium."

The guard nodded. "Yes, it was a great tragedy. The story appeared in all the newspapers. Women came here and prayed. Men wept. Children tossed flowers into the crypt. His parents built the crypt for them, so that they could always be together."

"How . . . how did they die?"

They had reached the gate. The guard unlocked it and Mercedez stepped through, back into the world of the living. He stood on the other side and said, "It was through violence. The celebration of the millennium, with fireworks, and fiestas all over Mexico City. During the festivities, men fired guns into the air, as we do in Mexico. It was the most horrible tragedy. The couple were, they say, kissing, hugging close to one another. He had lain down on the grass and she on top of him. A bullet fell from the sky. It pierced her heart, then his. The newspapers say they died instantly. It was a great tragedy señorita. An accident, but a great tragedy."

"Yes," she said.

Mercedez walked to the metro and took the train back to the Reforma. She spent the entire ride trying to make sense of her experience. Had she had sex with ghosts? Could that be? Maybe she was losing her mind.

But something told her that in fact she was gaining something, not losing, although at this point she didn't know what that could be. And oddly enough, she did not feel frightened by the experience, although part of her thought she should.

In the hotel room she checked for messages, but there were none. That was disappointing. Bill was on the phone all the time, and yet somehow he couldn't find a minute to call her? She felt frustrated. Not that she wasn't having an interesting time. Still, she did miss him and wished he were here with her. Maybe she was seeing ghosts and tour guides who disappeared precisely because she was on her own when she was supposed to be on this holiday with a man who had invited her.

It was close to eight o'clock and she decided to have dinner in the hotel dining room. She wanted to be with people, living people, but she really wanted to stay here where she felt safe and comfortable and was sure that the food would be good and the service what she needed at the moment. When she came back she would have a leisurely bath, shave her legs, douche, and undertake some of the beauty regimen that she knew was good for her. What helped her to look and feel beautiful. And that, she knew, was what made her attractive to others and helped with her self-confidence. And she would also plan her day for tomorrow. No more cemeteries! Tomorrow she would do something more touristy. Yes, she would explore other parts of Mexico City. She just hoped Bill would arrive tomorrow. Or at least call and let her know when he would be joining her.

CHAPTER *5.*

Mercedez woke bright and early the next morning. She stretched luxuriously on the satin-covered king-size bed. What opulence! The elegant furnishings, the lavish appointments, all of it delightful to behold. Until she realized that the bed was so large she felt dwarfed. If only she had someone in it with her. What a great bed for fucking!

She sighed and sat up. The room was filled with golden light from the sun. She snatched up her satin robe and walked to the window, moving the sheer curtain aside. Below the traffic was wild west again, as it must be every day here. Bumper to bumper chaos but somehow it kept moving. It was like looking down on an ant hill; tiny individual beings that moved with little or no rhyme or reason yet somehow the larger picture conveyed some sort of intelligence.

She ordered room service, coffee, and toast, which she ate with just a little cherry marmalade spread thinly on top. Then she showered and dressed in another sundress, the fabric splashed as if buckets of paint had fallen on it. She wore her espadrilles again, thinking she'd be doing a lot of walking today. She was bound and determined that she would enjoy the city, even if she was alone.

Just before she left the room she checked for messages. There were none. Deflated, she felt angry at the same time. This was no way to treat her! Surely Bill could have found three minutes to call and leave her a message, even if he didn't have time to talk!

At the reception, she handed the concierge a card for Pedro the cab driver. He phoned and Pedro was at the front of the hotel in less than five minutes.

Anger fueled her and she strode from the hotel, her long legs moving her quickly to the curb. Pedro hopped out and opened the door for her and she slid into the back seat.

"Buenos días, señorita! How are you this fine morning?"

"Well. And you?"

"Sí, I am well also. The sun is shining, music is playing, and I have a lovely señorita in my taxi. Who could not be well?"

Mercedez laughed, and her mood lightened.

"El destino?"

"Well, there are so many things to see here. What is Mexico City famous for?"

"Oh, too many places to name. You can go to shopping, to museums, to visit the zoo. . . . Mexico City is the capital of the country. This was the center of the Aztec empire, you know. We are the world's largest city. Here you will find culture, finance, nightlife. You can do anything."

"I'd like to go to a museum," she said tentatively. "Are there many?"

"Sí, señorita. La Museo de Arte Moderno, La Museo Nacional de Antropología—"

"That last one would be good. The anthropology museum. And shopping. I'd like to buy some good Mexican crafts."

"There is also la Basílica de Guadalupe. We are famous for this. The shrine of the virgin."

"OK, let's do all that. We'll start with the Basílica then shopping, then lunch and I'll go to a museum or two in the afternoon."

"Al-right!" Pedro said, imitating what he must have seen on American TV.

He cranked up the music on the radio and they sped through the traffic. Mercedez watched the lively street scenes all around her. So many people! Crowds didn't seem to bother them. She liked her space and didn't think she could last here long.

"What's that?

"Here is Zócalo. It is thirteen acres. What you call a 'town square,' the biggest in Latin America. The famous Montezuma had a palace that stood on this very spot. Most of these mansions and the public buildings you see are many hundreds of years old, built with the stones of Aztec temples that the Spaniards destroyed when they came."

They drove down tree-lined avenues with parks here and there, enormous sculpted fountains shooting water high into the air. Mercedez felt entranced by the beauty surrounding her.

"What's that song?" she asked, listening to the music on the radio. It was a classic Mexican sound but the words were harsh.

"They call this *narco corrido*. They are Mexico's forbidden songs. Ballads."

"Ballads? The lyrics are pretty violent."

"This is Mexican hip-hop. The songs are modern, about drugs and guns and guerrillas. I can change the channel if you like."

"No. That's okay. I want to get a good feel for Mexico."

"Your people come from here?"

"My father was from somewhere around Mexico City. I'm not sure where. My mother was born in Oaxaca but her mother and father moved to Texas when she was one. I was born there."

"Ah!" he said, nodding his head knowingly.

As they drove, Pedro pointed out some sites: The Palace of Fine Arts, the Metropolitan Cathedral, and many statues and monuments to Mexico's countless fights for freedom.

"We have arrived!" Pedro said, and Mercedez got out of the taxi.

She stood before a mansion but the sign out front said it was a mercado. "Will you come back for me in one hour?" she asked.

"Sí, señorita. I will wait right on this spot."

With that, he drove away, weaving skillfully through the traffic.

Mercedez entered the elaborate building and immediately the hubbub of the seemingly endless number of shops overwhelmed her. This was not like any Mexican mercado she had been to before. The closest was in San Antonio, and that was tiny compared to this. A sign said there were six floors of shopping available.

She moved through the aisles with tables and carts selling everything imaginable. Next to a stall of plastic buckets was an antique dealer with lovely vintage cameos and lockets. She inquired about prices and selected a locket for her mother and a tie pin for her dad.

Many shops sold clothing, the range going from designer knockoffs to traditional Mexican ponchos. And then there were the tiny skeletal figures. She knew these from the mercados in the United States. These Día de los Muertos skeletons were for the upcoming holiday, Day of the Dead, when the entire country would celebrate. Her grandmother had told her something of the holiday, but seeing it here in its home would be wonderful.

She spotted a skeleton that reminded her of Connie and bought it instantly. Then another of a couple with their little girl, and she had to buy that for Connie, too! Then there were sexy skeletons, lady skeletons in low-cut gowns or short skirts, men in formal dress. Several skeleton couples were engaged in "the act" and she bought several of those, in various positions, thinking these would be fun to display along her bookcase at home. A kind of Mexican Kama Sutra!

She looked for one that Bill might like, but none seemed to represent him. And then she saw a Muertos figure with a cell phone at his ear. "I'll take that one, too," she told the proprietor of the shop.

The floor above had more of the same, and she felt tempted to purchase a mirror, the frame of hammered tin, but carrying it around would be burdensome, and she doubted she could get it home without breaking the glass. No need to invite seven years bad luck!

One curious booth had a woman selling candles in glass jars. The colors were lovely. Most of the jars had an image on the front, usually of a religious person. One had the ubiquitous skeleton, and the woman picked up that jar and said to Mercedez, "This one, you must have this one, señorita."

Mercedez laughed and lifted her shopping bag. "I've got a whole bunch of skeletons in here."

"This you must have!" the woman insisted.

"How much?" Mercedez inquired, not really wanting to buy it, but maybe she could just get away by saying it was too expensive.

"Ten pesos."

"I—I don't think I want—"

"Señorita!" The woman stopped moving and stared at her, then crossed herself. "You risk too much. You must burn this on the second night of el Día de los Muertos. It is all that will save you."

Mercedez sighed. Ever since she had arrived in Corpus Christi, everyone had been warning her about everything! This was getting to be too much!

As she turned to go, the woman shoved the glass with the candle at her. "Take it. Even if you do not pay the small sum. I cannot allow you to leave without this. I must do what I can."

"Oh, alright!" Mercedez snapped. She pulled ten pesos from her purse and gave them to the woman, then shoved the candle into her shopping bag.

Her mood had shifted a bit. An hour had almost passed and she headed outside, hoping that Pedro was waiting. He was, and once she entered the taxi, they drove off immediately.

She sat back and closed her eyes, a bit upset by the encounter.

"Did you enjoy yourself?" Pedro asked.

"For a while."

"Here. I know what you will like." He changed stations and a lively Mexican *rocnrol* song came on. "Is familiar, sí?"

The music began to invade Mercedez' dark mood and she found herself tapping her toe and bobbing her head at the familiar Beatles-like tune, with a Mexican spin. Listening to the Beatles, riding in a Beetle, suddenly she felt light again.

They arrived at the Basílica, and Pedro was already saying "This is the new Basílica, constructed between 1974 and 1976 when the original old church from the sixteenth century began to crumble. This shrine is considered the holiest in the western hemisphere."

Surrounding the church was a virtual mercado of vendors selling religious scapulas, plastic holy water bottles shaped like the Virgin of Guadalupe, glow-in-the-dark rosary beads, candles, and all types of objects for the faithful.

Mercedez asked Pedro to wait for her. The path to the building was long and a special paved section that led to the door was for devotees, who crawled along on hands and knees. She reached the church and entered. The building was circular and the shrine to the virgin who wore multicolored robes could be seen from any position. The building was too new to have much charm, but she was impressed by the seven-foot doors.

As she left, she purchased a small statue of the Virgin of Guadalupe for her mother.

"What's next?" Pedro asked.

"Lunch, I guess. Do you know of a quiet café with good food? Maybe on the way to the museum?"

"Sí, señorita," and he drove along at a good clip.

Mercedez was feeling low again. It wasn't so much that she still felt bad about what happened at the mercado. It was more that she felt lonely. She should be seeing these things with Bill. Or with someone.

"Señorita, may I ask you a question?" Pedro said.

"Yes, of course."

"Why is it that a woman as beautiful as you has come to Mexico City all alone? I do not understand this."

"Pedro, I don't really understand it myself." She gave him a little smile as he looked at her in the rearview.

Suddenly she said, "Pedro, would you join me for lunch? I'd love to buy you lunch and talk with you. If you don't mind."

He stared at her for a moment then said in a serious voice, "Señorita, you flatter me. I am old enough to be your grandfather. If you still want to share food with me—"

"Food, Pedro, food!" she laughed. "Will you join me?"

"Sí, señorita!" He grinned and began singing along to the mariachi music on the radio.

He parked about one block from the Museo Nacional de Antropología, which she saw as they passed. The café's little tables were shaded by tall palms, and the tops of the tables were ceramic mosaics with an Aztec design.

Mercedez ordered a salad and a glass of fruit juice. Pedro had a plate of enchiladas and beer.

Somehow, sitting here with Pedro was very relaxing. She felt no real attraction to this man, at least not a sexual one, but he made her feel protected somehow.

"You know, Pedro, I really don't know my roots. Being in Mexico is kindling some sort of memory for me, not so much of anything I've experienced, but more as if I have an ancestry that's calling to me."

"Sí," he said, nodding, as if this were the most normal thing in the world to say.

"It's not as if I had a plan to come here. It just . . . happened. But now that I'm here, so many wonderful, even magical things have happened to me . . . I don't know what to think."

"Señorita, Mexico is a magical country. The land and the people are old. The blood of the people has saturated the soil so many times, we cannot be separated from our land and the land cannot be removed from us. It is good that you have returned."

She nodded and had a forkful of salad.

"Señorita, you still did not answer me. I cannot make sense of you being here alone. Do you not have a husband?"

"Well, there's a guy I'm traveling with. Sort of. He's in Cancun on business. He'll join me here . . . soon," but even as she said it, she didn't feel sure of when Bill would be with her.

"He is a fool!" Pedro declared. And Mercedez laughed. "A woman such as you should not be alone for one hour. You are beautiful, intelligent, a pleasant personality. What kind of man leaves such a woman alone?"

She didn't have an answer.

After lunch she excused herself to go to the washroom. When she came out and saw the public telephone, she made a call to the hotel to see if Bill had left her a message. Nothing. A small sadness engulfed her. How could he be so callous? Didn't he care at all? He was paying for this entire trip and yet he had abandoned her. She could understand him being busy with work, but no one was so busy they couldn't make a phone call! Unless something happened to him. That thought hadn't occurred to her until just now. Maybe she should try to phone him at the hotel in Cancun. She would do that when she got back to the hotel, if there was no message. Maybe something happened and he couldn't call her.

When she returned to the table she paid the bill and Pedro drove her to the entrance of the museum, a low, modern building. "What time shall I return for you, señorita?"

"Um, maybe two hours? That should be enough time to see most of the museum."

When Pedro left she entered the building, paid the entrance fee and picked up a brochure. Right by the entrance stood a small shop and she decided to see that first, even though it was a backward approach.

The shop had the usual assortment of Aztec T-shirts and oven mitts, books about the pre-Hispanic indigenous cultures, maps of the ruins around the country, ceramic tiles with Aztec and Mayan designs. Things she had seen elsewhere, or variations, but the quality was better here. Then she noticed tint boats in one glass case, multicolored, that reminded her of canoes. Each had a small skeletal figure sitting in each boat holding a paddle. She was fascinated by the figures and asked the price.

"They are eighty US dollars each," the girl said. "These are pieces of art created by Hernando Luis Martinez, one of our most talented artists, and there were just ten made. These are all that are left. He creates something special every year for el Día de los Muertos."

"They're amazing, aren't they?" came a sultry male voice from behind her.

Mercedez turned to see a startlingly handsome man with black hair and brown eyes, and skin with a slight tan. "Yes," she said. "I haven't seen anything like them."

"And you won't. Martinez is a one-of-a-kind artist. Nothing mass produced."

"You know his work then?"

"Pretty much. I come here for four months every year to work at the museum and I've gotten to know some of the country's artists, because of the displays at the shop here."

"Where are you from?" Mercedez asked.

"Canada. I divide my time between Toronto and here."

At first Mercedez had thought that he must work in the shop, but no sales clerk she had ever met split their work life between two countries.

"What type of work do you do?" she asked.

"I'm an archeology professor. I teach courses at the University of Toronto on Aztec and Mayan cultures, and come here to Mexico City to work at the museo, studying new artifacts that have been unearthed."

"Wow. That sounds fascinating."

"Oh, it's not glamour work. It takes forever to analyze a shard of pottery, or a fragment of bone. Still, sometimes we get amazing finds and then it's as if a whole toy box has opened up to me. Say, my name is Hugh. Hugh here in Mexico."

She laughed and as they shook hands said, "Mercedez. Here, there, and everywhere."

"Like the car?"

"With a 'z.'"

"Got it. So, have you been to the Museo Nacional de Antropología before?"

"No. I've never even been to Mexico City before. I'm from Corpus Christi, Texas, and just visiting. Where's a good place to start?" She held out the map of the galleries to him and he took her arm.

"Let me show you around."

"Oh, I couldn't do that! You're busy. You have work to do."

"I'm actually finished for the day. Our shipment just arrived and needs to be unloaded before I can do anything else. Come, let me show you the artifacts. If you'd like me to, of course."

"Would I ever!" she sang.

Mercedez couldn't believe her luck. Not only was Hugh a

nice man, and very handsome and sexy, but he knew all about the exhibits. She would get a tour most people couldn't even pay for!

Mercedez spent the next hours with Hugh, learning about the Aztec and Mayan cultures, their history, and the rise and spread of the Toltec warriors. The interior of the museum allowed them to move back and forth across the open hall and examine artifacts placed in settings that replicated the past.

She examined pottery, weapons, clothing, seeds, and even a few remains in the form of bones and skulls. Hugh interwove the connections between the various peoples who lived in Mexico from the earliest days when they were simple nomadic hunters through the glory days of the Mayan, Olmecs, Zapotecs, and Aztec empires. She learned how the conquistadors traveled from Spain to investigate and conquer the new world, gathering land to expand Spain's rule. In 1519, Hernando Cortés conquered the Aztec Empire and by 1520 Francisco Fernández de Córdoba and Juan de Gryalva were exploring the coasts of the Yucatán and the Gulf of Mexico.

"Did you know that by 1525 the Spaniards were in your home state, Texas, as well as all across northern Mexico?"

"No, I did not know that!" Mercedez said. "In fact, there's a lot I didn't know."

She looked at Hugh with admiration. "This is great. But you know, I'm descended from the Mayans. Did they get conquered, too?"

"Yes, and no. The Mayans excelled in sciences and mathematics. They were way ahead of the Europeans on that score.

And they were very good at recording their history. There are stone glyphs, and the Pop Wuj book."

"What's that?"

"It's a book written by the Mayans in the sixteenth century. The priests were desperate to preserve their culture and history during the Spanish onslaught. It's probably why the Mayan descendants still dominate the Yucatán today."

As they walked out of the gallery, Mercedez noticed that the sun had gone down, and the sky was just growing dark. She looked around. "We're the only people in here!"

Hugh laughed. "Well, the museum closed about two hours ago."

"You're kidding?"

"I am not."

"Oh, gee, I forgot I asked my taxi guy to pick me up at . . ." she checked the time on her cell phone ". . . uh, well about three hours ago."

"Don't worry about it. He probably realized you were still in here."

Mercedez hurried to the door. There sat the little green and white taxi, with Pedro napping behind the wheel.

"Well, he's still there. I guess I owe him a fortune."

Hugh laughed. "Listen, how about if we send him home for the day and you and I have dinner together."

"I'm not dressed for dinner," she said, looking down at her skimpy sun dress.

"You're wearing clothes, aren't you? Listen, come to my place, I'll make dinner and we can relax. What do you say? I'm a pretty good cook."

"Well . . . Let me call the hotel first."

"Sure."

"My cell doesn't work in Mexico."

He laughed. "You can use mine. It doesn't work outside of Mexico."

Mercedez found the hotel number and called. Bill might have been trying to reach her. Or maybe he was at the hotel waiting. "No," the desk clerk told her, "he hasn't checked in yet. And there are no telephone or written messages."

What was the point of going back to the hotel and spending the evening alone, dining alone, having a drink alone in the bar?

"All set?" Hugh said as she came back to the front door.

"Yes. I'm ready. I'm looking forward to some fine cuisine."

"Oh," he said, "you won't be disappointed. If I hadn't become an archeologist, I'd be a chef! And look, we can take your taxi. I never drive to work. The traffic here is insane. Have you noticed?"

Outside they had to wake Pedro from his deep sleep. Mercedez and Hugh slid into the back seat and for a moment Pedro looked startled and Mercedez felt she had to say something.

"Pedro, this is my new friend Hugh. He's an anthropologist, working at the museum each year for a few months. Hugh, this is Pedro, best taxi driver in the city."

Pedro turned and the two men made eye contact, Pedro looking suspicious for a moment, but then he put out his hand and they shook Mexican fashion. Pedro also nodded, as if in approval.

"Okay, señorita. El destino?"

Mercedez turned to Hugh and he gave the address. Pedro started the car. The radio was blaring and he pulled into traffic, singing along, a happy song that made Mercedez smile.

When they reached Hugh's place, a lovely block, a group of four haciendas circled by a pebbly driveway edged with brilliant flowers, Mercedez paid Pedro for the ride and the wait, handing over several hundred pesos.

"Señorita, what is this for?" Pedro asked.

"Because you waited for me."

"But, it was my pleasure! And my responsibility. You are, or were, a woman alone in Mexico City. You must be protected."

Mercedez smiled. "Pedro, are you married?"

"But of course. With three children. Well, teenagers now." He stroked his white hair.

"Then take this. Buy your wife flowers. And your children something special. Please. It would make me happy."

He paused for a moment, and then nodded. "Sí, señorita. I knew I was correct all along. You are a special woman." He bent his head down so he could see Hugh through the window. "And you will see her home safely?" It was more of a demand than a question.

"Sí," Hugh said.

"Alright." Pedro took the money and pocketed it. "Now I will go home to sleep. But first, flowers!"

Hugh led Mercedez inside a lovely apartment, furnished in Spanish modern. A large and lazy looking striped cat stretched itself as they entered, then, in her own time, got up and walked to Hugh and rubbed against his leg.

"Barbara," he said to the cat, "this is Mercedez."

The cat looked up at Mercedez as if she understood. Mercedez loved cats. "I used to have a cat when I was a child," she said, bending to pet Barbara, who eagerly came to her.

"Wine?" Hugh asked.

"That would be wonderful."

"Red or white? Or rosé if you prefer?"

"I like white."

"Me, too."

While Hugh made a pasta dish with Mexican salsa and artichokes, stir-fried, they talked.

"So how did you decide to become an anthropologist?"

"I fell into it naturally. I was interested in my heritage."

"Then why didn't you study Canadian history."

"My Mexican heritage."

"You're Mexican?"

"Aztec ancestry. My father was from here, my mother from Ireland, they met in Montréal, and I live in Toronto most of the year, and Mexico City for some of the year." He laughed. "An international mish-mash. Anyway, Mexico's history has always fascinated me and it was natural that I wanted to study cultures here. I'm a cultural anthologist, but really, I'm pretty broad-based in my interests. And you?"

"Me, well, I've done a lot of things, including going to school for photography. I'm inclined toward the arts and I guess you'd say I'm still a dabbler. I like to do so many things and I'm not sure which discipline I want to commit to for the long-term."

"It's good not to lock yourself into anything until you're

sure. I have friends who regret their career choice. And even their choice in a spouse. Speaking of spouses, do you have one?"

"No. Not really. I was married but it didn't work out. I met a guy in Texas and I'm only here because of him. He wanted to bring me along on this trip but so far I've spent more time alone than with him. He's still in Cancun. I've only known him a few days, so it's nothing serious—he's a friend of my brother-in-law's, a coworker."

"Ah," Hugh said. "Well, spouses are hard to get and harder still to hold onto. I had one. She died in a car accident five years ago."

"Oh, I'm so sorry!"

"It's been a while. Life goes on. I can't say I've forgotten her, but I'm not stuck in the past. I'm open. It's just that nobody else has come along that has really interested me." He looked at her over the candlelight as they sat at the table.

For a while they both dug into the pasta and salads. "This is great!" Mercedez said. "You really do know how to cook."

"Told you!"

Once dinner was over, they sat together on a hammocklike swing, on the enclosed terrace, surrounded by mosquito netting, and sipped tequila. Around them, Mercedez heard the call of a bird reverberate through the silent night. "Sitting here, I'd never believe I was in Mexico City. It's so quiet and peaceful."

Hugh slipped his arm around her shoulder. "You know, Mercedez, you're a lovely girl. Smart. Beautiful. Intelligent."

She laughed. "You're the second man who has said that about me today."

He looked surprised.

"The other was Pedro."

They both laughed. The laughter faded as they drew closer. She could smell his scent, not just the aftershave, but the maleness of him. Their lips met, first tentatively, then with more intention. She placed her hands on his chest and slid one beneath the Mexican cowboy shirt he had changed into. His arm that surrounded her pulled her close and his other hand moved up and down her arm, then her body, sliding over her curves, rising and falling, and back again.

Mercedez felt so excited by him. It had been a long time since a man excited her in such an emotional way.

Hot kisses on the lips, then the neck, the chest, his hand slipped down her dress and his mouth found her breast.

All the while she unzipped his jeans and her fingers wormed their way inside the opening. He didn't wear underwear! She found that really sexy!

The warmth of the evening surrounded them and her flesh felt caressed by the air as well as his hands. Suddenly he stood and reached out a hand. She took it and he pulled her to her feet and led her inside to his bed.

They stood beside the bed kissing, fondling one another, stripping off the remainder of their clothing. Somewhere along the way they fell onto the bed, but Mercedez didn't remember exactly when.

They moved as a unit, it seemed, sliding around until her mouth faced his cock, and his lips met her pussy. She took him in, the full length, and his mouth loved her clit, that was clear. He made her burn, and she made him hard as a rock.

When they both were panting, they turned again, simultaneously, without spoken words to direct the action, and faced one another. He lifted her hip over his thigh and slid down so he could penetrate her with his cock. She came instantly as the hard hot flesh slid deep into her wetness.

He stayed inside her, not moving for a moment while she shuddered, then they kissed more, their passion building again. This time he fucked her hard and fast and she was breathless. His rod was on fire inside her and he had the energy of a god, stoking her fire until she built again and the flames overwhelmed her, with only his hot liquid shooting from his hard cock to quench them.

They fell asleep uncovered, holding one another, Barbara curled at their feet, as the Mexican night closed in on and enfolded them.

CHAPTER 6.

*T*hey awoke leisurely, snuggling and cuddling in bed that turned into soft and sweetly satisfying sex. Afterward, Hugh made Mexican eggs with refritos on the side, strong coffee with rich cream, and toast. They dined with the large window open facing the lush courtyard.

"It's so amazingly beautiful here," Mercedez said. "I'd love to live in a place like this."

"Well, you can rent this one for eight months if you like."

"What do you mean?"

"Like I said yesterday, I head back to Toronto for eight months, and then I'm back here next fall."

Mercedez felt a lump in her throat. Finally she had met a

nice man, a decent man, and they seemed to click. And now he would be leaving soon!

"So, when do you fly back?" she asked, trying to sound casual.

"Actually, later in the day tomorrow. I was hoping we might spend some more time together tomorrow before I go." He reached over and took her hand. "I like you, Mercedez. You're a special girl."

"I like you, too," she admitted.

"Well, let's hang out today and tomorrow, okay with you?"

"Sounds good." But even as she said it, she was trying to prepare herself mentally and emotionally for ending something good that was just beginning.

After breakfast, they took a swim in the pool. Hugh assured her that all of the eight apartments had tenants who worked at high-powered jobs, and none of them would be around to see them swim naked—and most of the tenants swam naked from time to time anyway.

Sunlight glinted off the water as she crouched at the edge of the pool and ran her hand through the warm liquid. She dove in, feeling the water glide along her skin as she submerged herself fully.

A second later Hugh joined her, also naked. They met underwater, facing one another, and their arms opened simultaneously and their lips met.

They floated to the surface and only broke apart for air. Slowly, both of them laughing, Hugh backed her into the corner of the pool. Suddenly he slipped under the water and when he came up again it was close against her body, and his penis entered her from underneath, deep.

Mercedez gasped. She held the edges of the pool and propped herself up so he could thrust up into her.

"Don't want me to drown?" he asked when she lifted herself higher.

"Not until you're finished!" They both laughed, eyes sparkling.

She loved the feel of him inside her. Her body shook with the tension of holding herself up while being impaled. Her nipples hovered at the surface of the water as her breasts bounced up and down. "Yes!" she cried as he moved faster.

"Oh, please, fuck me!" She rarely called out when she was having sex, and she felt thoroughly shameless in her wantonness. His cock was so big, so long, and thick enough that it rode her walls. His movements were precise. Determined. But creative. She couldn't get enough of him.

And when they came together, their mouths met and their cries entered one another.

Afterward they lay on lounge chairs by the pool letting the sun dry their bare skin. Hugh reached out and grasped her hand. She looked over. His eyes were closed but he brought her hand to his smiling lips and kissed her palm.

They had been in the sun for about thirty minutes, luxuriating in the warmth of the day, when Hugh asked, "Would you like to go somewhere for lunch? I know a great little restaurant that serves serious Mexican cuisine. Not the fast food tacos, but the real haute cuisine of Mexico."

"Sounds great, but I really need to go back to the hotel and shower and change my clothes."

"Well, let's make it dinner, then. Alright with you?"

"Yes, absolutely."

"Good. And bring a change of clothes so you can stay here tonight. That is, if you'd like to."

"I would like to."

They both laughed and hugged and their lips met, building warmth and romance into desire just inside his front door. Soon they were on the floor, fucking, hard this time, full of energy and hunger as if both of them had gone without great sex for a long, long time.

She got onto her hands and knees and he knelt behind her, thrusting into her doggie-style. She bent her head to the floor, savoring the deep penetration, the long hard cock rubbing the flesh inside her until it swelled deliciously and pulsed in time with the thrusts and they came together once again, his cock plowing deep and staying there.

It was four in the afternoon before she arrived at the hotel. Pedro had picked her up when she phoned, and the moment she entered the taxi he said, "Ah, señorita, you look much happier, more alive than you did yesterday. I am happy for you."

"Pedro, you're a dear," she told him. "Did your wife like the flowers?"

He turned and grinned at her wickedly. "Sí, señorita," and Mercedez laughed.

She rushed up to the room, pulling her clothes off as she went, and stopped suddenly when she saw the bag on the bed. Then she heard Bill's voice on his cell. Apparently he hadn't heard her come in.

"Honey, come on, I phone as often as I can. I'm busy down here. No, it's all work, no play. No, I'm in meetings all the time."

Mercedez held her breath. Clearly he was talking with a woman, and it sounded as if they were intimate. She didn't know if she should keep listening, or if she should make a noise and let him know she was there.

She didn't have to decide because suddenly Bill walked into the room, the cell still at his ear. He looked a little startled to see her, or maybe she imagined that. But he smiled and held up one finger, telling her she should wait, he wouldn't be long.

He turned and walked to the balcony and went outside, closing the door behind him.

Mercedez threw her purse on the bed. She felt awful. Of course, he had a right to be with anyone he liked, since they weren't lovers, just "fuck friends." Still, that he was on the phone with another woman while in *their* hotel room, that bothered her. She knew she was being grossly unfair. Hadn't she just come from Hugh's place? This arrangement was so odd. She and Bill were supposed to both be free, but somehow the freedom didn't sit quite right with her. And yet she had to admit that between the two of them, she preferred being with Hugh. Yet she liked Bill, and did feel he had been inordinately generous and kind to her. It was all very confusing and she decided to have a Jacuzzi to relax her nerves.

She ran water in the tub and when it was the right temperature, she immersed herself in it, sliding down as the bubbles from the jets rushed against her muscles. She put her head back and closed her eyes, letting her breasts bob on the surface. There was no point worrying about all this. Hugh was leaving. She and Bill would part company in a few days. She would just try to relax and have a good time for the remaining days here. But it nagged at her that she had a dinner date with Hugh, and had promised to spend time with him tomorrow. How could she do that? Would Bill mind? If he minded it would bother her and if he didn't it would bother her. It was all so confusing!

Suddenly she felt the water slosh forward and opened her eyes. Bill, naked, was sinking down into the Jacuzzi next to her. He slipped an arm around her shoulders and planted a big kiss on her lips, sliding his tongue in deep. Meanwhile, his other hand felt for her breast under the surface and played with her nipple.

When they broke apart, he smiled at her. "Miss me?"

"I did. For a while. But you were gone so long."

He removed his arm. "What is it with women? I told you I have work to do here. Believe me, if I could just play, I would."

"I'm sorry," she said. He really did have work, she knew that.

He glanced at her and his face relaxed. "Come here," he said, and she moved on top of him. They kissed and soon her hand fondled his cock until he lifted her up to sit on him as their lips played.

Suddenly his cell phone rang.

"Damn!" He broke away and picked it up from where he'd left it on the floor near the Jacuzzi. He looked at the number then placed a finger over his lips indicating Mercedez should be silent.

"Yes?" He listened, and Mercedez thought she could hear a voice coming through that sounded female. "Of course! Don't be silly!"

His tone altered to one of mild annoyance. He lifted himself out of the tub. "Having a bath."

He grabbed a towel from the rack and half wrapped it around his hips as he headed for the door.

Mercedez splashed water loudly and hit the restart button for the Jacuzzi.

Bill hurried out the door and closed it behind him, Mercedez thought, *to block the noise.*

"This is ridiculous!" she said aloud. Here she was, pretending to be invisible. What was it with this guy?

She washed herself and headed to the shower to rinse off. It took time to dry her hair and apply some makeup, but there was no sound from the other room. Eventually she opened the bathroom door and stepped into the bedroom. He wasn't there. She went into the living room and checked the balcony door. He didn't seem to be in the room anywhere. She found the wet towel on the floor and a note on the table. "Gotta go. Catch you later. Love, Bill"

Mercedez ripped it in two. What kind of a man can't stick his head into the bathroom and let her know he's leaving? Was she supposed to wait around the rest of the day for him? When was "later"?

She took her time and dressed well, in one of the new outfits she'd bought, and then called Hugh. "Hey, I'm ready. Are you ready?"

"Always! Want me to pick you up?"

"No. Just give me the address and I'll meet you there."

"How about drinks first, then dinner? There's a nice bar on the same street."

"Sounds good."

Mercedez scribbled a note to Bill. "Had to go also. Later.

M." She didn't write the word "love" because she wasn't feeling it at all. She was feeling angry. Abused in some way. Maybe she wasn't cut out for casual relationships. Maybe she liked to have deep intimate sex with a man she could get close to.

Well, even if she did, so what? Right now she had two men who were in various stages of leaving. Bill, she suspected, had someone else. Hugh, well, she didn't really know him yet. Either way, it left little for her but the moment, so she might as well enjoy it.

The bar, el Lagarto Loco—The Crazy Lizard—was decked out in Day of the Dead décor, glittery tin and wood bobbing skeletons, sugar skulls, colorful tissue paper cut into the shape of grinning skulls and draped around the room like crepe paper at a child's birthday party. The clientele was a mixture of well-heeled Mexicans and tourists.

Hugh spotted her and stood up from the crowded bar and waved her over. Once she had squeezed past the dozens of patrons between them, he reached out to pull her the last few feet, into his arms. He kissed her long and hard, as if they hadn't seen one another in a year. It was nice.

"What would you like?" he asked her above the din.

"How about a margarita. Strawberry."

"You got it!"

Hugh ordered and they sat on bar stools listening to the lively mariachi music from the three-man combo at one end of the room, and trying to talk above the noise.

"How was your day?" he asked her.

"Good. You?"

"Fine. I went into the museum and the shipment still hasn't

been unloaded, so I guess I won't get a look until next year. I finished up a few things so I have all day tomorrow free, from about noon on."

Mercedez felt a bit ill at ease. She didn't know what to say. Surely Bill would be expecting to spend time with her, too. Did she owe allegiance to either of these men?

"These are wacky decorations," she said, changing the subject to something safer. "I used to see things like this in Corpus Christi but my family didn't participate in the Day of the Dead."

"You should check it out while you're here," Hugh told her. "It's a holiday like none anywhere else on the planet and its history goes back to the Aztec and Mayans and their rituals. It was Christianized, of course, tied in with saints along the way when the conquistadors came here, but the roots are still pure native. But, you know, Mexico City isn't the place for it. If you get a chance, go somewhere smaller, where they still celebrate it fully."

"Like where?"

"Guanajuato isn't far from here. And Oaxaca."

"Oaxaca. That's where my mother's from!"

"See! Is your dad from there, too?"

"No, he's from around Mexico City, but I don't know the town."

"Maybe he's descended from the Aztecs. That would give you a lot of strong blood!"

"Strong and hot!" she said, and they both laughed.

They left after one oversized drink, and walked a block to a chic little restaurante that had a tiny layered sign that read *el pirámide* on the door.

"What is this place?" she asked.

"It's a secret," Hugh grinned, and winked at her.

Once they entered and were seated at a small table in a hidden cove, she looked around at the cute interior. "It's like we're on top of a pyramid!" she said, laughing. "I just did this, in Chichén Itzá!"

"Exactly like we're on top of a pyramid. They have it down pretty good."

She could see the view "below" as they sat at a table by a Choc Mool, head turned in their direction. The grassy fields were just like Chichén Itzá; they were seated on a clear glass platform and the "view" was the basement. Every floor of the five in the restaurant was made of glass. "This is very nice. And unusual. What a great concept!"

"The food is good, too. I recommend the el pollo en el chocolate."

"Chicken in chocolate? Is that a meal?"

"Yes, and a very good one, in honor of the Choc Mool!" He waved a hand at the statue. "The chicken is coated in rich chocolate and baked until the skin is almost black and crackly. The meat is the most tender you'll ever eat. I can almost guarantee it. Do you eat chicken?"

"Yes, I do. Okay, I'll have that!"

Hugh ordered Mexican wine which was surprisingly good and they lingered over the meal—"This chicken is amazing!" she admitted—talking about his work, the culture past and present in Mexico, what they liked to do in their downtime, the courses Mercedez had taken, and the ones she still hoped to take, about Los Angeles where she lived, and about

Toronto, where he lived. "You should come up and visit me," he told her. "You're welcome any time."

Normally she wouldn't have been so straightforward, but these were extenuating circumstances. And she really did like Hugh. "So, is there a Mrs. Hugh?"

He laughed. "My last name is Murphy. Strange, huh, for a half Aztec guy. And no, there's no Mrs. Hugh or Mrs. Murphy. And I know what you're thinking: this guy is thirty-three years old, well-heeled, handsome, debonair"—they both laughed—"and he's never been married. Why?"

"Maybe he's gay," Mercedez said, getting into the game.

"Do you think his hairstyle is that good?" Hugh asked with a raised eyebrow.

"Well, yes, but he doesn't act gay, if you catch my drift."

Hugh nodded.

"But he could be a serial killer."

"Uh, he's too crazy, I think. And not nearly organized enough."

"He's good with knives, though. I've seen him. But maybe you're right," she said. "But is he a control freak?"

"Could be. Most men are. Would you hold that against him?"

"Probably not. Do you think he's a confirmed bachelor?"

"I doubt it," he said. "More likely, he hasn't met the right woman yet. At least until now."

The waiter came by to ask if they wanted dessert. Mercedez ordered a fresh fruit salad and Hugh had a coffee with Triple Sec.

"This was so good. I haven't had such a great meal in a while, although I did have some terrific fish in Cancun."

"Well, that's the place for fish, by the ocean. So, tell me about this guy you're traveling with."

Mercedez shifted uncomfortably. "Like I said, he works with my brother-in-law. He said he was coming here on the company expense account and offered me a chance to travel in Mexico with him. He's got the best accommodation, and has footed the bill for everything. He's a nice man."

"Are you sleeping with him?"

Mercedez head snapped up and their eyes met. "I did. I'm not sure about now, though. He didn't want anything more and neither did I."

She didn't like how this was making her sound, as if she was some kind of gold digger, traveling on Bill's dime, fucking him so he'd pay for things. That's not how it was, how she saw it, and especially now that she'd met Hugh, she didn't know how to translate it for him.

"You know, it's not a complicated thing. I had some time. He's a nice man. We hit it off in some ways, and he's basically busy with his business, so I get to just hang out. We've had sex, but it isn't serious at all."

"Hey, you don't need to justify yourself to me."

"Are you sure? I have the feeling you asked for a reason."

"No, just curious. Besides, I told you this guy we were discussing is probably a control freak!"

They both laughed, breaking the tension.

"Listen, do you like to dance?" he asked.

"Do I? Dancing R US! And I'm pretty good at it, they tell me. I've won a few competitions."

"Great! There's a Latino club near my place."

Mercedez began feeling uncomfortable. She wanted to go dancing. And she wanted to go to his place. But she really wasn't sure she could just cut out on Bill like this for the entire night.

"Let me make a call first," she said.

"Here, use my cell." He handed it over and she searched in her purse for the number of the hotel, asking for her room. It rang and rang. No answer. She didn't bother to leave a message.

"Alright, let's dance!" she said.

El club de salsa was jammed. The lively music filled her with its enchanting rhythms, like the shining sun, and they took only a moment to find a table then Mercedez jumped up with Hugh on her heels and they headed to the dance floor, caught up in the magic of the soul sound. They spun together. Hugh caught her about the waist and she threw back her head, raised her arm above her, and bent one knee so that her shoe touched her thigh. Hugh was a great dancer, and his body knew the Latin rhythms well. Mercedez loved this type of dancing, and they were on the floor for at least an hour before taking a break.

"Wow!" she said at the table, plunking down. He ordered tequila for both of them. "Did you study this here?"

"Nope. In Canada. It's very popular up there."

"Really! Hot music in a cold climate."

"Go figure! The weather might be cold but the people aren't."

"I've never been to Canada."

"Come and visit me. I have a large apartment overlooking Lake Ontario. You'd like it. Come for a weekend. A week . . ."

He left it open-ended.

They spent the night until well after midnight at the club dancing, laughing, and talking. The hot music had them dancing side by side, her hip swinging toward his hip, her hand on his chest, his arm pulling her in front of him, dancing eight steps to the up tempo's six beats. Just the movements alone were so sexy, they both looked and felt hot and alive and passionate.

Everything was going really, really well. But Mercedez felt she really couldn't just leave Bill out in the cold. She had to at least go back and tell him she would be spending the night and the next day with Hugh. Maybe he wouldn't like it. More likely, he wouldn't care. But Mercedez wanted to be clear about things. She valued honesty and truth and felt she needed to be upfront.

"So," Hugh said, "we'll catch a cab to my place."

"Uh, listen. I didn't bring a bag with me."

"That's all right. I've got a spare toothbrush."

"It's not that. It's . . . I need to go to the hotel and straighten things out with Bill. Look, I'm really not sure where things stand. He . . . we both said we would keep it casual, that we were both free to be with other people. But I like to lay all the cards on the table. I just want him to know that I won't be back tonight, and that I'll be with you tomorrow. I owe him that."

Hugh just looked at her. "You know, you're really very special. I can't believe how lucky I am, that I've met you. Do you want me to go with you?"

"No, I better do it alone."

"I can wait in the cab."

"I don't know how long I'll be. Bill wasn't there when I phoned, and he might not be back yet. Listen, I can always call Pedro. He said, any day, anytime, he'll come and pick me up. I hope you understand."

"I do. And listen, if you end up having to stay the night, don't worry about it. Call me in the morning and we'll get together for breakfast."

Mercedez smiled. "Okay, that sounds great. But I'm hoping to get to your place later. I really want that."

"Call if you need me. Here's my card."

"Hugh, you're pretty amazing yourself."

"We aim to please, ma'am."

They kissed and hugged and fondled one another on the street corner but eventually Mercedez hailed a taxi to the hotel.

It was 1 A.M. when she got in, and Bill was out, although she could see that he'd been back and changed his clothes. She took a Sol from the bar fridge and sat in one of the winged armchairs with the balcony door open, watching the night.

The sky was clear, dotted with a million stars. Despite the size of the population here, somehow the lights did not overwhelm the heavenly bodies. She thought about Hugh, and Bill, and about how being here in Mexico had been important to her in some way she couldn't yet identify. It was a magical land, full of synchronicity. In some strange way she felt she was reaching deep down inside herself, finding her most passionate roots.

As she stared at the heavens and thought about the excitement of being here and all that was opening to her, one star seemed to outshine the rest. She stared at it as it went from white-hot to a yellow that resembled the sun's yellow, and grew in size. Could this be happening? Was she imagining it? Too much tequila?

The midnight sun seemed to fill the sky now, and the heat of it came down from the heavens. She felt it caressing her flesh and then penetrating under her skin, into her muscles, beyond them, through her organs, deep into her bones. The heat built inside her, making her entire body throb. She moaned, ecstatic with the temperature, the trembling of the light that had entered her as her body built to a climax with that hot light, that golden light—

"Are you awake?"

Mercedez opened her eyes. She felt full of passion, moist, sultry, full like a flower ready to release its pollens.

"Hi, Bill."

He took a seat before her on the footstool. Behind him, out the window, the sun was rising in the sky. "I got your note. Saw you were going out, so I took myself to dinner with a colleague." He checked his watch. "Time flies. Did you have a good evening?"

"Oh, I did. I was at the museum and met an archeologist there and he invited me to dinner and dancing and—"

Bill stood. "No need to explain. What you do is your business."

Somehow his lack of interest felt cold to her, hardening the moisture within her, chilling the passion she had a moment before felt filled with.

"Yes, well, he's invited me over for the night."

"That's fine," Bill said, like a father to a daughter, not the way a lover speaks to a lover. "It's six A.M. though, but if you want to go, by all means."

Mercedez knew it wouldn't be good to race over to Hugh's place at this hour. It made sense to sleep and then call him in the morning.

"Well, maybe tomorrow morning I'll get together with him for breakfast."

"As you like." Bill headed for the bathroom.

Mercedez picked up the phone to call Hugh, so that he wouldn't be up all night waiting for her. There were messages and she played them. Both were from women, and both for Bill.

"Honey, I'm home. Call. Anytime."

"Hey, lover, when are you gonna phone me? I've been waiting all night. Gimme a shout, okay."

The first could have been Mexican, speaking in English, but the second was definitely a southern United States accent.

She was still holding the phone when Bill returned. "There are a couple of calls. They're for you."

Without a word Bill took the phone and played the messages. When he finished, he hung up without a comment.

He climbed into bed then pulled back the covers on her side and patted the mattress.

Mercedez felt annoyed with him, for so many reasons, and she couldn't even say why. She liked Bill, was mildly attracted to him, but she absolutely preferred Hugh, so why should it matter that Bill had been calling or even been with other women? It was all so confusing. She switched off the light and got into bed.

Bill slipped an arm around her shoulders and pulled her to

DAY OF THE DEAD

him. She wanted to resist, but being touched seemed to bridge some of the distance that had grown between them. His hands moved skillfully over her body, riding the wave of her hip, down her thigh, up over her mons, and further up her stomach to her breast, then back again. "Turn over," he said, "I'll give you a backrub."

She did and his hands kneaded her shoulders and the large muscle of her back with great skill. The massage began to relax her almost instantly and she drifted off. Somewhere along the way Bill lay on top of her, his penis against her bottom, and he slipped it inside her from the rear, entering her pussy deep.

She was so sleepy. It seemed that penises were the same but different, this one long and thin, Hugh's thicker and longer. But they all did the trick, stimulating the sensitive folds of skin inside her, making her cry out for more, making her want this fucking that went on and on, building her up until she thought she couldn't get any higher but then did. And finally, when she came, the last thing she saw was that the sun was higher in the sky and Bill's hand rested in a proprietary manner on the fleshy swells of her ass cheeks.

CHAPTER 7.

M ercedez woke alone in the big hotel bed. She
looked around but it seemed the room was empty.
She'd had a lot to drink last night, that was for certain. She
rolled her head with just a bit of dizziness and faced the clock.
It read 5:00. Should the sun be up at 5 A.M.? It took her a
moment to regain enough consciousness to realize that the
little lighted dot on the clock next to the numbers was for P.M.
She sat bolt upright.

"Five in the afternoon?" She looked around. Bill's clothes
were here and there, but his briefcase was gone. She saw a note
on the table in the living room and tumbled out of bed to read it.

"Gone for business meetings all day. Go see your friend. I'll be out for dinner and will be in late. I put the Do Not Disturb sign on the door; call housekeeping when you're up so they can fix the room. Love, Bill."

"Oh my god, I forgot to phone Hugh!" It crashed down on her all at once that she had been so exhausted last night that once she'd picked up the messages and Bill took them and then everything that happened after that, she totally forgot to phone Hugh. It was five in the afternoon. What must he think?

She ran to her purse and pulled out his card with his cell number and dialed. A brief message came on asking her to leave a message, which she did. "Oh Hugh, I'm so sorry! It was late when Bill got here last night and by the time I got to sleep—I guess I'd had too much to drink with you because I *just* woke up and it's five! Call me. Please!"

She put the phone down with a low moan. He was leaving today! This was her last chance to see him and she may have blown it!

Why was everything suddenly a mess? Why did she let herself get so tired, and then stay up all night with Bill? How could this have happened? She went over the evening and realized that she did, indeed, have a lot to drink, and she normally didn't have more than one glass of wine in a night.

She tried Hugh's number again, and at the last second realized that he didn't even know which hotel she was staying at, or her last name, or the name on the registration, so there was no way he could have contacted her. She told him she was at the Meliá and the room number and asked him to phone.

Meanwhile, she showered quickly, leaving the door open so she could hear the phone. Once she was out and drying off, she called housekeeping and asked for the maid to come and fix the room. Then she ordered coffee and toast from room service.

She dressed quickly, thinking that maybe she should just grab a cab to Hugh's place. Once the coffee and toast came and was eaten and the maid arrived, Mercedez called Pedro. "It's an emergency. Can you pick me up right away?"

"Si, señorita. Five minutes, no more."

She left Bill a quick note that she had gone out and would be back as soon as she could, then headed to the lobby.

Pedro was already there and she told him she needed to get to Hugh's place, "Pronto!"

He drove like the wind, looking up from time to time into the rearview mirror. "Señorita Mercedez, tell me. Is everything alright?"

"No, Pedro, it's not. I've been foolish."

"Do not be so hard on yourself, señorita. Life has a way of moving us from one place to another despite what we intend."

"Life is what happens when we're busy making other plans, huh? What John Lennon said." Still, she felt miserable. Hugh was leaving today. What if she missed him and he was already gone!

They arrived at his apartment complex and the lights were off at his residence. She rang the bell anyway, but, no answer. Just then, a stylish older woman with well-coiffed silver hair came out of the next apartment and smiled. "Are you looking for Hugh?"

"Yes, I am. Do you know when he'll be back?"

"I'm afraid he's already left for the airport."

"Oh no!" Her shoulders caved in. "I can't believe this. What time did he leave?"

"Well, I was just getting in from shopping, so I'd say roughly five o'clock."

A low groan escaped Mercedez' lips.

"You know, it takes so much time now at the airport for international flights, I'll bet you could have him paged. Come in. My name is Esmeralda. You can use my phone."

The woman unlocked her door and Mercedez hurried to the phone. She checked the number for the airport and called information. Within minutes they had taken down the information and assured her they would be paging Hugh Murphy on a flight to Canada.

Mercedez left Esmeralda's phone number and hung up. She waited impatiently for the phone to ring.

"Let me offer you some tea," Esmeralda said.

"Thanks. I don't want to be any trouble."

"I'm having some anyway. I'll just bring a pot."

Maybe his flight had already left. It was nearly seven now. Oh, how could she have let this happen?

Esmeralda came back with a large coral blue pot with Aztec triangular markings around it in earthy colors, and two teacups that were clearly of English origin, possibly bone china. She poured the tea, and Mercedez recognized the scent. "Jasmine?"

"Yes. My favorite. Do you take sugar?"

"No. I like it as is."

"So do I."

While they waited and sipped tea, they talked about things in general, but soon, somehow, the conversation swerved toward personal territory and Mercedez was pouring out her heart to this stranger, telling her about her life and about the trip with Bill, how she had met Hugh and now through her foolishness she was letting him slip away.

"You know," Esmeralda said, "sometimes we think we have lost when we have really won. Only time tells us the truth."

"That's pretty much what my taxi driver, Pedro, said. I'm just afraid that Hugh will misunderstand. He'll think I just didn't want to call him, or come back, and it wasn't that way at all."

"If he thinks that, then he misjudged what transpired between you two, in which case, he might not be the right man for you, Mercedez."

Mercedez wasn't so sure about that. She wasn't sure about anything much, other than that Hugh was gone. She could feel that in her bones, as if they were psychically linked.

She waited one hour, then stood up. "Thanks, but I don't think the phone will ring now."

Esmeralda stood as well and took her young hands in her gnarled old ones. "If it was meant to be, it was meant to be. Sometimes what we need we must work to find. The sun is brilliant, the gold appealing, but don't always trust it. It can blind you."

Mercedez felt she had heard that before, or something quite similar.

She thanked Esmeralda and made her way across the lawn to the taxi where Pedro sat patiently waiting for her. He took one look at her face and said, "No luck, señorita Mercedez?"

"No. I was too late."

They drove back to the hotel in silence. As Mercedez was exiting the taxi, Pedro said to her, "Señorita, perhaps you should visit another place in Mexico. Get away. Here, it is busy all the time. In a smaller place, you can think about things."

Absently she asked, "Where's a good spot?"

"Guanajuato. Tomorrow, if you like to go, I can pick you up and drive you to the bus. It is only one hour or two from here. The town is small, old, and beautiful. My people are from there. You will like it."

"I'll think about it," she said.

She paid him, giving him a large tip, and went straight up to the room. Her note sat where she had left it—Bill hadn't returned. There were no messages on the phone. This was grim. And it could not go on! Maybe Pedro was right. She should go somewhere new, a quieter place. Likely she needed to get away by herself and think about things.

There were magazines and maps in the room and she found one of the entire country, although without much detail. Guanajuato was not on the legend but when she measured what would be one or two hours from Mexico City, she finally found it, to the northwest, a dot on the map, and yet the information inside the book said it was the capital of the state. She didn't know why she should want to go there, but two people had mentioned this place to her. Maybe. She'd see what plans Bill had.

Mercedez turned on the TV. She ordered dinner, lobster, sent up to her, and a half bottle of white wine. There was a hair salon in the hotel, open late, and she took herself down there to have her hair trimmed and her nails done.

While the manicurist was working on her cuticles, she

heard one of the women in the salon asking about Guanajuato. Everybody was talking about this town! She looked at the manicurist and asked, "So, what's in Guanajuato?"

"No idea. Never been."

After the haircut and manicure, Mercedez took a little walk around the hotel. The Reforma area was quiet, but then it was a weeknight. The air, still warmed by the sun that had only just set one hour ago was dense and pungent with the wafting scents of flowers and food.

Finally, Mercedez went back to the room. Bill still hadn't returned. There were still no phone calls. She decided to phone Connie, and then realized she would still be away. Maybe her mother, but she wasn't up for any conversations that might lead to what her future plans were.

Restless but a little down, she tried the TV again. A travel show in English came on when she flipped channels and of all places, it featured Guanajuato! It was the tail end of the report, but the city did look charming.

Finally, still exhausted from the marathon day and night and day and night that led to this disappointing day, she napped in the big armchair facing the balcony window. And dreamed of men in golden suits of metal with golden eyes and hair and helmets, and a dark voice warning her not to trust the gold. "Fool's gold," the voice said. "Only a fool could love it. You are not a fool, just a sleeper. A sleeper sleeping."

She woke with a start to hear Bill say ". . . sleeping?"

Groggy, a bit stiff from the awkward chair, she stretched a bit and yawned. Bill was just putting his briefcase down onto the table.

"Did you have dinner?" he asked.

"Yes. Earlier. You?"

"I ate with a colleague. Have a good day?"

"Not especially."

"Oh?" He paused. "Did something happen with your friend?"

"He'd already left for home. Up in Canada."

Bill opened his briefcase, saying, "That's too bad. I didn't realize he was leaving today, or I wouldn't have kept you up so late. I'm sorry."

"Don't be. It's not your fault. It's nobody's fault. Things happen the way they do," she said, standing, awed that she was now saying the things that had been said to her.

"So, listen, I've been thinking," Bill said. "I'm bound to be tied up here for another day or two before I can get a full day free. I hate to do this to you. I thought I'd have more free time but it's not turning out that way."

Mercedez felt her spirit sag. She'd come here, thinking she'd be with Bill. It was okay traveling alone, doing everything alone, but it was more fun for her to be with someone, sharing experiences, which is what she thought would be happening.

"There's a place not far from here," he was saying, pulling out a map and opening it up. "I've been there. It's a fascinating little city, and I think you'd like it. What I was thinking is, you might go there tomorrow. Either come back tomorrow night, or stay over and return the next day. It would give you a chance to see a place you might not otherwise have seen. The city is—"

"Let me guess. Guanajuato?"

Bill looked at her. "How did you guess that?"

"I think I'm psychic."

They spent an hour sitting on the balcony watching the stars, Bill drinking a Scotch and soda, Mercedez having a Perrier, hell-bent on giving her stomach a chance to settle down, since it had been upset all day. Once they climbed into bed, they made love, Bill all tenderness and concern, eager to please her as much as himself. It was the missionary position, and Mercedez liked it because her clit got very stimulated that way. She orgasmed three times before Bill finally allowed himself to come. He was asleep in minutes, but Mercedez lay awake, thinking about life in general, and her life in particular, and wondering if she would ever see Hugh again.

They both woke early, and Bill was up and dressed and heading out the door with a quick kiss on her lips and a fleeting, "I've left you money on the table. Go to the terminus heading northwest. All the taxi drivers will know it. Buses leave every hour. Have fun!"

Mercedez got out of bed, did her morning ritual, and ordered coffee and eggs today, thinking she would only eat again in Guanajuato. While she ate, she looked at the money Bill had left for her, wondering if he was rich. There must be another $700 US there. Maybe she would end up staying the night, so she decided to take it all with her and return what was left to him.

When she was ready, she phoned Pedro and asked him to pick her up.

As he left her at the bus terminal, he handed her a piece of paper and said, "Here, señorita. This is my cousin. She has a hacienda in Marfil and rents rooms. It is just outside the downtown, in a beautiful area beside the water. It is lovely, and you can rest there, undisturbed by the noise. You will like it."

"Thanks, Pedro. You've been wonderful."

"Smile, señorita Mercedez. Life is short. The dead tell us this."

And with that, he was gone.

Mercedez bought a ticket and didn't need to wait long for the bus. When she handed her ticket to the driver as she entered, the woman standing beside him reached into a basket and brought out a sandwich and a drink which she handed to Mercedez.

The bus was modern and large, and had curtained areas, window shades, and a movie screen at the front. Mercedez was one of only six passengers. The requisite lively Mexican music played for the first ten minutes and then they pulled to a local stop on the side of the road to pick up more passengers.

Seven or eight people boarded the bus, which pulled away from the dusty wooden bus stop the second the last person stepped in. Two Mexican cowboys were among the new passengers. They were twins, dressed identically, faces, and haircuts, even down to their sideburns. They took the double seat behind Mercedez, who was sitting alone, and who nodded as they passed her.

Cute guys, she thought. A bit younger than her, but still legal.

The music died suddenly and the video monitor flickered to life. It was an old movie, *really* old. A John Wayne western. She sat back and tried to get into it. The sound was off, though, and had been badly dubbed into Spanish. The film was that weird coloring they used in the 1960s—an ex-boyfriend had been a film student and pointed out Technicolor movies to her. It might have been a good movie—she found it hard to focus.

At least this was someplace else. She didn't have to worry about balancing Bill and Hugh. Hugh. She missed him terribly. But it was over, that was for sure. She had no phone number for him in Canada—he would have given that to her yesterday, if she hadn't slept the day away and missed him. Bill was a nice man, and he'd been good to her. But he was older, not interested in a relationship, and it seemed he had a few other girls on the side. Still, he was living up to his part of the bargain—a trip to Mexico, all expenses paid. She even got sex out of it, so it wasn't bad by anybody's standards. But it wasn't love, that was for sure.

Suddenly she was aware of a hand gripping the seat beside her. Her seat was reclined slightly and the hand gripped the other seat from behind, on the inside. Large fingers, a few dark hairs between the joints, short nails that were clean. She stared at the hand wondering what those calloused fingers would feel like on her body. Silly fantasy. These cowboys weren't interested in her, just in watching the film. At least she figured they were.

Mercedez leaned forward and peered through the crack between the seats. The twin behind the empty seat stared at her with soulful dark brown eyes and grinned. He had a tooth missing at the front. She looked back at the seat behind her and saw a mirrorlike image that grinned, too, a tooth missing on the bottom. She sent them both a smile with all thirty-two teeth, and sat back.

Out of the corner of her eye she noticed another hand, on the window side of her seat, then one on the inside of her seat. While she pretended to watch the film, she slid her hand up between the two seats and was able to touch both the hands between the seats at once, and with her other hand she touched the one near the window.

She rubbed her fingers up and down over theirs. Their fingers stroked hers, and then stroked her palm, and Mercedez felt sensations ripple through her. On the screen John Wayne was about to mount up.

The three spent the next thirty minutes on the bus, hand to hand, and Mercedez began to feel warm and wet from this skin contact. She had never experienced such a sensation before. Sure, guys had touched her hands and she had touched theirs, but it was nothing like this long stimulation.

The bus pulled off the highway again and the driver announced that they would have a fifteen minute rest stop at the cantina.

The two hands retreated. Mercedez picked up her purse and stood, smoothed her skirt, then headed for the front of the bus to exit.

The cantina had a variety of snacks but she just wanted a soft drink. She knew she should use the ladies' room while she could, although the bus had a restroom. She headed to the back of the cantina. As she was about to enter the women's washroom, the two cowboys came out of the men's room close by. All three stopped in their tracks.

Mercedez gave them a smile and entered the ladies' room. When she finished using the toilet, she flushed and opened the stall door to come out and found the boys waiting for her, grinning sheepishly. She held open the door invitingly, and the slightly taller of the two entered the stall with her, then the other one came in, too.

Hands flew to her body, four of them, feeling her thighs, her arms, her chest, riding the swells of her hips and breasts, her ass. One cowboy got behind her, the other in front. She closed her eyes as they touched her, letting the sensations ripple through her body, driving her confusing thoughts away, feeling the heat spread through her. Her dress was lifted above her head, her panties lowered. She reached in front and behind her and simultaneously unzipped two flies, then felt two identical penises, both rock-hard, the balls beneath tense; she pulled the genitals into the open. She stroked them both, making them harder, and the cowboy in front took a nipple into his mouth while the one behind reached around and caressed her other nipple. She couldn't help but moan.

Suddenly they heard someone else in the bathroom. The cowboy in front put his finger to his lips and both Mercedez and the one behind grinned and nodded in understanding. They continued as they had been, all the while the woman in the next stall peed, wiped, and flushed, then exited and washed her hands before leaving the bathroom.

The cowboy in front grasped Mercedez by the waist and lifted her until the head of his cock was at her pussy opening. Arms trembling, he paused while the twin behind positioned his cock at her bottom hole. She couldn't believe they would both poke her at once. But, slowly, she was lowered, impaled evenly on both poles.

Her head fell back and she panted, struggling to not cry out—she didn't want to draw attention to this washroom, she didn't want this interrupted.

The hands at her waist lifted and lowered her and the ones behind grabbed onto her buttocks and did the same. They fucked her with piston precision and timing. She was hot and wet and tight, the rubbing inside her cunt and her asshole stimulating her to new sensations, the wall between so thin she could feel them both apart and together. She felt completely filled and expanded, and the two together felt like the biggest cock in the world. She could not believe how wonderful this felt!

They fucked this way for a long time, and then suddenly the cowboys stopped, in unison. They zipped up and handed her her dress and panties and said something about the bus and hurried out of the washroom. She followed a bit slower, glancing in the mirror at her bright eyes and flushed cheeks, trying to look presentable for reentering the bus.

She was the last one on and the driver made a comment that she was making them late. She took her seat, the bus started up, the lights dimmed, and the movie continued where it had left off.

Mercedez was grateful for the air-conditioning, which cooled her off. She was alive with fire inside. Her pussy and her asshole both throbbed with unfulfilled desire. She wanted so much to touch herself.

Suddenly from behind, hands reached for her, sliding down inside her dress, one for each nipple. They toyed with them, twisting and turning and pulling the nubs to the hardness of fleshy beads. Moisture poured from her cunt. The divine torment lasted another forty minutes until the bus pulled into the next stop.

Mercedez raced to the washroom and her cowboys followed. She wasn't sure, but it seemed this time the taller was in front and the other twin behind. Again, she was lifted and the two cocks planted into her two orifices. This time, she was so close to orgasm that she came almost instantly, and the cowboy in front clamped a hand over her mouth to keep her from screaming as the hot hard cocks went deep inside, filling her to the point where she thought she would go crazy, shooting hot cum inside her two holes, washing her with scorching maleness.

The cowboys zipped up and exited, and this time Mercedez made it back into the bus on schedule. Somehow, the John Wayne movie had finished, although she only remembered him riding that horse fast and hard into the hills. Now, the lights were fully on, and the music started up again. She saw a road sign that read Guanajuato 5 kms.

It was a sunny day, not yet noon, the world looked bright and alive again, and she had a whole new place to visit without the worry of two men who had been so important in her life until the recent addition of two other men. Twins she wouldn't see again, but this meeting had been fine by her, as it likely had been for them.

She squiggled in the seat, her pussy and asshole still hot and tingly from the fucking. What a wonderful day this was turning out to be!

CHAPTER *8.*

M ercedez exited the bus, waving good-bye to the twin Mexican cowboys who, from their seats, waved back. The bus left her in its dust.

The bus stop was on the highway, not in the small city surrounded by snowcapped mountains. Fortunately a taxi sat idling and she poked her head in. "Hi. Can you take me to Marfil? I'm looking for the Ex-Hacienda del Antiguo Camino."

"Sí, señorita. Hop in!" he said in broken English.

Once inside the taxi, which was a battered old beige Toyota, except for the trunk and the hood which were brown and red respectively, the driver took off at a slow speed along the highway for perhaps half a kilometer, then turned left.

"Where you from?" he asked.

Mercedez looked at him in the mirror. "The United States. But I just came from Mexico City."

"Big. Noisy. Too much people. Too much cars."

She smiled at the face in the rearview, which seemed to be a younger version of her Mexico City taxi driver, younger by maybe ten years.

"You stay here long?" he asked.

"A day or two. Is Guanajuato a nice city?"

"Sí, señorita. Mucho nice. You will like it very much." He handed her a card with the taxi name and number. "You call me, I pick you up and take you where you like to go."

Mercedez stared at the card and raised an eyebrow. "So your name's Pedro."

"Sí."

They arrived in the suburb of Guanajuato and drove through the quiet narrow streets.

"Where are all the people?" Mercedez asked.

"Siesta," Pedro said.

"Ah!" Mercedez had forgotten about the afternoon siesta. Mexico City was crowded during the afternoon, and she hadn't been in Cancun long enough to experience it.

He drove up to the iron gate of a large two-story house. The stone walk was surrounded by flowers, and more multi-colored blossoms climbed the stone and stucco walls. There were cute four-paned windows with filigree grillwork over the bottom half and a huge curved door with wrought iron fittings.

She walked the little path to the side of the building and

found that it sat on a stream that flowed to the city of Guana-juato, just a stone's throw away—she could see it from here. There she found another door and pulled the rope to ring the old-fashioned bell hanging above it. The door opened imme-diately and an exquisitely beautiful woman in her forties with gleaming black hair pulled into a braid that ran down her back answered, "You are Señorita Mercedez."

Mercedez' mouth dropped open. "How did you—"

"My cousin, Pedro. He telephoned me to say you were arriving today. Please, come in."

Mercedez entered the air-conditioned office. The woman, whose facial features and body shape were, if not perfect, very close to perfect, introduced herself as Francesca. "Please, be seated, she said, "I will need your passport to fill out the registration."

They did the paperwork and then Francesca led Mercedez to her room, another suite, really, a full living room with a comfortable looking sofa and chairs, a dining area, and a sep-arate bedroom. The space was all Spanish arches and iron lamps, the décor brass-hammered plates and crossed swords above a huge king-size bed with a classic red and gold tasseled cover. The washroom was modern and spacious, and there was even a minibar. It had all the amenities of a good hotel with the charm of a privately run establishment.

"This is just lovely," she said, and Francesca smiled.

"Señorita Mercedez, if there is anything you need, please, just ring the bell outside."

"Thank you. I think I'll unpack, have a quick shower, and then head into town. Is it walking distance?"

"Guanajuato is close but on the other side of the water, so you must go around, which makes it far. Pedro will drive you."

Mercedez closed the door and flopped down onto the bed. She felt good. The encounter on the bus was unexpected. And now that she had arrived in this smaller, less hectic place, she was feeling much more relaxed. Somehow, being alone in a major city made her feel lonely. Here, in a place closer to nature, she felt right at home. In some ways, it reminded her of Corpus Christi. She wondered if her dad was born somewhere around here.

She unpacked at a leisurely pace, and then jumped into the shower. The water smelled earthy and it washed away the travel dust. She decided to not dry her hair but to let the sun do that naturally.

She had brought along two dresses, plus the one she wore on the bus, an extra pair of shoes, and undies for two days in her overnight bag. She didn't know how long she would stay, but it wouldn't be more than two days, that was for certain, although maybe she'd want to be here for a week!

Once she'd run a comb through her long, dark hair and checked her face in the mirror—she left off the makeup—she picked up her purse and straw hat and headed out, prepared to go to the office and phone for this particular Pedro. But when she stepped outside, he was already seated at a table drinking a red drink with Francesca.

"Señorita Mercedez, please join us," Francesca said.

The table held several empty glasses and Francesca picked one up. "Do you like sangría?"

"Very much."

Francesca poured Mercedez some of the wine, and then

spooned a bit of fruit into the glass, her movements languid and sensual. Pedro watched her, a gleam in his eye. Mercedez wondered if these two were lovers. Dark eyes shining, Francesca handed Mercedez the glass.

She took a sip. "This is very, very good!"

"The fruit is local, of course, and the wine is from Mexico."

Mercedez sipped again. "I don't think I've had red Mexican wine, just the white. I'm impressed."

"So tell us, señorita, what brings you here, to our small city?"

Mercedez felt comfortable with these two, as if they were parental figures, or more like a supportive aunt and uncle. "I'm here visiting and I wanted to see places that are not so frequented by many tourists."

Pedro said, "There are many tourists here, but most of them are Mexicans."

"That suits me fine."

"But why are you traveling alone?"

Mercedez thought to herself that every Pedro got right to the point. "Well, I met a man—"

"Ah," said Francesco, eyes gleaming, nodding, as if this story would be interesting.

"It's not like that. He's a nice man, but it's not love. . . . Anyway, he invited me to come along while he's here on business—"

"But you are unhappy with the arrangement."

Mercedez smiled sheepishly. "Sort of. He's always busy. But I'm not sure I'd want to be with him all the time anyway."

"Because there is another man."

"How did you know that?" Mercedez asked, astonished.

"She is *bruja*."

"A witch?"

"I prefer," said Francesca, straightening in her seat, "sorceress."

"Can you read tarot cards and crystal balls?" Mercedez blurted out.

"I read people. Oh, and palms. Give me yours."

Mercedez opened her hand to Francesca, palm up, and the gorgeous woman took it in both of hers and studied the lines for a long minute, tracing some with her fingertip. Finally, she released Mercedez' hand and sat back in her seat.

"What? I hope there's nothing horrible there."

Francesca said nothing, just stared at Mercedez, her face very serious.

"Did you see illness? Death?"

"Life is full of both, and death is always a door to change."

Mercedez began to feel unnerved. "Are you saying . . . I'm going to die?"

Francesca began pouring herself another glass of sangría. "I would never say that to anyone."

"But it's what you saw. Tell me!"

"I saw in your future great changes. You have a large door to pass through."

"That's cryptic."

Before she could probe more, Pedro stood and said, "Señorita, siesta is over. If you would like to go into the town, I will drive you. Otherwise, I must wait for the next bus at the highway."

"Okay," Mercedez said. She picked up her hat and purse and said. "Thanks for the sangría."

Francesca nodded without looking at her, which upset Mercedez even more.

In the taxi, she asked Pedro, "So, is Francesca always accurate with her predictions?"

"Usually. But you must understand that she sees things in a very big way, not how you and I see things. It is good to listen to her and then to keep what she tells you in a small box at the back of your thoughts."

They traveled a few blocks to the highway, then back to the dusty bus stop. A road from there led to the city itself.

"Tell me what's good to see in Guanajuato," she asked.

"First of all, señorita, I must tell you that there are very few cars on the streets. Guanajuato is built over underground tunnels, the Calle Miguel Hidalgo, which are the roads that the cars travel on. The tunnel is three kilometers long and follows the Guanajuato River—the same river you will sleep beside tonight. Here and there throughout the tunnels are steps leading up to the city above. I will let you out at the steps in the heart of the city. From there, you must walk the streets and discover for yourself."

No sooner had he said this than they entered a winding tunnel of two lanes of one-way traffic and high stone walls. They drove around the S-curves for what must have been three or four blocks. Suddenly Pedro pulled to a stop on the right near a stairwell. Mercedez handed him money and got out, traffic whizzing by on the other size of the taxi. She had just closed the cab door and turned away when she turned back again, about to ask how she would find a taxi back, but Pedro was gone. She guessed she would need to come down here into the dark tunnel and hail one.

She took the high stone steps up and found herself on a footpath with a stone railing that overlooked the tunnel onto which this colonial city had been built.

Without direction, Mercedez began to stroll the narrow streets that all seemed to end at the steps to the tunnel. Instantly she was charmed by the buildings of many colors and many heights, like layers of a cake. Flowers and plants draped the iron balconies. It seemed that hundreds of alleyways crossed the more major streets, and she came to one called Callejón del Beso or Alley of the Kiss, and stood for a moment, staring at the sign, wondered about the name.

Suddenly she felt someone behind her and turned. The handsome young man said, "Excuse me, señorita, but I see you are wondering about the name. It is this: This callejón is very narrow. It is said that lovers can stand on the balcony, one on each side of the callejón, and kiss."

"That's romantic!"

"Unless one falls off a balcony."

Mercedez laughed politely.

"If you wander this callejón in the evenings, you will hear musicians who stroll the lanes with guitars, serenading the residents."

"Thank you. That was very kind of you to stop and explain all that."

"For such a beautiful señorita, it is a pleasure. Buenos días," he said, nodding and turning.

Mercedez wandered the romantic little street full of children playing, mothers hanging laundry, old people sitting on the sidewalks. What a beautiful place to live, she thought.

She had brought along a tourist book and once she reached the main square, full of cafés, shops, and a gorgeous cathedral with a fountain in front, she perched on the edge of the fountain and scanned the book. Guanajuato's original name meant "Place of Frogs." The indigenous tribes thought it fit only for frogs. Then, when the Spanish came, they found rich veins of silver, which they extracted, and built the magnificent city with the profits. There were only a few tourist spots in this university city, like the Iglesia de San Cayetano, the church built in the mid to late 1700s; the silver mines; a museum devoted to that history; the el Pipila monument dedicated to the independence hero who burned down the door of the granary; the Museo de las Momies. She wasn't sure what she would do tomorrow, but for today she just wanted to relax and stroll the lovely streets that were filling up with people as if everyone had come out of hiding. She watched families strolling across the paved and cobbled streets, popping in and out of shops, making purchases. The temperature here was pleasant, not as hot as in Mexico City, and she wondered if the surrounding mountains were responsible.

Mercedez felt peaceful here. The mild temperature, the buzz of humanity, the leisurely pace of the populace, the music, and, she realized, the lack of tourists, all of it helped her relax. And she needed to relax. As great as this trip had been, it was a whirlwind. A lot of people like to spend six days in seven countries, and Mercedez knew that could be fun. But there was something about slowing down, getting to know a place and its people that appealed to her. It was the reason she came here, before her emotions got all tangled up around men.

Eventually she stood and wandered up the little hill behind the square and found more streets, some surrounding a large park, and eventually ended up on a wide main thoroughfare full of shops selling everything. She stopped to look at silver jewelry, and also noticed the abundance of clear taffy candy in many of the stores. There were fabric stores, clothing shops, hardware and mini–department stores, and many many restaurants and hotels behind the facades. She ventured into one little corner shop that sold vegetables, most of which she didn't recognize, some of which looked like cactus displayed in bushel baskets and along shelves. She was admiring a box of okra and suddenly realized that above and behind the veggies were small coffins, and she gasped. She turned and looked around, astonished. This store sold vegetables and coffins! How bizarre! There were small frilly white coffins for children apparently, decorated with white ribbons and satin roses, and elaborate, mauve, satin-covered rectangular boxes that she thought might be for pets. "Are those pet coffins?" she asked the proprietress.

The woman with two children playing at her feet looked up and frowned. "They are for bones."

"Oh," Mercedez said.

Out on the street, she suddenly realized that there were shops along the way that sold coffins, including one store that was almost a museum, full of photographs from the past of horse-drawn hearses. Interspersed between the caskets were Día de los Muertos figures. Another reminder that the holiday was very close at hand.

When she emerged she found that the sun was down but

the sky still light. And she realized that she hadn't eaten since breakfast. The bus sandwich was still in her purse, but it wasn't what she wanted. She surveyed the restaurants on the main street and finally found a cute one, the quiet patio of Las Embajadoras, a hotel. There she dined on enchiladas with green sauce and drank mescal, then had a chimichangas for dessert, banana slices, butter, brown sugar, and spiced rum all rolled into a burrito and deep friend. The calories would kill her but this was one dessert her grandmother had made when she was a girl, and she hadn't had since. She sat over the scrumptious fare, lingering, letting the taste create memories of the past.

When Mercedez emerged from the hotel, the sky had darkened and the ornate street lamps were lit. The city was still alive with pedestrians and she imagined that the night life would continue until ten or eleven, and then the populace would sleep until dawn. She wondered if she needed to get back to the Calle Miguel Hidalgo to catch a taxi, although she did notice there were a few cars on the street, but not many, and no taxis. The weather was still mild, and she decided to walk off the calories. She headed back up to the city hall at the end of this street. Maybe she could find her way to the tunnels from there.

She had just reached the fountain when a familiar voice said, "Did you hear them yet, señorita?"

She turned to find the young man who had stopped earlier to tell her about the street named Kiss. "Hear who?"

"The musicians," he said.

"No. I think I'd have a hard time finding my way back to that street."

"Come with me, then. I will show you."

They walked through the narrow streets filled now with people and life. "What a beautiful small city," she said. "Are you from here?"

"I am a student. I came here to study death."

Mercedez stopped in her tracks. "Death? Are you serious?"

He smiled. "Yes, I hope to be a forensics specialist."

They reached Callejón del Beso just as a small band of musicians turned the corner ahead and came toward them. Three men and two women sang a lovely sweet song, about life and death and love being what makes it all worthwhile. One of the males strummed a small guitar.

Mercedez and her escort stood at the corner until they passed. As they did, one of the girls gave Mercedez a white flower and a beautiful smile.

They were soon out of sight, their song just a memory. "That was lovely," she whispered, putting the flower into her hair.

"Señorita, would you do me the honor of accompanying me to a café?"

What a quaint, old-fashioned way of asking, she thought. "That sounds lovely." They turned and walked uphill to an area where she hadn't been before.

The small café was not for tourists, it seemed. Only locals sat in the seats, and her host seemed to know the man behind the counter. He came back with two glasses of tequila, and a bottle of water. Mercedez raised her shot glass as he raised his and they clinked lightly. "A su salud," he said.

And Mercedez echoed him, "To your health."

"So," she said, "my name is Mercedez. What's yours? And don't say Pedro."

He laughed but looked confused. "I am Roberto."

"Nice to meet you."

He was a sweet young man, university age, and over the next hour she found out that he was from Mexico City, in his second year at school, and had wanted to study at this particular university because of their program.

They chatted easily. He told her bits and pieces about the history of this city, about his life, and Mercedez was an enthusiastic listener. Finally, three tequilas later, when she noticed that the café had pretty well emptied out, Mercedez said, "I guess I'd better find a taxi to take me back to where I'm staying. Do I go down into the tunnels?"

"I can drive you back," Roberto offered.

"Oh, I don't want to put you out."

"It is no trouble at all. Where are you staying?"

"Marfil."

"Just across the water."

They split the bill—she insisted—and he led her three blocks uphill to a lot where his was parked. The lot was full of Volkswagens. "Does everyone in Mexico own a Volkswagen?"

His face split into a boyish grin. "It is our national car. But seriously, it is one of the most economical cars, and works perfectly in our climate."

"Which one is yours?"

He pointed to a moped, and she laughed. "Even more economical."

"Yes," he agreed.

He climbed on and she behind him. They drove in silence but for the sound of the small engine.

When they arrived at the Ex-Hacienda, the lights were out but for the one over her doorway. "Listen, I don't have anything to drink, but there might be something in the minibar, if you'd like to come in for a while."

"Of course," he said, following her to the door.

Inside the room she switched on all the lights in the living room area. "Please, have a seat." Then she headed to the minibar and opened it.

"Well, let's see. There's beer, and there's beer. And one small bottle of tequila. Shall we have this?" she asked, holding up the bottle.

"Yes."

They split the little bottle and Mercedez drank water with hers, always mindful of not wanting to get too drunk.

They talked easily, and in fact she realized that chatting with such a young man was relaxing. There was nothing flirtatious going on, well, maybe mild flirtation, but if anything came of this, fine, if not, it didn't matter. She wasn't in this town for a sexual encounter, although she wouldn't pass it up if it felt right.

It must have felt right because somehow they made it to her large and comfortable bed. He was young and strong, virile, the muscles of his back and shoulders hard, and she knew he worked out at the school gym. He stripped off his clothes immediately and began undressing her in the no-nonsense way of young men. Then he pulled her to him, and his full lips met hers. His lips slid down her face, down her neck, down the middle of her chest to her belly button. He looked up. "You are tattooed!"

"A small one. Not like yours."

In fact, his back was covered with the tat of a large scorpion in black with grey shading. Still hugging and kissing, she asked, "Why did you get a scorpion."

"My astrological sign is Scorpio. And sex rules my sign."

That's pretty hot, she thought.

The next thing Mercedez knew, he slid off the bed and stood at the side of it, gesturing with his finger for her to come closer. She did.

Roberto said, "Lie down, with your head here." He pointed to the bed just in front of his groin. She did, and he bent over and pushed his cock down. She took it into her mouth.

"Bend your knees." When she did, he grabbed her ankles and pulled her legs up to his chest, then higher, and pretty soon he had her lifted upside down into the air. She wrapped her legs around his head, which he bent so that he could eat her pussy while she sucked his cock.

They ate and sucked each other and he held her up by the legs, his tongue sliding deep down into her, making her cunt hot with desire as she dangled against his body, taking that long, strong cock deep into her throat.

Suddenly he flipped her onto the bed and she thought he would fuck her doggie-style, but again he grasped her ankles. This time he held her by the ankles and lifted her off the bed, sliding his cock into her pussy. She bent her head, giving her ass the most elevation.

His body was strong and hard and he thrust fast and deep,

leaving her nothing to do but moan into the mattress. The fucking lasted through her first orgasm, then through her second, then through a third, until she felt delirious, out of her mind, limp and swollen with expectation and desire, a vessel for his relentless cock. And oh how she wanted that cock fucking her!

Roberto fucked her until the sun came up, and then they fell into a sleep and she awoke with his fingers deep inside her, her body on fire, her nipples swollen, every inch of skin alive and hungry. And then he fucked her again.

When they finally greeted the day, it was almost noon.

The room had a little coffeemaker and Mercedez made some while Roberto showered. Then she got into the shower, and pretty soon she wasn't alone. *This guy is a machine!* she thought, but she didn't mind. Sex where she had to exert herself a lot was fun from time to time.

While water rolled off her back, he lifted her up with those powerful arms of his and sat her on his cock from behind. She braced her hands against the shower stall wall and got a good long fucking until she screamed out her pleasure.

After she'd soaped up again, rinsed and then dried herself, she came back into the room. Roberto said, "If you like, I'll give you a ride into the city."

"Okay. Let me just slip into something. Don't you have classes today?"

"In about an hour," he said, checking his watch, and then checking her out.

She took a pair of thong panties out of her suitcase and slipped them on. Before she could even get to her dress he was all over her, and soon she was on the bed, on her back, and he was on his knees between her legs, which he lifted to his shoulders. Once again, she was fucked silly by this university stud muffin.

While she turned onto her side and lay in a daze, he dressed and said, "Let's go!" and slapped her playfully on the butt, making her skin tingle there.

Somehow, she got her wildly fucked body up and dressed, got a brush through her hair, and moved as quickly as her rubbery legs could carry her out the door after him. There was no sign of Francesca or Pedro, and she was just as glad.

The sun burned the sky as they rode, her pussy bouncing on the seat of the moped, her crotch up against his ass, both of them singing a Britney Spears song and laughing wildly. It was fun being with Roberto. She felt nineteen herself.

"Where do you wish to go?" he asked.

"Well, what's to see?"

"There are many places. But I know one you probably would not go to on your own."

"You never know. But why? Is it dangerous?"

"Not at all."

"Well, then, take me there," she said recklessly.

They bypassed the tunnel and instead took a winding dirt road up the mountain that curved again and again, the road rough, her pussy getting another workout as her clit bounced against the seat until she orgasmed.

When she got a grip, she looked up and saw a tree that at first seemed to have weird black leaves, but when they passed it she said, "Those are bats hanging from that tree!"

"Yes. Fruit bats."

"Glad they're not the bloodsucking kind."

"El Chupacabra. Not around here," he laughed.

Eventually they pulled into a parking lot in front of a building with high walls. "What's this place?"

"A museum."

"Really? What do they exhibit?"

"Mummies."

She got off the moped, turned and looked at him. "You're kidding."

He shook his head. "Guanajuato is famous for this museum. There are a hundred and two mummies on display."

"Mummies? You mean like Egyptian?"

"These are Mexican mummies. People who were buried in the adjacent cemetery. When the families could not pay for the upkeep of the resting places, they were disinterred and it was found that a percentage were mummified."

"You're kidding!" she said again.

Roberto only laughed. He looked at his watch. "I must go. I can pick you up, but not for about four hours. There are usually taxis around here, and you can always call one from inside. Here is my cell number." He scribbled it on a napkin he found in his pocket.

"Okay. Thanks for the lift. And for, well, everything. And for bringing me here, I think."

He kissed her gently on the lips. "You will find it fascinating in there. Let me know if you want to see me later."

Mercedez waved good-bye. She found herself standing alone in the parking lot, no cars or mopeds, no buses, nobody.

Some museum! Maybe it wasn't open. But when she went to the door she found it unlocked, and entered.

She walked into the cool darkness and soon came upon a ticket booth, but there was no one inside. "Hola!" she called. Nothing. There was no sign for prices, hours, or anything like that. She wasn't sure what to do since there seemed to be no one around.

After a few minutes, she pushed through the turnstile, thinking there must be someone inside. The turnstile led to a small, dark corridor that split right and left. She couldn't see what was left but to the right there were exhibits, so she headed that way. It was a very small circular room with a walkway that went around the inside of the circle, close to the display cases. She began on the right. There were mummified animals, a bat, a rat, and some larger mammal that she didn't recognize. A brief description in Spanish accompanied each item. She also came upon a coffin with sharp looking wooden spikes coming up from the bottom, dozens of them. The write-up said something about torture. "No kidding!" she murmured. Near it was a chastity belt from the Middle Ages and she wondered how that got here, if the Spanish had brought it over, if there had been an inquisition in Mexico.

Finally she was at the end of this room, where she began, and there, in a long, wide case were the mummified remains of what was described as a witch. The woman's hair was intact, and clearly she had been an older woman. Remnants of clothing, the colors faded, the fabric rotting away, and bunches of dried herbs and colorful pottery was in the case with her. The eyes were long gone and the empty sockets that were left seemed to stare straight at Mercedez. With a shiver, she left the room and poked her head back over the turnstile. Still no ticket-taker.

Now she ventured into what turned out to be the main part of the museum. What she saw astonished her. A room of wood and glass cases filled with mummified children, most dressed in festive attire. They wore christening outfits, and little fancy dresses or satin suits for promenading around the squares. Their flesh had dried to leather. Some had their eyelids closed, others displayed the empty sockets of the witch. Each had a piece of parchment in the case with a little story attached to it, talking about the history of the child, if known, and when and how it had been found. There was also a tall case with the mummified body of a woman and next to it what was described as the world's smallest mummy, a fetus, taken from her body when she was exhumed.

A part of Mercedez felt that she should have been revolted, even horrified, yet she had never seen anything like this, and it fascinated her. Somehow, these had once been living, breathing human beings. How did they get to this state?

At the end of the first room was a case with a tall mummified man wearing the remnants of a suit. The card said he was the first mummy found, a French doctor, two hundred years old, who had lived and worked in the area.

Finally she stumbled onto an information sheet, which gave her facts she needed about this museum in order to understand how these mummies got here. Roberto was right—they were disinterred when the families could not pay for upkeep of the grave. The paper said most of the mummies were not on display, only 108, in various states of mummification. Adjacent to the museum was the cemetery from which they had been exhumed, not from the ground, which seemed to hasten decomposition, but from the shelves in the walls aboveground. It was thought that a combination of the temperature and the humidity of this area encouraged this condition. The paper also stated that relatives frequently came to visit their ancestors, and that many of the visitors were classes of school children from the State of Guanajuato.

Armed with knowledge, she felt better able to wander the corridors of this museum, and moved on to the next of what turned out to be dozens of rooms. Here she found horizontal cases of people in mummified states. There were men and women, young and old, clothed, partly clothed, but oddly most were wearing socks! One or two cases held couples, and she thought that was sweet, that they were together for eternity.

Somehow the hours passed, and going from room to room and seeing so many of these mummies put her into an otherworldly state. Time stood still. Her perceptions altered. Reading about their lives, about their deaths, she began to feel she was getting to know them, and imagined the lives they led, their loves and hates, joys and sorrows.

She also noticed the bodies and how different they were. There was one very large woman, who looked as if in life she might have weighed in at over two hundred pounds, from the bulkiness of her remains. Then there was the petit man who had died at the age of forty, who wore the remnants of a tie and white shirt. Several of the females had flattened, dried breasts, and one man the shreds of an erect penis! She stared at him a long time—this was the only mummy with a penis.

What must he have been like? There was no card to identify him.

"He is exceptional, no?"

Mercedez spun on her heels, a hand to her chest. "Oh! You startled me!"

"I'm so sorry," the attractive thirty-something woman said. "I thought you heard me coming."

"No. It's so quiet in here. I guess I got lulled by the silence."

"Yes, I understand. I have had the same experience."

"This one," she said, nodding at the case, "died young. He was not yet twenty."

"Really? That's very sad."

"Yes, it is. He attended university here in the city, and I believe he hoped to be a pathologist. They say he died on the Callejón del Beso. Do you know it?"

Mercedez nodded.

"He was standing on a balcony and leaning over to kiss his lover on the opposite balcony and fell to his death. This was not so long ago, perhaps twenty-five years."

Mercedez didn't move. "You . . . you wouldn't know his name, would you?"

"I believe it was Roberto, but I am not certain. I can check the records if you like."

Mercedez gasped. "No . . . no, thank you. That's alright. I was just curious."

"Many are curious about this one, with the genitals still

intact. They say his ghost still haunts the Alley of the Kiss, as if searching for a lover to fulfill himself."

Mercedez shook her head. No, it couldn't be. A coincidence, that was all. "Um, listen, I never did pay. There was nobody at the gate."

"You can pay on the way out. Our guard at the exit, Pedro, he will take your money. Tell him that Marianna told you to pay him."

"Alright. Thanks. Is this the way out?"

"Yes, just follow the corridor to the end, and then you will see the *salida*. I hope you enjoyed the museum."

"Yes, I did. Very much. I'm surprised, though, that there aren't more visitors."

"Oh, you were fortunate. We have two busloads of school children who have just arrived!"

Mercedez heard them in the distance, coming through the turnstile.

Marianna said, "Come back. Anytime. Buenas tardes."

"Good afternoon," Mercedez said, and headed down the corridor, the voices of the shrieking children growing louder as they entered the main part of the museum and reacted to the mummies as only school children can.

Before the short exit corridor, she found a washroom and a telephone. Quickly she pulled out the card with Roberto's phone number written on it and dialed. A message came on in Spanish: no such number. She hung up, shaking her head. Things had certainly been strange since she came to Mexico, and now they were getting stranger. Yet somehow, she did not feel frightened. It all seemed to be building. Leading somewhere.

At the exit, she found an old, hunched man seated in the sun on a low stool. "Are you Pedro?"

"Si, señorita. May I assist you?"

"Yes. Marianna told me to pay you, since there was no one at the entrance when I came in."

Pedro told her the fee and she gave him the pesos, and then headed out into the courtyard, now packed with cars, taxis, school buses, and vendors, selling all types of crafts. She passed the booths and tents of wares but nothing struck her until she came to the candy man. "Souvenir candy?" he asked.

She stared at the twisted taffy and an image formed in her mind. "Is that what I think it is?"

"I do not know what you are thinking, señorita, but I know what this is meant to be. The candy is shaped like the mummies."

"Mummy candy? Sure, I'll take some!" She looked them over until she found one that resembled Roberto.

CHAPTER 9.

Mercedez entered the hotel room at the Meliá in Mexico City sucking on mummy candy. She found Bill at the desk, writing on his laptop.

"Hi honey! Did you have a good trip?" he asked absently, still typing.

"I did. It's a fascinating city. And you? How's the world of business."

"As usual. Ups. Downs. Watching all the time that your throat isn't being cut by the competition."

Somehow talk of the mundane business world brought her down to reality fast. She had had such a weirdly exciting time in Guanajuato and was so eager to talk about it, but there was no one interested, or so it seemed.

Mercedez tossed her overnight bag on the bed. She pulled out a clear cellophane package of the twisted honey-colored candy and placed it onto the desk next to Bill.

"What's that? Oh, it's mummy candy. Strange, huh?"

Even this was a letdown. He'd obviously been there, had that, and knew everything. There was nothing to share, or so it seemed.

"Let me finish this invoice and I'll take you to dinner." He turned in his chair to look at her. "Alright by you?"

"Sure," she said. "Why not?"

He turned back and began typing.

As she unpacked, he said, "Oh, and there's a message for you on the phone. Your friend, I think."

Mercedez' heart leapt in her chest. Did he mean Hugh? She kept herself from racing to the phone, fearful of hurting Bill's feelings, but apparently he didn't seem to have any feelings around this.

She punched in the code, and listened. It was Hugh's voice, assuring her that he would have called if she'd given him her last name and the hotel and that he was so glad she'd left a message. "I picked it up at the airport, just before boarding, so I didn't have time to phone you. I'm back in Toronto now. Listen, here's my number in Canada. Mercedez, call me!"

She jotted down the number, folded the paper carefully, and walked to her purse, sliding it into a secret and safe compartment in her wallet to make sure she didn't lose it. She would call him later, when she had some time alone. She really wanted to talk with Hugh. She wanted to tell him how much she missed him. But she wanted privacy.

Mercedez finished unpacking and stored her bag in the closet. She looked at her dresses and said, "Are we going to a dress restaurant, or casual?"

"As you like," Bill said.

What about what you like? she thought. *Just answer me. Why does everything have to be so . . . diplomatic?* But she said nothing, just scanned the dresses again, trying to pick something that would work for either environment.

"Honey, there's a package over there with your name on it."

Still watching the screen before him, he pointed to a chair in the corner. Mercedez went to the bag with the designer name and opened it. Inside was one of the most beautiful pieces of lingerie she had ever seen, a sheer red-gold negligee, low-cut front and back with spaghetti straps, and slits up the sides, front and back almost to the crotch. The gown was edged with a border of Mayan symbols in beadwork.

"Oh, Bill! This is beautiful!" She turned the gown over and over, staring at the fine details. Then she turned to him, greatly touched that he had been thinking of her after all.

He half turned in his chair with a small smile on his face and she came over and sat in his lap and kissed him full on the lips.

"Honey, I'm so sorry I've been unable to be with you. All this damned work. I know I've left you alone too much. I just wanted to try to make amends."

She kissed him again, longer, and he returned the kiss eagerly, as if he had been fasting the entire two days she was gone. They kissed long and deep and then he said, "Why don't you go try that on, and I'll just finish up my final paragraph."

"Okay," she said eagerly and ran to the bathroom. She stripped off her dress and panties and slipped the gown over her head. Her breasts sat in small cups that allowed the cleavage to be well displayed and the fullness to nearly over-flow. The sheer silk clung to her hips, her thighs, and fit her waist perfectly, as if this had been made for her. She looked at herself from all sides. Everything about the gown cried designer. She had never owned anything so wondrous. And the color suited her skin and hair perfectly! It must have cost him a fortune and she felt very touched.

She spent some time refreshing her makeup, fixing her hair, and spraying her body with the rose eau de toilette that she loved. If only she had some fuzzy red mules to go with this! She'd get some tomorrow.

When she opened the door, Bill was standing by the bal-cony doors, a drink in his hand. He turned, and the look on his face was priceless. "You are gorgeous!" he said, and his eyes reflected his words.

"Come," he said, and Mercedez joined him. He opened the balcony door and they stepped out onto the private terrace. She stood at the railing and he behind her, his body up against hers. The sky had darkened and the city below them hummed with the life of a world-class metropolis.

Mercedez felt the slight breeze ripple the fabric around her legs and dance across her skin. She turned to Bill and slid her hands up his chest, then her arms were around his neck and she was kissing him on the lips, letting her tongue slide into his mouth, tasting him, the liquor he'd just been drinking.

His hands moved around to the back of her waist, then down over her silky buttocks. She loved the feel of his hands sliding the silk over her ass.

"Stand up here," he said, pulling the low patio table to the railing.

She stepped up onto the table and he said, "Lean over the balcony." She looked at him for a moment. "You trust me, don't you?"

"Yes."

"Then do it. I'll hold you up."

She turned and gripped the railing which was normally chest high but now was waist high and leaned over, thrusting her ass up and spreading her legs at his urging until they were wide apart. Bill moved close behind her. Slowly he lifted the silk skirt of the negligee, sliding it up the backs of her thighs. Then her ass was open to the air, and he placed a palm on each cheek and spread her ass wide.

Soon she felt his breath at her slit, his tongue working the folds of skin of her pussy as she dangled from the waist over the railing. She let go of the rail and allowed her arms to wave free. Her long hair hung over her face, blowing around her in the breeze, and her breasts broke over the little cups of the nightie and dangled like ripe fruits high above the city.

Bill's tongue worked her clit, lashing it mercilessly, making her pant, and her legs tremble. He held her firmly about the waist, and she let herself respond to that tongue, allowing it to build her up and up until she thought she would lose her mind. Then he stopped, leaving her breathless, quivering with desire.

His tongue slid back and licked her bottom hole, making the anus warm and wet, creating sensations where they were usually few. He licked her repeatedly and she trembled anew, her eyes blinking open and shut. The clouds in the sky seemed to lower and come toward her as if the gods were inviting her into their realm. The clouds formed shapes: the Choc Mool, and the winged serpent Quetzalcoatl in all his manifestations.

Suddenly the tongue entered her asshole like a cock and she cried out, the sounds from her lips blending with the city sounds, and her rectum spasmed in orgasm.

Her whole body trembled as she screamed. And when she was finished, he entered her cunt, his cock serious and direct, plowing her deep, in, out, over and over, quickly, warming her cunt fast, bringing on the trembling muscles again, causing her breasts to bob in the air like melons shaken on a vine. A warm light rain began to fall, but it only burned her, stoking the fire as her flesh ignited. His cock wouldn't let up. She didn't know how much higher she could go, but she soon found out.

While the cock fucked her, he slid a finger into her behind and at the same time fucked her asshole. She spread her legs a bit wider and he inserted another finger. Everything inside her was tightening, contracting around him, eager for him to finish her off, and he fucked her hard and quick in both holes.

The rain came in earnest, with lightning streaking the sky near her, then thunder overhead close behind, then the downpour, the sky lighting up again and again, mirroring the passion as the thunder boomed and shook the air.

"Fuck me!" she cried. "Yes, fuck me!"

His whole body tensed as he shot cum deep into her cunt and his fingers impaled her. Lightning cut the night as she screamed, the sound blending with the boom of the thunder.

And when it was over, and as she stood on the small table on the terrace floor, leaning over the railing, Bill behind her, in her, holding her as they watched the storm recede, Mercedez could only think, "I'm so glad to be alive!"

They dined in a fabulous five-star restaurant near the hotel, the ambiance quiet, elegant, and romantic in an upscale way. Bill ordered for both of them, snails, beef in a rich spicy Mexican sauce with wild rice and strips of a green vegetable she was unfamiliar with. They lingered over the food, sipping wine, and Bill ordered a second bottle of the expensive vintage.

Somewhere between the main course and dessert, Bill got a call on his cell. He answered then said, "Hold on. I'm in a restaurant and I don't want to disturb the other patrons." He put the caller on hold and raised his hands at Mercedez, saying what-can-I-do?

Bill left the table and she really didn't mind. Let him talk to all the women he wanted to talk with. That was fine with her. They'd had great sex, she felt alive, more so than she ever remembered feeling. Nothing could bring her down.

At least that's what she thought. Bill was gone a long time, so long that all the tables around her had emptied and she was sitting alone in the restaurant. At one point she got up and went into the foyer to look for him, but he was nowhere to be found.

"Your friend, he asked that you wait," the hostess said with a smile.

Mercedez went back to the table. She had a second coffee, knowing it might keep her up all night. Maybe she should have a drink. No, that would just put her to sleep at the table.

Her mood soured. A glance at the clock told her that Bill had been gone an hour and a half. "What time do you close?" she asked the waiter.

"We've closed," he told her, an implication that maybe she should go on home so that he could.

She sighed and opened her purse. She'd left the cash at the hotel, but she had her trusty VISA card. "Why don't you bring the bill," she said.

He did, she paid, and then she walked back to the hotel, wondering what the hell happened to Bill. Her mood was as dark as the streets, and she passed a number of rowdy types that annoyed her, and was nearly hit by a drunken driver as he sped around the corner and went through a red light.

By the time she reached the hotel she was upset. Whatever had happened, there could be no excuse for this. She would just pack her bags and go home, something she should have done already, if she'd had any sense.

Bill was not in the hotel room. She tossed her old clothes into her suitcase and left the things bought with his money, the gifts, everything else right here. He could give them to one of his other women. She didn't need gifts that were bought at the expense of mistreating her.

Suddenly she remembered the call from Hugh. Should she phone him? What time was it in Toronto? She phoned the desk to ask. It was after two in the morning Toronto time. Was that too late? Yes, especially if Hugh had to be at work. She wanted to talk with him when they both had time, when they were both relaxed. On the other hand, maybe she could phone and see if he was working yet. Maybe he wasn't and now was a great time to call.

Before she could pick up the phone again, it rang. "Honey, it's Bill. Listen, I'm so sorry. I had a real emergency. One of my colleagues is in the hospital. I phoned the restaurant but you'd already gone. I was so tied up with the chaos that I couldn't really call until now."

That dampened her anger some. Still, she felt annoyed, justifiably or not. "Is it serious?"

"Yes. She tried to kill herself."

"A woman?" Mercedez blurted out. "Is she someone you work with?"

"Hold on a sec . . ." After he came back on he said, "Okay, things have gotten a little worse, so I can't talk now. I'm going to be here all night. And then tomorrow I have a full day of meetings again. Uh, listen. I think you should fly to Los Cabos, get some sun. Go for the day, and when you get back tomorrow night, I'll be finished with Mexico City and we can just spend all our time together."

"But, I can stay here, go with you to the hospital."

"That wouldn't be a good idea. This woman is very fragile. You're a stranger, she doesn't know you. I've got to do this alone. And like I said, tomorrow I'll be at meetings all the damned day. Look, there's some cash in my my suitcase, in the pocket. I've already called Mexicana Airlines and reserved a spot for you at 8 A.M. Just take as much money as you need—don't stint. Use it to buy whatever you need."

"So you've already bought the ticket."

"Yes, while I was waiting here. I think this will be messy, and it would be better for you to be away from all this. Go. Have fun. I'll see you tomorrow night. Look, I've gotta run. Take care, honey. See you soon."

When Mercedez got off the phone she sat down, stunned. How could all this happen? And why was he at a hospital with a colleague who tried to commit suicide? A woman? Maybe he wasn't even *at* a hospital. He didn't say that, she'd assumed. Maybe this was just a ploy. More than likely one of his women was freaking out and he ran to her side. Mercedez wondered if she was being uncharitable, not to mention paranoid, in thinking that. But everything had been so wonky, all the secretive phone calls, being in so many meetings he couldn't even contact her, and now this.

She wasn't sure what to do. She didn't *have* to go to Los Cabos tomorrow if she didn't want to. She could stay here, in the city. But then she'd be wandering around Mexico City by herself again, and she had always heard that Los Cabos at the tip of the California Baja was an amazingly beautiful place. The ticket was bought. It was an opportunity. If she was going to spend the day alone, why not on the beach?

Okay, she thought, I'll go. She jumped up and packed a large beach bag with a towel, makeup, and the bikini from Cancun. She placed the bag by the door and phoned the desk for a very early wake-up call. Then she phoned Pedro and asked him to pick her up at six for the airport. She wondered if she'd have time to phone Hugh in the morning. Or if he'd even be there. Maybe he was already back at work.

She could always call him from Los Cabos. After all, she'd have the entire day there, lounging on the beach. Surely they had phones.

Bill's suitcase had a stack of money that made her eyes glaze over. There must be thousands of US dollars. She had no idea how much the trip would cost, and took $300—she could put the rest on her VISA, although that meal would set her back by more than $300. Still, she had a bit of money left from the contest.

Well, they could sort out the money later. Bill had said he'd pay for everything, and other than that meal, he had. He was as good as his word. He hadn't really lied to her about anything, but she did get the feeling that the truth had been stretched and wrapped around corners a few times, and tonight might have been one of those times. Still, they were "fuck friends." Despite the dynamic sex, she felt that more and more. Whenever they got close emotionally, he seemed to pull away. Hugh was the opposite. He was there. With him, it was Mercedez who managed to screw it up all the time.

She couldn't shake the feeling that everything happening here in Mexico was happening for a reason. If only she had some sense of what that reason was. Surely it would come to her eventually. It had to. In the meantime, she would just try to go with the way the current flowed.

Lying in the dark under the soft sheets, her last thoughts

were of the sun, that powerful energy that fueled life. It could warm you or burn you. Maybe that's what so many people had been telling her lately.

CHAPTER *10.*

O kay, Mercedez told herself once she was seated in the
Mexicana Airlines 747, an orange juice before her on
the tray, headed west to Los Cabos, I will have fun!

No matter how strange things had gotten, every up had
been met by a down, every connection breeched by loneliness,
still, she could always rely on herself. She was headed to a sun
spot, one she had always been curious about, and now she was
getting a chance to explore it. All this was good, and the
important part. This was jet-setting at its finest—off to Los
Cabos for the day—then she'd be back in Mexico City tonight
and she and Bill would do something together tomorrow. She
had to hold on to the positive.

Besides, she had Hugh's phone number with her; it was a Saturday so the chances of catching him at home would be good. How could any of this be bad?

But even as she gave herself a pep talk, another part of her was thinking how hard it was, being away from places that are familiar, with friends or family available that you could hang out with. How difficult it was, not knowing what man to rely on, not to mention which man to trust! Normally she could run her worries and fears by her girlfriends. But she was alone here, everything was new, every second of the day she was required to adapt—that's what traveling was about. She felt a bit on overload.

Bill was solid, there in one way, but always, always, always busy. Hugh was someone she got along with perfectly—they had so much in common—but he was now *very* far away. And really, she didn't know him well. Yet.

Mercedez picked up the in-flight magazine and began to read an article on Los Cabos and grew enthusiastic about where she was headed. The name translated into "The Capes." It was a region at the southernmost part of the California Baja Peninsula—although the land belonged to Mexico—and was the southern tip of the longest and probably the most majestic peninsula in the world. It was also home to two bustling towns, Cabo San Lucas and San José del Cabo. Amazingly, it wasn't until the 1970s that tourists even knew about the area because until then it was too difficult to reach. The peninsula itself over millennia has been sliding westward and because it sits on the San Andreas Fault, it is expected that one day this peninsula will be an island. It is what the writer of the article described as home to the biologically richest body of water on earth.

But the most intriguing information had to be its history. Cabo San Lucas was discovered in 1537 by Francisco de Ulloa, Cortés's navigator. Soon pirates discovered the peninsula's tip on their trade routes and used it as a safe harbor. Too many pirates and ultimately the area found itself frequently under siege. San José del Cabo was founded as a Jesuit mission in 1730.

Pirates! Her imagination went wild, with visions of Johnny Depp in swashbuckler regalia expertly swinging a sword off of which the sun glinted.

It was a short flight and in no time she had instructed the taxi driver to take her to the most beautiful but deserted beach. Changing behind a rock into her bikini, and carrying her large beach bag in one hand and the large bottle of water she had purchased in the other, she strolled along this pristine white sand, listening to the waves of the green water gently break. Above, she heard gulls cry. Ahead and behind there was no one, and she anticipated a full day of lazing in the sun before she had to get back to the airport and the return flight to Mexico City.

She walked for what felt like a couple of miles, the warm sand beneath her bare feet. This was nature at its finest. Just Mercedez and the sun and sea, connecting her to herself. Allowing all the chaotic thoughts to evaporate like mist on the water.

Here and there as she walked she found seaweed, and the odd crab, but few shells—maybe it was the time of year and the tides. Along the shore were rocky coves. Enormous boulders jutted out into the Pacific, and she knew there must be underground caves there.

She checked her cell phone. It was about noon. She had many hours to enjoy herself. She stopped and stripped off the bikini and let the warm sun bake parts of her that were rarely exposed to sunlight. She could feel her ass muscles as she walked, the gluteus maximus stretching and relaxing. The sun stroked her nipples and the areolas which rarely felt its warmth. She wondered if nipples could get sunburned! She'd probably find out.

At some point she felt the need for a little rest and opened her large beach towel and sat on the sand facing the water. It was only five hundred years ago that people thought the earth was flat, and she could see why. To stare out onto the horizon was to see a pencil line drawn straight across. Under the line, blue green. Above the line, the milder blue of the sky with barely a white cloud in sight. Cortés and the other early explorers may have claimed this land as their own, and ruined ancient cultures, but no one could contest that they had expanded the perception of the earth as one large village, the inhabitants all of humanity.

Mercedez lay back on the towel and put her hat over her face to give her eyes shade. The warmth of the sun heated her bones, lulled her, and stimulated her at the same time. One hand cupped a breast, holding it as if offering it to the sun gods. Her other hand slid down her belly, caressing her skin on the way, slipping down her thigh and up between her legs. She rolled and writhed beneath the golden globe, fingering her clit as she opened the folds with her fingers to the sun, pinching and twisting a nipple, letting moans freely escape her lips. She lifted her legs up into the air, spread them wide, then brought her knees to her chest close together, and then spread her legs open again from that position. The hot sun licked her wet slit and she felt the heat penetrate that tender, vulnerable skin, and the puckered flesh around her asshole.

She rubbed her nub lazily, feeling the pressure build, the tension rise, and the heat increase. A large smile spread across her face from the delight she felt, the endless time, no pressure, the power to please herself, the elements of nature that contributed to her pleasure.

Finally, the energy moved beyond that fine line and she wanted release. She rubbed harder, slipping fingers inside her twat, rubbing the G-spot along the vagina that made her burn with desire. She threw her legs over her head to get the maximum heat from outside and was just able to lift her head enough to take one of her own nipples into her mouth and suck and nip it.

Suddenly, she exploded. Her cries interwove with the sound of the waves and the gulls, sending her pleasure into the air, air that would, eventually, find its way around the world. Taking a part of her passion with it.

Afterward, she flipped onto her stomach and let the sun burn into her bottom, her back, the backs of her legs and arms, and drifted into a calm and relaxing sleep.

The voices she heard like echoes woke her enough that she lazily opened her eyes a little. A man and a woman of equal height walked along the beach holding hands, talking, laughing, and coming her way.

The woman wore a blue, purple, and white bikini, with a matching sarong tied at her waist that moved gracefully as she walked. The man wore rolled-up beige cargo pants, and a black tank top. Both had medium brown hair, good tans, and were shoeless. And must have been six feet tall, both of them.

Mercedez was aware that she was naked, not sure of the rules about nakedness on the beaches here, but then they were so isolated, and this couple had already spotted her.

As they neared, they both looked at her body, their eyes lingering on her ass, and Mercedez lifted herself up onto her forearms and ran a hand through her hair at the top, pulling it back from her face, waking herself up. Exposing one naked breast. She saw their eyes focus on that.

"Hi!" the woman called.

"Hello," Mercedez answered. "Beautiful day."

"Isn't it?" the man said.

They stopped before her and asked, "Can we join you?"

It seemed like a strange request, given there was so much empty beach.

"We usually come here, right near that boulder, pretty much every day," the woman explained. "We're very attached to it."

"Sure," Mercedez said, "join me."

She reached for her bikini but the man said, "Oh, don't dress on our behalf. We usually strip down."

And they both did, the woman unknotting the sarong as the man removed his tank. Then the woman slowly peeled the bikini bottoms down her thighs, exposing a bush of hair the same color as that on her head. While she reached behind and unhooked her bra, the man unzipped his pants and let them drop to the sand. He had a long slim penis, and pubic hair that reached to below his belly button. Both bodies were in excellent condition, lean but muscular, and Mercedez thought they were both pretty sexy.

All the while they undressed, they looked at Mercedez, smiling. Weird people, she thought, but they seemed harmless. And they were *very* attractive.

The woman's slenderness did not preclude curves. Her full breasts were very rounded, like melons, with hard, pert nipples, very pink. The man had workout muscles, his legs, abs, arms, and, when he turned, a tight butt. She noticed a fish tattoo above his well-hung genitals. She also noticed that his cock was getting hard.

They plunked down onto the sand beside Mercedez. "Where are you from?" the woman asked, pulling her shoulder length curly hair back from her face and thrusting her nipples at Mercedez as if asking her to suck on them. This woman had the most remarkable pale blue eyes, otherworldly, and Mercedez wondered if she was Scandinavian.

"Well, recently from California. I've been traveling in Mexico for about a week now. I'm headed back to Mexico City tonight. You?"

The couple looked at each other and the man took the woman's hand. He, too, had startling eyes, the color of the sea that framed him. "We came from California by boat," he said. "A small yacht. A twelve footer."

"How exciting!" Mercedez said, pulling the water bottle out of her bag. "That must have been quite a sail down the coast." She took a long swig and then offered the large bottle to the couple, but they both declined. It was only then that she noticed they had carried no bag with them, no towels, nothing.

"It was," the woman said softly, glancing at the man. "We had a wonderful time coming down. We really did. We traveled to here, then over to the mainland, to Acapulco, then up to Puerto Vallarta—you should go there. It's an amazing place. You'll find something you're missing there."

Mercedez thought that was an odd thing to say, but then people had been saying odd things to her lately.

"And then we sailed up the Gulf of Mexico then back down and ended up back here," the man said. "We did a lot of exploring. But this was our favorite spot. We want to stay here forever. That rock face there," he said, pointing to a cliff down the beach where the boulder extended so far out it was close to the waves, "there's an underwater cave there, around the other side. And see that big flat rock there, out in the water?"

"Yes."

"They're not far apart from the cave exit."

"You mean that rock is part of the closer one?" Mercedez said. "I wouldn't have thought that."

"They're not connected, just not far apart," the woman said. "The underground cave is a shortcut. Would you like to see it?"

"Absolutely!" Mercedez said, jumping to her feet.

The couple did likewise, and the man said, "Race you girls! I'll even give you a head start!"

"We don't need it!" the woman said, but grabbed Mercedez' hand and the two women ran down the beach, breasts bobbing, laughing, Mercedez' strong legs moving her out in front quickly so that she was pulling the other woman along.

She turned briefly and saw the man catching up, his cock hard, bobbing a little as he raced after them. She let go of the woman's hand and ran with all her might, her strong dancer's legs carrying her fast and far as her strides lengthened. She was almost there. One more second. Her hand slapped the rock. Another hand slapped her bottom, and she snapped her head around at the man who had smacked her, about to confront him, when the woman finally reached them and smacked the man's butt. Now the three were laughing, doubled over from breathing hard, and Mercedez could feel the little sting across her ass cheek that must have burned a little in the sun.

Once they stopped gasping, the woman led them around the rock. Here, the ocean came up so close there was but twenty feet of beach. "When the tide comes in," the woman said, "there isn't a beach here. Just water."

Mercedez thought she looked a little wistful.

On the other side of the large boulder there was a hole, an opening into the boulder. "It's a sandy bottom and we can walk through all the way to the exit into the ocean," the man said. "Are you game?"

"Sure," Mercedez said, not quite certain what to expect, but she could use a little excitement.

The man led them inside the opening, only slightly higher than he was tall, but wide enough for two people. Inside it was dark, since they were inside a rock. He reached back behind him and Mercedez took his large hand, then she reached back for the woman behind her.

They walked along the sand in the darkness, the only light behind them. Mercedez heard water lapping. "We'll be at the ocean soon," the man said.

They were walking down now, the sand beneath their feet sloping, and Mercedez felt the thrill of the unknown. Somehow, she didn't feel afraid, although she was in utter darkness.

Suddenly, the woman behind clicked on a lighter, and for the life of her, Mercedez didn't know where she had hidden it, since she was naked and had no bag. All around were walls of striated sandstone, hardened by millennia, the stone eroded smooth by water so that it curved and flowed like the ocean itself. "It's lovely," Mercedez said.

"Yes." The woman looked at the rock and reached out to touch it. "The first time I saw this I thought it was one of the most beautiful places I've ever been."

Mercedez made a quick look ahead before the lighter went out. She saw water ankle height; already her feet felt wet.

"Are we going into the ocean?"

"Can you swim?" the man asked.

"Yes. But how far?"

"We're three-quarters of the way to the end now. The water will rise as we go. When we're chest high, we'll dive and swim to the end. The walls narrow from here so basically you can't get lost, just swim straight ahead, and you'll surface in half a minute. When you exit the cave, your hand will touch a black coral reef. That's when you should surface. But you'll notice a change in the light anyway as you come out of the cave.

This sounded easy, and at the same time Mercedez felt it

was a bit risky. But, nothing ventured, nothing gained, she knew, and she wanted to do something different. This was *very* different.

The water did rise, to her knees, her crotch, her waist, just about to her breasts. "Uh, my chest level isn't yours," she told the man, who was at least six feet.

"Uh, right," he said. "Okay, this is where we dive, then. "You both alright with this?"

"Yes," the woman said. "I'm ready. Always."

"I *think* I'm ready," Mercedez said.

The woman lit the lighter again and Mercedez watched the man dive beneath the water which looked level and calm, but because the sea floor was lowering she knew she would be underwater in a few more steps.

"How long to the end?" The guy had said half a minute but she wanted that confirmed.

"It's not far. You won't lose your air."

"Okay," Mercedez said, assuring herself that she could always turn around and come back.

She inhaled a deep breath and pushed herself under the water. It was cool in here, no doubt from the darkness. She opened her eyes once, but the salt water would ultimately bother them, and there was nothing to see anyway. Mercedez employed the butterfly kick, using her strong legs to propel her forward quickly. When her foot hit a wall, she knew this was where the cave walls narrowed and she switched to more straightforward kicking.

The walls narrowed further and she could feel them if she tried to fan out her arms, so she did a paddleboat type of crawl, kicking madly, using her hands on the walls to propel herself forward. The fleeting thought crossed her mind that if she wanted to go back it wouldn't be easy.

She wasn't out of breath, seemed to have plenty of air, but . . .

Suddenly she moved out of the narrow darkness and with a blink realized that it was lighter here. Her hand touched something rough and she knew this was the coral. Time to surface.

She used the coral as a launching pad and pushed herself up with her hands, breaking the surface quickly.

After letting out the stale air and taking in a big breath of fresh air, she looked around. The man dogpaddled close by, and suddenly the woman surfaced behind Mercedez, spitting water from her mouth. The three grinned at one another.

"Let's swim to the other rock," the woman said, once she'd caught her breath.

The man pointed at the large flat boulder out in the water, about two hundred yards away. "Can we all swim that far?" he asked.

"No problem," Mercedez said.

They swam leisurely, warm water gliding over their glistening bodies, and when they reached the rock climbed on top, helping one another. This boulder was definitely large enough for them. It could have accommodated another ten people. From here, the shore looked so far away—Mercedez saw her bag and towel down the beach. She turned and looked out at the ocean from this vantage point. The shoreline in both directions stretched for eternity, as did the horizon, or so it seemed.

"It's beautiful here," she said. "Thank you for showing me

this." She turned to find the man and woman kissing and fondling one another's genitals.

At one point, the woman stretched out an arm, inviting Mercedez to join them. She moved into an embrace from both.

They sandwiched her between them. The woman crouched down slowly, sliding her tongue over Mercedez' chest, licking and sucking her breasts. Behind her, the man also began to lower himself. The two moved in tandem, so that they were at about the same height. Hot lips and tongues pressed against Mercedez' flesh, and hands rode her skin, stimulating her back, arms, legs, stomach, every part of her, reaching up her throat to touch her face, fingers entering her mouth . . .

Her head fell back, her long hair lowering down her back, and the man stroked it and her buttock at the same time.

The woman tormented her nipple for a long time, sending Mercedez into aesthetic little spasms. Only when she felt limp did the woman lower herself still, her tongue darting in and out of Mercedez' belly button, circling the small tattoo near it, then down further, the man at the same level still.

Mercedez spread her legs wide. The man kissed her ass all over, his tongue sliding down the crack and stopping at her bottom hole. Meanwhile, the woman was at her pussy lips, sucking and licking her clit, the hot tongue occasionally darting into her slit.

Mercedez held both of them by the head, front and back, letting them take her completely. Her legs trembled as the tension built, tongues inside her slit and inside her asshole, hands stroking her everywhere. Two hands grabbed her ass cheeks and spread them wide, and two other hands spread her pussy lips wide.

"Oh, my god!" she cried as the orgasm hit her, rocking her, nearly knocking her off her feet as they lashed her with those sensitive tongues.

No sooner had she come than the man pulled the woman around behind Mercedez and laid her down on the rock, himself on top of her, his long cock sliding deep into her pussy. Mercedez watched them fucking, the woman moaning each time the cock shoved deeper into her. Soon, Mercedez sat on the rock, her pussy up against the woman's head and that head turned and lifted and the tongue started again on Mercedez' pussy as she leaned down and the man lifted his head up and they kissed.

The woman orgasmed twice before the man came. Then the three rested.

Soon, the two women were touching again, their bodies pressed together, nipples to nipples, pussy to pussy, rubbing and writhing as they faced one another. They rolled over, Mercedez on the bottom, and then rolled again and the woman was on the bottom. At some point the man stopped them with Mercedez on top. He spread their legs and got between them. Then he lifted himself up with his muscular arms and slid his cock into Mercedez' cunt, then out, then lowered himself in a modified pushup and slid his cock into the other woman's cunt, then out, then back to Mercedez, then the other woman, and she found this incredibly erotic, him fucking them both like this.

Both women's hands lowered and they fingered each other, rubbing clits in time to the fucking so that they were never unstimulated. While the cock was in Mercedez, plowing deep inside, she rubbed the woman's clit. When the cock entered the woman, she rubbed Mercedez' clit.

The three went on this way until their pace quickened and the man, with superhuman abilities, fucked one then the other in rapid succession and the fingering increased in speed until both women came together. Mercedez felt her vagina contract around the cock, then it left her and her burning pussy kept contracting as her clit button exploded, then the cock was back in her again.

When they were finally done, the women lay side by side on the rock watching the man masturbate himself for a while until the woman sat up and bent low over him, taking his cock into her mouth. Mercedez had an idea, and joined her. The women took turns with the cock, just the way he had fucked them, and each woman took one of his balls into her hand. When Mercedez' mouth had the cock, the other woman squeezed on the ball she held. When the other woman took the cock down her throat, Mercedez squeezed the tight ball.

The cock hardened and when he came the women were just changing and the hot cum splashed into both their faces and onto their chests as it shot into the air.

They all laughed and hugged and Mercedez realized that the sun was low in the sky. Her eyes roamed the beach and she noticed that her bag and towel were very close to the water's edge now, about to get wet.

Her eyes moved to the cave where they had entered. The rock on the shore was surrounded by water now. Suddenly she realized that the rock they lay on was lower in the water as spray wet her body. She walked to the edge of the rock. It, too, would be submerged soon.

"Hey, guys. We'd better go," she said, turning. And she found herself alone on the rock. "Guys? Guys? What the fuck?"

They were nowhere. Had they jumped into the water and left her? Surely she would have heard a splash. Just to assure herself they weren't playing a game, she walked around the edge of the rock. If they had slid in, they would surface soon. She waited a few minutes, but they were not there.

"Okay, this is weird," she said to herself, goose bumps on her skin. Surely they couldn't have gone back to the boulder. The water was too high. They couldn't swim back through the cave because the entire cave was now underwater. But whatever had happened to them, she didn't have time to dwell on it.

She dove into the sea, letting the waves carry her toward shore, using her legs and arms to guide her to the area where she'd left her belongings. Soon she washed up on the sand. Her towel was already half wet from the incoming tide. She picked up her bikini, donned it quickly, then her towel and bag and looked around. The couple was nowhere. And she could see that the rock out in the water was now underwater. The rock that housed the cave was more than half submerged. The beach itself had narrowed considerably with only about two yards of dry sand left.

There was nothing to do but go back, and to go back quickly, and try to find help. If that couple had gone into the cave . . . she didn't want to think about it.

When she reached the marina where she had started along this beach, she found a guard seated on a chair reading a newspaper. She ran to him.

He listened patiently while she told him not the whole story, and certainly she omitted their sexual escapades, but that the couple was out on a rock and might be stranded. "You've got to call the police. Get some help. They may be stranded."

The guard folded his newspaper carefully and slowly.

"What are you doing? Do something! They might be dead."

"Señorita, they *are* dead. That couple is famous here. They died five summers ago when they came down on their boat from California. As the story goes, they moored their boat here, right at this marina, and walked down the beach, so far that they were alone. There is a rock face there with a tunnel, and you can swim out into the ocean from there when the tide is low. This is what they did. They then swam to the rock you described, very flat, several hundred meters from shore. When the waters began to rise, they were forced to try to swim back through the tunnel and were trapped underwater. There, they drowned. Their bodies were never recovered."

"But . . . but then how do you know this?"

He looked seriously at her. "Because, señorita, you are not the first person to tell me this story. Others, not many, but you are the fourth I know of, tell of meeting them on the beach, following them into the cave and swimming to the rock, then finding themselves alone on the rock, the tides having risen, and returning to shore alone." He looked her up and down. "Most of the others became intimate with the ghosts."

Mercedez said nothing. She turned toward the town, slipping her dress over her bikini as she went, and strapped her sandals onto her feet when she reached the street.

She felt in a quandary and didn't know what to think, what

to do. Should she go to the police? Would they think she was crazy? Had others really had this same experience?

She saw a stand selling drinks and magazines and newspapers and stopped to buy a fruit juice because she was thirsty and out of water. Then she spotted the headline: "Anniversary of Ghost Couple and el Día de Los Muertos." She bought the paper, and took herself to a small café for a meal of fajitas and read the story of the couple who had died five years ago, the romance of it, the horror of it, and the writer tied it in to the upcoming Day of the Dead celebrations which would begin just a few days from now.

The photograph with the article was grainy but Mercedez recognized them. Their names were Janet and Greg Hutchison, from San Diego, California. The article talked about their yacht and the trip down the coast, just as the couple had related it to Mercedez. And just as the guard had said, the two were now a part of the legend of Los Cabos. They had walked up the beach and because her bag and their beach shoes were found near the underground cave when the tide went out again, it was thought they swam through the tunnel into the ocean, stayed too long, and tried to swim back, drowning in the tunnel. When the waters receded, their bodies were pulled out to sea.

Mercedez trembled. She had been on that rock. She might have tried to swim back through the tunnel. She might have drowned.

Apparently, the writer said, the ghosts had returned to the beach every year since their deaths to make contact with the living. It was a ritual, the article declared. So far, no one else had succumbed to the lure of the deep.

"Will they haunt you this year?" the writer asked. "Will you be the lucky recipient of their erotic favors? Will you have a special invitation to visit the land of the dead?"

Mercedez folded the paper and shoved it into her bag. She had about two hours before she needed to get to the airport. She spent her time wandering the cute seaside town in a bit of a daze, mainly browsing in shops, just trying to get herself calmed down. When she saw the black coral earrings, she knew she had to have them and bought them. Two long curvy abstract pieces of coral, one on each hook. One resembling a tall man, the other a tall woman. She bought them to remember this place by. A memory of the dead.

CHAPTER *11.*

$\mathcal{M}$ ercedez stood at the airport waiting for her flight. After hours of getting used to the idea that she had been with ghosts again, she began to feel not so much unnerved as inspired. Somehow, she felt she was on a quest of some kind. Everything that had happened to her in Mexico had been like a puzzle piece. She had collected many of the pieces so far but didn't know how they fit together yet.

One thing that kept coming back into her thoughts was what the woman said to her when they first met: *Puerto Vallarta. You should go there. You'll find something you lost.*

An announcement came over the loudspeaker that her flight for Mexico City was boarding. She hesitated. She had told Bill she would be back tonight, or rather, he had made the arrangements for her flight back. But why? Every time she'd come back from somewhere he was out, or going out, or had meetings the next day, or was on the phone, or had a suicidal colleague he had to deal with, if that was true. . . .

This was not good. She felt compelled to return, and that didn't make sense. She should be returning to Mexico City of her own free will, but right now it felt like an obligation.

She went to the desk and asked about flights to Puerto Vallarta. "Yes, we have one in one hour."

"Book me," she said. "And can I rebook my flight so I fly from Puerto Vallarta to Mexico City?"

"Yes. If you don't know when you want to leave, you can book it in Puerto Vallarta."

While waiting for the new flight, she used the pay phone to call the hotel in Mexico City. When the room rang, Bill picked up immediately.

"Mercedez, honey! Are you at the airport already? I thought your flight didn't get in for a while yet."

"I'm at the Los Cabos airport."

"Oh? Was there a delay?"

"Not with the plane. Listen, Bill, I want to go to Puerto Vallarta."

"Gee, I'm sorry, it's not on the itinerary—"

"I know that, but I'm paying for it."

"That's not what I meant. I mean that time-wise, there are no more days in this area. Tomorrow I'm in meetings all day and then the next day we fly south."

He's in meetings tomorrow. Just what I thought, Mercedez

mused. "Well, I figured you might be tied up with business tomorrow, so I thought I'd just go from here to Puerto Vallarta, see that place, and then fly to Mexico City tomorrow night."

"I had plans for us tonight," he said, sounding stiff.

Now she was feeling a little guilty. "I'm sorry, Bill. I didn't know. You didn't say anything. I've already canceled my flight and booked one to Puerto Vallarta. I'll fly in from there tomorrow night."

There was silence on the other end of the line. Finally, Mercedez said, "How's your colleague?"

"My colleague? Which one?"

"The one who tried to kill herself."

There was a pause, and Mercedez had the distinct impression that he was going over in his mind what he had told her. Finally he said, "She's doing well. Much better."

"I'm glad to hear that."

"I wish you'd told me before canceling your flight."

And Mercedez thought, *I'm glad I didn't.* She might have been pressured into returning tonight, just to spend a couple of hours with Bill and then be left alone again all day tomorrow!

"Well, it's already done. And I really do want to see this place. You're busy anyway tomorrow and—"

"That's not the point. The point is, we had a plan."

"*You* had a plan. Which you didn't tell me about."

"Wasn't it obvious? I booked your return for a reason."

"How was I supposed to know that? You're always working so I wouldn't really know what that reason was."

"I'm not always working. We've had plenty of time together. But I'm here for work. You know that."

"Yes, I do. And that's fine, as long as I can do what I like the rest of the time."

"You make it sound as if when you're with me you're not doing what you like."

"That's not what I meant. Of course I like being with you. What I meant was, I guess I didn't know you'd be working so much. Now that I know, I'm trying to plan for myself so I can do things I enjoy when we're not together."

That seemed to calm him a bit.

"And yes, I could have flown there and we could have had dinner together tonight, but then you're off at the crack of dawn, and I'd really rather see the smaller places. It's not that I don't like Mexico City, but I want to see the people, how they live, how they are. Can't you understand that?"

"Of course I can. Look, why don't you book the next flight here, stay overnight, then fly out tomorrow morning and—"

While he went on with *his* plan, Mercedez closed her eyes and sighed softly. Why couldn't he see what he was asking? All that effort for a few hours together. It's not as if they were anything more than "fuck friends." "Bill, that's too much. I wouldn't even get in until midnight and by the time I got to the hotel it would be one thirty, maybe two in the morning, and you'd be out of there by seven. What's the point?"

"To be together?" he said stiffly.

"For five hours? And most of that you'd need to sleep."

She heard the call for her flight. "Listen, I have to go,

they're calling my flight. I'll be back tomorrow night, at a reasonable hour. We can spend time together then."

"Please be here by eight o'clock," he said tensely. "We need to leave the hotel and catch an early flight the next morning and I don't want to be worrying about where you are, and I can't miss that flight."

"Alright. I'll be there. I promise. Don't worry. And Bill, relax. You sound like you could use a rest from all the work. And I'll see you tomorrow night, okay?"

"It will have to be, won't it?"

That annoyed her. But she didn't want to argue anymore. "Okay, see you by eight. Bye." And she hung up before he could say anything more.

This didn't feel right. Not at all. The relationship was growing toxic and she didn't really know if it had ever been anything more. Certainly since they had left Cancun things had gone downhill.

While she boarded the plane, she fumed about Bill and how unreasonable he was being. Yes, he had paid for everything, but he had offered that. Did that make her some sort of purchase? A barter: she would do everything he wanted when he wanted it in exchange for him paying for this trip, which supposedly was "no strings attached" and since they were "fuck friends" both of them could see anybody they liked? She had thought they were, above everything else, friends, without the entanglements of anything more than casual sex, which he wanted, and she had come to see made sense. Bottom line: he was not really relationship material.

Which suddenly reminded her that she had not called

Hugh again! She had meant to call him from Los Cabos but everything that happened there had erased that from her thoughts. Had erased almost everything from her thoughts. And now, once again, it was too late, with the time difference, and not having access to a phone except on the plane and she didn't want to be talking with him on a plane.

The flight was quick. She wished it was daytime so she could see Puerto Vallarta from the sky. She'd have to change her ticket for an earlier flight tomorrow, and would do that before leaving the airport here, just to make certain she got into Mexico City on time. She did promise that.

But the airline was sold out for the flight she needed and she had to book on a small regional no-frills airline. At least she got a flight!

She looked for an information booth but found none open. It was getting late. She hailed a taxi and asked the driver if there was a Holiday Inn in the city. There was and he took her there, the hotel located, he told her, on Banderas Bay. She'd read about the bay, a twenty mile horseshoe-shaped clean beach with calm waters, that had been formed by volcanic craters.

She booked a small room for the night, paying with her credit card. At this point, she didn't want to be beholden to Bill. "Can I get a late checkout?" she asked, and the desk clerk put her down for 2 P.M.

She had a long hot shower and washed her hair and let it air-dry while sitting on the balcony overlooking the water. Even from here she could see the beach littered with little jewels, protoplankton, the tiny creatures that whales live on.

And the sky, so large, strewn with stars. She felt good being here. Somehow, it felt right.

It had been a long day, full of adventure of the most unusual sort, and Mercedez climbed into bed gratefully and slept deeply.

At the crack of dawn Mercedez woke and ate a leisurely breakfast on the hotel's patio restaurant overlooking the ocean. She spent most of the morning lying on a beach chair by the pool, occasionally going for a swim to cool off. Around noon, she swam up to the pool bar, which had seats underwater, and ordered a piña colada and chatted with the bartender, a beautiful girl in her twenties with moist-looking skin and lustrous black hair. She wore a sky blue bikini that accentuated her curves and Mercedez frankly admired her body, as did everyone else at the bar.

"How long are you here?" the bartender asked.

"Just today. What are some of the good things to do?"

"Well, we have great tours of nearby islands with snorkling, of the jungle, and there's a tour of movie stars' homes—a lot of the famous movie stars had houses here, like Elizabeth Taylor and Richard Burton when they were married. The first time they were married, I think. There's the beach, of course, and—"

"I want to shop. Are there some good places in the town?"

"Excellent. You can find some amazing bargains here on embroidery, clothing—"

"Any unusual stores? I guess I'm looking for something that is truly Mexican, but not run-of-the-mill. I like the unusual."

"Well, there is one place. . . . It doesn't really have a name and it's not always open, but if you're lucky, you might find the door isn't locked. It's in an alley just behind Our Lady of Guadalupe Church, at the square. There's a skeleton in the glass of the door made of tin, very small, up in the top right corner. That's about all I can tell you, there are no windows."

"What do they sell?"

The bartender paused. "They sell the heart of Mexico."

She was called away by other customers, and Mercedez took her drink and left the pool, wandering down the few steps to the beach for a short stroll.

Pale-skinned hotel guests were lined up on beach chairs and loungers, cool drinks by their sides, cooking under the glorious sun. The water here was another beautiful green blue, the sky clear, and every so often as she walked she would meet a vendor selling everything from drinks to hats to iguanas—as if the tourists could get those across the border! She went over for a close-up look at an exceptionally long iguana wrapped around the shoulder of a teenager, just to touch the skin, which wasn't as abrasive as she expected. One of the large eyes on the side of its head seemed to stare at her as she spoke softly to it.

The iguana began nodding his head rapidly and the boy said, "He likes you, señorita. He only does that when he is competing with me for the females!"

They both laughed and with a final pat on the back to the iguana, Mercedez left.

She decided to skip lunch and instead had a shower and checked out of the hotel. It was fortunate she didn't have luggage, just her beach bag, but it would have been nice to have another dress to wear today. If she had thought about it, she could have rinsed this one out last night. But it was a holiday. No laundry! She decided to see if there was a dress she could buy, and found a green sundress with a miniskirt in the hotel's shop.

A taxi was dropping off a couple and she snagged it to el Centro, the center of town. Puerto Vallarta proved to be a lovely little place full of charming shops and cafés, and buildings resplendent with old Spanish architecture. Many shops were closed, because of siesta, but she didn't mind wandering the cobblestone streets.

Our Lady of Guadalupe Church was easy to spot, the tallest structure in the town. The peak of the tower was an enormous crown, and she found a brochure in the church entrance that said the crown was a replica of that worn by Carlota, Empress of Mexico in 1860. The original crown on the church had been silver, but an earthquake required a replacement. This wasn't one of the oldest churches, just a bit more than one hundred years since construction had begun, but they had taken time with details, like the eight angels at the base of the building holding hands.

After exploring the church, she wandered behind it, searching for the shop the bartender had mentioned, with no luck. Frustrated, she followed Rio Cuale to the Mercado Municipal, a two-story maze of shops that, as the bartender also had said, sold everything. She found a lovely silver armband and felt playful enough to bargain with the vendor, getting it for one-third the price he first quoted her. She slipped it up her arm to her bicep. It fit perfectly and she knew it looked hot. Wouldn't Connie be jealous!

She passed the T-shirts, leather goods, painted masks and

all of the usual and unusual items sold in Mexico. The larger mercados like this one brought in goods from everywhere around the country, and she found hammocks from the Yucatán and black coral from Los Cabos. And a variety of the Day of the Dead figures, some of which she had seen before, and others that were intriguing. There was a skeletal couple waving from a boat, and Mercedez picked it up and decided she had to buy this, just to remember Janet and Greg.

Her flight was at six and it was now three. She stopped and bought a fruit ice and ate it on a bench in the town square, admiring again the beautiful church, this time from a new angle, a bit to the side.

Suddenly, she saw a door, and intuitively knew, this was The Door! The one the bartender had told her about. It was like a mirage in the desert, and although she had walked around the church several times searching, she had not seen it until this moment, when she wasn't searching, just relaxing.

She finished the fruit ice and stood up, heading for the door. It was made of plain wood that had once been painted a red that had faded from the sun. The shop had no windows, and the glass in the door was so dusty she couldn't see inside. But up in the right-hand corner a small tin and wood skeleton hung. If she hadn't known about this place, she would never have suspected it was anything more than an empty shop. Even the little skeleton in the door window would have just been a reflection of the upcoming Day of the Dead holiday.

She tried the knob and it turned. The door opened to darkness. "Buenos días!" she called.

"Hola!" came a male voice from the darkness. "Come in, señorita. I have been expecting you."

"You have?" Mercedez stepped through the door hesitantly.

"You may close the door," the voice said.

"It's too dark in here. I won't be able to see," she said, knowing that the only light was from the sun behind her.

"Please, señorita. It is about to rain."

She turned to look out the door and the day had turned dark. Within seconds large drops began to fall from the sky, pelting the sidewalk like hail.

She closed the door behind her and stood in darkness for a moment until suddenly a match flared. Behind it she saw the hand that had struck it light a candle, then another. While she watched, the illumination showed that the hand was connected to an arm which connected to a torso. The room and the man came alive with light.

By the time he was done, thirty candles had been lit, giving the chamber a cathedral-like appearance.

"I—I was told about your shop," she said, looking around. There were rough wooden shelves that held all types of oddities lining the whitewashed walls. Right away she saw animal bones; some skulls with teeth that looked like they were from a lizard or a fish. There were also other bones that reminded her of arm bones, but she didn't believe anyone was selling human bones. There were metal objects, and items made of old leather, some with exotic looking feathers attached. She also saw a wall that seemed to contain spears and shields, the markings either Aztec or Mayan.

"Do you see anything you need, señorita?"

"I don't know. I'm not sure what all of these things are."

"Perhaps it is not necessary to understand, but more to feel their importance to you."

Mercedez moved closer to the periphery of the room and began walking slowly around, looking at objects. En route she picked up a candle and carried it with her so that she could examine everything. "This place is like a Mexican curio shop," she said in awe.

"Exactly," the man told her.

She still couldn't see him clearly, at least his face, but the candlelight reflected off his rock-hard body, and it was a superb body, that was for sure. He wore pants low on his hips, tied with a rope, but no shirt. The man was short and of a muscular build, with tattoos across his chest, from upper arm to upper arm, and another on his stomach that came up from his groin and spiraled inward toward his belly button, stylistically a bit like the snakes at Chichen Itza. Most of the inked images were abstract but she recognized some as Mayan and Aztec designs. All were black, at least in this light.

Once she had scanned the shelves of bones, she moved on to pottery. There were fragments, and also complete bowls with faded colors. "When are these from?" she asked.

"They were made by our people before the conquistadors came here, before the Aztec and Mayans civilizations came to be. Before the world as we know it formed."

"Shouldn't these artifacts be in a museum?"

He said nothing.

Mercedez crept around the room slowly, examining pieces of fabric, beaded necklaces, metal and stone tools. This place was wonderful, just like a museum. "These things must be very expensive," she said, more to herself than to him.

"They are priced according to the need."

"That's cryptic!"

Again, he said nothing.

Once she had gone around the room twice, she turned and looked at him. His face was still obscured by shadow and she really wanted to see what he looked like. She stepped toward him and the face she saw made her gasp. It was the most alive face she had ever viewed. The brilliant dark orbs that were his eyes sparkled with a light of their own. His straight dark hair hung sensually around his shoulders, and his face looked almost sculpted, as if he had been carved in stone.

"Have you found something you need?" he asked, his voice rich as chocolate, warm as blood.

She could only stare up at him and say, "I—I don't know."

"Come," he said, offering her a hand.

She didn't know why she took it. She felt compelled to follow him. He led her behind a fabric curtain into a smaller room, just as dark, with only her small candle for illumination. Here, when she lifted the candle, she saw different items on the walls: masks, small statues on shelves, larger ones poised on the floor. Some she recognized: the snakes and the Choc Mool from Chichén Itzá, an angular-faced figure similar to one she had seen at the archeological museum in Mexico City that was Aztec. . . .

"These are . . . amazing. Where did you get them?"

He didn't answer her question but said, "You appear to be attracted to the Mayan culture."

"I am! My blood is Mayan. But I don't know much about it. I know they made human sacrifices, and killed women, children, warriors in the name of their gods."

"Their gods were the old gods that demanded sacrifices in order that the people could continue. You must not judge the past by the present. That is meaningless. We can only see ourselves in history as in a dream, and remake ourselves into the future as a premonition."

"Wow," she said. "That's pretty complex. But I think what you're saying is true. I just don't know how to see myself in the Mayan past."

The man took a small cylindrical object from a shelf and handed it to her. It was like a tube for mailing, but no more than six inches long, the diameter two or three inches at best. The ends were covered. She held it up to the flickering candle flame to see it better. There were markings along the shaft, Mayan from what she could tell, painted in what might be fading red and green over turquoise. The tube felt like light wood, the ends were stiff, and stitched to the tube.

"Is this . . . is it a drum?" she asked, not knowing what to think.

"It is, one used by women. It calls the spirit world to enter them and to bring them fully to life."

"Really?" She felt skeptical. "How does it do that?"

"Play the instrument and see for yourself."

She set the candleholder onto a shelf with nothing above it.

Before she could begin, the man took her hand and turned her palm upward. Quick as a blinking eye, he stabbed her palm with something sharp.

"Ow! What are you doing?" she cried, stepping back in horror, but not before he pushed the little drum onto that palm.

"Why did you do that?" She was beginning to wonder if this was such a good idea, being here, alone with him, in this room, in a shop nobody could find easily, during siesta when no one would be on the streets to help if she screamed. . . .

"Do not fear me," he said. "The drum must drink your blood in order to call on your behalf."

"O—kay. Now what do I do?"

"Follow your heart."

She looked down at the drum, barely visible in the minimal light in the room. She felt her hand pulsing and wondered if she would end up with some infection from having an open wound touching this old and probably dirty object. But soon her hand throbbed with heat and the drum felt like some living creature she held, and she wouldn't have been surprised to feel it move.

Instinctively she tapped one end with her fingertip. Then the other. Remarkably they made a different sound, one high, one much lower. She liked the tones very much, and spontaneously tapped one, then the other, at first alternating, then with more of a pattern, more at the high-pitched end, less at the lower pitch, then changing, and soon found herself with a rhythm that seemed to reverberate through her arm, into her torso, and down her legs. Suddenly she was aware that she had been dancing, moving her feet to her own rhythm. The sounds from the drum seemed to fill the room and she began to smile, a broad grin that pulled her lips wide. Laughing, she whipped her hair around her head.

The man before her came into view, and it was as if the room was lit fully. His face was the most beautiful she had ever seen, every feature even and smooth, a fine blend of primitive Indian and modern sophistication. He aligned his movements with hers, moving around her, embracing her but not touching her body, his arms encircling her, and she felt the heat of him as she happily beat the drum.

Her body soared with inner fire, alive, churning with an energy that rivaled a thousand suns. Suddenly the man did touch her, his hands on her hips, holding her from behind, as she rocked and swayed and hopped to the music she created and he aligned with her.

Every part of her tingled, ringing with living cells, calling for a mate, and he answered. As they moved together in perfectly harmonious, snakelike movements she thought she could hear hissing. His cock slid up inside her wet cunt from behind and an image formed in her mind's eye of the stone snakes at Chichén Itzá, the vision serpents, those that opened the doorway to Quetzalcoatl, the deity at the center of the world.

She felt filled as never before with the largeness of this organ that seemed godlike to her. Her hot juices bathed it, lubricated it, allowed it to press up against the deepest part of her, and he stayed inside her as they hopped and swayed and she felt heat escalating to incineration level.

Now they were on the floor, writhing together in the dirt of the jungle, two snakes, using muscle to move around, copulating snakes, joined in an eternal mating that evoked the creator. It was a savage fuck that left her helpless, submissive to something larger than either of them, and she could only acquiesce to the demands that overwhelmed her, and for which she felt grateful.

Suddenly she became unaware of her hands beating the drum, unaware of her body moving in dance. She had become the drum and the snake dance, and the only thing that was not her was the hard cock impaling, refusing to release her, and she did not want to be released. She wanted it inside her forever. Her walls closed around it, contracting and expanding, and she screamed as her body convulsed in an orgasm that lasted so long she wondered, hoped it would never end. Only that cock—so full and hard, so steady inside her—that was the only thing not her in this eternal moment. And at the magic second when they merged, it too became her.

When it was over she got to her feet trembling, her eyes closed, sweat dripping from her body. Her legs were rubber, barely able to hold her up. She gasped for air as if she had run a marathon. Her mind felt clear as crystal, her body heavy in an earthy way.

Slowly she opened her eyes. And found herself out in the square, staring at the water as the brilliant sun bounced along its surface; the streets around her were drying after the down-pour. She was not alone but surrounded by throngs of tourists and locals going about their business. No one looked at her strangely, although a few people smiled.

Mercedez looked down. She was fully dressed, her bag slung over her shoulder. And in one hand she held the small drum that was indeed turquoise with pale red and yellow Mayan markings. She rolled it toward her fingers and saw the scar of a wound—how could it scar so quickly?

Then she turned and stared beyond the church, searching for the door.

She hurried along the side of the church, around to the back, searching for that door. Where had it been?

This is crazy! she thought. *I was just there. I have the drum! I have the wound. It has to exist!* But it was like the first time today when she had tried to find it. Every shop—and they were now all open—was not the right one. She raced in and out of the specialty stores, past straw and leather goods, sundresses, jewelry, lacework, but no matter which way she went on the street, the store was no longer there.

Finally, in desperation, she asked one of the shop owners, "Where's the store that sells old Mexican artifacts?"

The owner looked at her strangely. "Perhaps over at the mercado—"

"No, no, it was here! Right about where your store is. No, next to it. Between this store and the next one!"

"That cannot be, señorita. My shop has been here for twenty or more years as has the one next door, and as you can see, there is no room for another shop."

"But . . . I was just in it."

"Señorita, it is a hot day. Perhaps the sun—"

"I'm not loco!" she cried, feeling a bit crazy. "I'm sorry. It's just that I was there a few minutes ago, and now I can't find the shop. I got this there," she said, holding out the little drum.

"Ah, it is very beautiful. And very old, señorita. I would say very rare. If there was such a shop that sold something like this, I would know of it, but there is none. I'm sure you are mistaken and it was another street."

"Maybe," Mercedez said, knowing that she was not mistaken, that the shop had been here, as if it had existed in the space between this shop and the next, as if a crease in time had appeared and she had entered another dimension, but that was impossible, surely.

And yet, she had the drum in her hand. And the owner confirmed that it was old.

I didn't even pay for it, she thought. But then some part of her remembered the man's words: *the price is according to the need*. She didn't know what that meant, but obviously she had needed this. And perhaps she had given him something.

Carefully she placed the little drum into her beach bag and headed for the airport. She had been told to come here, to find something she had lost. Was it the drum, or was it her passion? Either way, she was grateful that she had had the luck to find the shop. She felt that in some way it would change her. Maybe it already had!

CHAPTER *12.*

Mercedez had just boarded the small plane, a margarita before her, when the flight attendant leaned over the seat, one of her lush breasts accidentally brushing up against Mercedez' arm. "The copilot was wondering if you'd like to see the cockpit."

"Really? That's so nice of him. But aren't there regulations and security issues and all that?"

"Well, on a flight this empty, we sometimes offer passengers special services. It's not exactly in the rules but it's not against them either. Yet," she smiled.

"That's great. Lead the way!"

Mercedez had noticed that she was one of only three

passengers on the twin-engine propeller plane. An old man sat at the back in the last row sleeping soundly, his snores rivaling the engines. A pregnant woman sat in the middle looking pensively out the window. And Mercedez had taken a seat near the front. They had been flying so low she could count the cars on the main highways.

The door to the cockpit opened and inside was the smallest space Mercedez had ever seen for housing two men and a wide panel of dials and levers plus overhead controls. When she stepped in, the flight attendant came with her.

"Buenas tardes, señorita," the captain said. He was an older man with white hair and a white handlebar moustache waxed at the ends to points, but still striking.

"Good evening. It's very nice of you to invite me to see the inner workings."

The copilot introduced himself. "I am Ramón, and the pilot is Captain Rodriquez."

"And I am María," the flight attendant said. "We welcome you aboard."

"It's a short flight," Ramón said. "We should arrive in thirty minutes. Hardly time to show you around. Here, sit in my seat for a moment."

He eased out of his copilot's chair and the space was so narrow that Mercedez had to brush against him full body in order to sit down. She could feel his erection through his pants.

She looked out the window at the sky, which was so much closer than even the tallest hotel room. And the clouds they passed through, gray fluff on this clear night. "It's so different up here. You see the same things in the cabin but it looks, I don't know, more amazingly up-close as you head into it."

"This is true," Captain Rodriquez acknowledged. "I have been flying for twenty-five years and it has never been boring."

"I'm very impressed with that," Mercedez said in earnest. "I respect people who enjoy what they do."

"Here." Ramón leaned over her, a hand on her shoulder, the arm reaching across her body brushing the side of her breast as he placed her hands on the stick. "We're on automatic, but you can get a feel for what we feel."

He wrapped his hand around hers and the plane descended a bit, then he pulled back and the nose ascended.

"Oh! I thought you said we were on automatic!" Mercedez shrieked.

"We were. The captain let you fly."

They were on automatic again. Mercedez could feel that, since the stick didn't alter the position of the plane. Her two seconds of flying had been spectacular, brief, and over.

"That was fun. That's so much." She stood to give Ramón back his seat but instead of sitting down, he slipped an arm around her waist.

María, still in the cockpit, excused herself and went out to attend to her passengers, leaving Mercedez alone with the pilot and copilot.

In the small, cramped space, she looked up into the handsome face of Ramón. He was a playboy, that she could see. He liked to flirt. To tease women. Well, she would show him where his teasing would lead.

Rather than push away from him, she pushed into him.

"You're used to flying," he said with a grin.

"I've done my share."

Captain Rodriquez kept an eye on the dials and another eye on the two of them.

Mercedez felt bold. Outrageous. She reached down and grabbed Ramón's crotch. His eyes and mouth opened wide, then his lips spread into a broad smile.

"Hands up!" she said, pointing a finger at his chest as if it was a gun, pretending to be a hijacker.

He laughed and raised his hands above his head, as far as the low ceiling would allow. Captain Rodriquez nodded and smiled at this game.

Mercedez unzipped Ramón's pants, reached in and pulled out his firm cock. She grabbed it as she had the navigational stick and moved his cock the same way. He laughed and tilted his body as the plane had moved, forward, backward, and then he bent down on his knees a bit until she moved his cock down and he straightened. All the while he grew harder.

Mercedez slid down his body, still grasping his penis, and when she got to her knees she pulled his cock forward again. She opened her mouth wide and looked up at him. He grinned down at her. "Fly me, baby! Right to the moon."

Suddenly Mercedez closed her mouth, the tip of his cock just half an inch from her luscious lips. She looked up at him with large, innocent eyes. "Beg me."

Captain Rodriquez burst out laughing and said in Spanish, "She has your number!"

Ramón flushed with embarrassment. This was not how a macho assistant pilot acted, but he was clearly titillated. He said in a controlled voice, as though it didn't matter to him, "Okay, yes, please."

"I said, beg."

Now he looked even more embarrassed. The cockpit filled with silence.

This time it wasn't just his words that changed. His voice also altered. The tone became less aggressive, more submissive, and he said, "Please. Please suck me off."

"Again."

Even as she said it, his cock grew harder, the vein protruding even more. She still held it, and slipped two fingers underneath, sliding them back and forth between his tight balls and his raging erection.

He had grown hungry, she was sure of that. "Please. I beg you. Suck my cock."

Mercedez grinned herself. She moved her lips close to the head of his penis and lightly kissed it. His body trembled, his cock trembled, and his balls grew tauter. She was afraid he'd come instantly.

"Please."

Mercedez moistened her lips with her tongue, taking her time, while he watched her, and all the while she ran her fingers from his cock to his balls and between his balls to his anus, then back again. Finally, when she heard him panting, she opened her lips just a little and began to slide them very slowly over his cock.

His body trembled again.

She used her fingers to encircled his nuts, squeezing hard, creating a vice grip, a fleshy cock ring to keep him from coming.

He groaned.

Mercedez felt the Captain's eyes on her and turned her head slightly, mouth full of cock, to wink at the older man, who again burst into laughter.

Slowly she licked the rock-hard cock from base to tip and back again, the top, the underside, then slid her lips over the entire penis, taking him deep into her throat. All the while his groans grew louder and more frequent. "Yes. Yes. Please . . ."

She licked the throbbing vein, and then let her tongue circle the head of his cock over and over, all the while squeezing his balls tight, and his cock felt so hard she thought he might explode.

Now she sucked him in earnest, using her mouth like a vagina, fucking him orally, pumping hard on his swollen organ as she took it into her throat.

In a moment of intuitive clarity, she released the grip she held on his balls.

He cried out and arched his back and thrust his prick at her, deep down her throat. She felt the pulsing as the fluids slid out of him and tasted hot salty cum that she swallowed down greedily, licking his cock clean afterward, and then licking her lips.

"This is the captain speaking," Rodriquez said, his voice deep. "All passengers return to your seats and fasten your seat belts. We are about to land in Mexico City. We hope you've had a pleasant and exciting flight. I know I speak for the co-pilot and myself when I say that for us this flight has been a true pleasure."

Mercedez jumped to her feet. She patted the copilot on the

cheek while he tried to recover himself, and bid the pilot good-bye, and then hurried out the door and to her seat.

She had just buckled up when the plane began to descend. The lights out the window of this enormous city twinkled in the growing darkness. She hoped to have time to phone Hugh tonight, if it wasn't too late. A lot depended on Bill and what plans he had. She might need to wait until she returned home to phone Hugh—

"Be careful."

Mercedez snapped her head around. A woman sat next to her. She glanced around: the old man in the back was still sleeping; the pregnant woman still chewed her nails to the quick. Mercedez didn't remember seeing this woman on the plane before and certainly she hadn't been seated here.

Then she looked closer. "I know you."

The woman in black nodded.

"You were at the mercado in Corpus Christi!"

"Where is the charm?"

"I—I left it in the hotel in Mexico City."

The old woman shook her head as if resigned to a terrible fate for Mercedez. "You are foolish. You are almost at the end of your journey and now more than ever you will need protection."

Mercedez felt upset. She had meant to bring the charm with her. In fact she'd taken it everywhere, but for some reason had left it at the hotel when she went to Los Cabos, maybe because she had been so upset. She'd just forgotten it. She stared out the window in despair. The old woman unnerved her. She wasn't superstitious, or at least she didn't think she was, but something about the charm, and this trip . . .

She turned back to say, "Look, I'll get it as soon as I—" but the woman was gone.

"I must be losing my mind!" she said aloud as the flight attendant walked to the front of the plane. "Excuse me; is there an old lady in black on this plane?"

The flight attendant looked confused. "No, señorita. There are just three passengers."

To herself, Mercedez said, "Why should I be surprised that someone just appears and disappears? Happens all the time!"

They landed smoothly and Mercedez waved good-bye to the flight crew of three.

There were plenty of taxis at the airport but she felt the need to see a familiar face and dialed Pedro's number. He arrived within twenty minutes.

"Señorita, did you enjoy your trip to Guanajuato?"

"Yes. But Pedro, that was three trips ago. I've also been to Los Cabos and today I was in Puerto Vallarta. I'm a real jet-setter!"

Pedro nodded. "It is good that you are seeing Mexico. There are many more places to visit. Like Oaxaca."

"Well, as a matter of fact, we're leaving tomorrow morning for Oaxaca, for a day I think, and then we fly home."

"Oaxaca is a good place. I have people from there. You must stay for two days. It is the festival Día de los Muertos."

Pedro heard a song he liked on the radio and cranked it up, another narco corrido tune from the lyrics.

Mercedez sat back suddenly sobered. She would be leaving Mexico very soon. That was so hard to believe. It seemed as if she had just arrived. As if adventures were just beginning. She had gotten used to this life of spontaneous adventure. It made her sad that she would be going home. And then she heard the silly lyrics of the shoot-'em-up drug lord song, about tattooed girlfriends who liked to ride the horse all night, and she laughed out loud. Pedro looked at her in the mirror and catching the gist of it laughed with her. They laughed most of the way to the hotel.

CHAPTER *13.*

$\mathcal{M}$ercedez arrived back at the hotel room five minutes before eight. Bill was waiting for her. Although she was pensive, he opened his arms to her, obviously not holding a grudge, and she didn't either. They kissed for a while, but then he said, "Listen, honey, I've got reservations for dinner and we're meeting friends."

"Oh? Who?"

"Well, one is my colleague—"

"Not the one who—"

"No. This one is male."

"And the other I suppose is the girlfriend."

"Something like that. Anyway, it's a chic place, so dress to the nines, okay? We should really go all out for our last night in Mexico City."

Mercedez showered and did her hair and makeup flawlessly. When she came out of the bathroom, Bill was already dressed in a dark blue suit, the pale blue shirt she had bought him when she first arrived, and a contrasting tie. He looked smart. She hadn't seen him dressed up before. "Lookin' great!" she called over as he was buffing his shoes to a mirrorlike shine.

He grinned at her.

Mercedez sorted through the closet and took out the red dress she'd bought. The crepe slid over her body and clung to it like a second skin. She stared into the full-length mirror, admiring the lines of the dress, the asymmetrical hemline which was so fashionable, and the low neck that showed a lot of cleavage. The little peplum accentuated her narrow waist. Her breasts sat in the bust of the dress without a bra, and the tops swelled slightly over the bodice. Her erect nipples pushed against the fabric.

She also wore the red stilettos she'd bought to go with it and the black coral earrings and silver bracelet she had found on her trips. She wished she had something nice to wear around her neck, but she only had the gold cross and didn't want to clash metals; better to leave her neck bare.

Now that she was dressed, she realized she should have bought the purse that matched the shoes. She only had her shoulder bag with her and her beach bag. Well, she'd have to take the shoulder bag, that was all there was to it.

Warm breath on her neck. "You look spectacular. You are one of the most beautiful creatures I've ever seen."

She smiled at him in the mirror.

"Too bad you don't have something for around your neck."

"I didn't think about the whole outfit when I was shopping," she said. "I have a gold cross, but, well, it's not right for this dress."

"Maybe this will work better."

Bill handed her a small beaded purse, somewhere between a clutch and a coin purse in size. She unzipped it and found inside a silver chain. Dangling from the end of it was a black pearl. She lifted it out of the purse saying, "My god, Bill, this is gorgeous! It must have been incredibly expensive!"

"Not so much. In fact, it didn't cost me anything. One of my business associates gave it to me."

"Really?" she turned and stared at him, not knowing if this was a joke.

He took the silver chain from her hand and put the necklace around her neck, fastening the clasp at the back. The pearl nestled between her breasts. It was a rich, deep black, like onyx, and went well with the black coral earrings.

"Perfect!" he said.

She turned and threw her arms around his neck. "Bill, you're amazing. This is so wonderful of you. I'm sure you have women you've known longer you could give this to."

"But none quite so lovely. You two belong together."

They kissed briefly, and then he patted her on the bottom. "We gotta go."

She used the beaded purse, which was better than her shoulder bag, and stuffed into it a bit of money, the room key, a credit card, comb, lipstick, pressed powder, and it was full.

Then she remembered the charm. She had to take it. She rummaged in the inside pocket of her suitcase until she found it and managed to stuff it into the little purse and somehow get the zipper closed.

They breezed through the lobby of the Meliá, many heads turning in the direction of such a gorgeous well-heeled couple. Mercedez knew she looked dazzling. She felt spectacular. She'd been preparing herself for problems when she returned, and it was so wonderful that they were getting along. It would be a total shame to end this amazing trip on a bad note.

They caught a taxi. It was not one of the Volkswagen minitaxis but a Lincoln, plush interior, and quiet. Bill gave the address and they were whisked across town.

Seeing Mexico City from this rarified perspective was different than anything she had done here so far. All the hustle and bustle remained outside the vehicle, visuals with no audio counterpart. It felt like watching a movie, being so removed from the reality around her, but she enjoyed it.

They arrived and the driver pulled to the curb of a restaurant with a name that was a number, "4", in brass beside the door. A long awning like the type they use a lot in New York ran from the door to the curb, and there was a red carpet on the ground.

Bill helped Mercedez out of the taxi and wrapped her arm around his as he led her to the door; the doorman couldn't take his eyes off her. Inside, the place was all elegance, the woods of the foyer old and well-oiled. They were greeted at once by the maitre d' and escorted across the sedate and crowded room. En route Mercedez glanced at everything on the walls and whispered to Bill, "It's as if this stuff belonged to the conquistadors!"

"It did," he said.

Her mouth fell open. Suits of golden armor stood in corners, round gold shields, long breastplates, and heavy-looking swords decorated the walls, leather banners with Spanish writings hung from the ceilings, cases of leather-bound books and golden goblets filled the shelves of walnut bookcases, wrought iron chandeliers hung from the ceilings. . . . She could hardly believe that these were real antiques, here, in a restaurant!

They reached a table where a man and woman sat. The man stood at once, shook hands with Bill as they exchanged verbal pleasantries, but all the while he stared at Mercedez.

"This is Mercedez, whom I told you about. Mercedez, John Smith from the Omaha office."

Smith extended a hand that engulfed hers. He was as big as a sumo wrestler, and it was all muscle, no fat. Tall, maybe six foot eleven, he towered over both of them. His hazel eyes were playful, with crinkle lines at the corners, and his thin lips spread across most of his rounded face. She liked the fact that the brown hair he had left was unkempt—it made this larger-than-life man very human.

"My fiancée, Annie Lewis," he said.

Once both Bill and Mercedez had shaken hands with Annie, they all sat, the waiter helping Mercedez with her chair. He then draped a linen napkin across her lap and Bill's.

She thanked the waiter, who she caught looking down her dress, and when her eyes returned to the table she saw that the slim, petite Annie was staring at her chest, too, a lustful smile playing on her full, sensuous lips. She ran a hand through her short white-blonde hair, spiky at the front, and arched a black eyebrow. A slightly wicked smile played on her lips that Mercedez found intriguing.

The four chatted amiably for several moments until the waiter handed Bill the wine list. He ordered a bottle of Artadi 2000 Grandes Anades. "It's from Spain," he told the others when the wine steward had departed. "It goes well with both meat and fish. I think you'll like it."

They chatted a bit more and at one point Annie leaned forward and down a bit, her low-cut dress exposing a lot of fullness, as she said, "That is a *lovely* pearl. Is it one of the ones from Mexico?"

"I—I don't know. Do they find pearls in Mexico?"

Before Mercedez could say more, Bill jumped in. "Actually, she doesn't know much about it. I just gave it to her about an hour ago."

He turned to Mercedez. "Black pearls have been used as barter in Mexico even before the conquistadors came here. The ancient Mayans and Aztecs traded in pearls and the first black pearls were harvested from the Pacific Ocean."

Mercedez held the little pearl in her fingertips and looked down at it, then up at him. It felt so cool and perfectly round. That it had once been a grain of sand that had become an irritant and grown inside an oyster like a kidney stone was astonishing to think about, really.

The wine came and Bill tasted it, nodding his approval to the waiter. Mercedez didn't know for certain but she thought this must be an expensive bottle.

Once the wine had been poured, Bill lifted his to the table and the others joined in for the toast. "To an exciting evening."

"Absolutely!" John said.

Annie chimed in, "Yes. I'm so looking forward to it."

"Cheers," Mercedez said, having the feeling that the other three had discussed the evening and she was at a bit of a disadvantage.

When the oversized menus came, Mercedez noticed there were no prices listed, another indication that this restaurant was one of those "If you have to ask the price, you can't afford to eat here" places. She told herself to make sure Bill didn't leave her here again, because she suspected the bill would max out her credit card.

The appetizers looked scrumptious as did the main courses being served around them. None of it looked especially Mexican, although clearly the chef had tried to add a Latino flavor to each dish, like the filet mignon with a piquant sauce.

Bill suggested the snails but Mercedez wanted to try the baked brie with jalapeños for an appetizer. They both decided on the pheasant. Annie had fish and John a steak, well done.

"So, Mercedez, have you been in Mexico often?" Annie asked.

"I was here once before. But this trip is amazing. I've seen a lot of places, thanks to Bill."

"Yes, Bill is a generous guy," she said, giving him a look that Mercedez couldn't fathom. Bill looked back at her briefly and smiled.

"I'm partial to the beaches," John said. "We don't have 'em back home and whenever I'm here on business I like to get as much surf and turf in as I can. And I mean that for food, too!"

Annie laughed, and the action lightened her up and Mercedez suddenly found her quite lovely and charming.

Throughout the meal they talked about Mexico, about the business that John was in—import/export—about Bill's job which Mercedez had heard little about, but it seemed it took him around the world. Annie worked as a receptionist in Bill's company. "That's how we met," she said.

"When are you getting married?" Mercedez asked, nodding at the large diamond on Annie's ring finger.

"Maybe a year, maybe two. We're in no rush. We've been together for two already. We live together now."

"That's a good approach. Get to know one another. It makes a lot of sense."

"What about you?" Annie asked, and suddenly the men, who had been talking politics, became quiet.

Mercedez put down her fork and looked around the table. "What about me? What do you want to know?"

"Anybody special?" Annie asked, a little nod of her head in Bill's direction.

Mercedez definitely did not feel comfortable talking about this. In her mind, she and Bill had become even more "fuck friends" than when they began this trip, and there was even less potential for a real relationship. If anybody waited in the wings it was Hugh, and she hadn't had a chance to call him, nor had he called again—she'd checked the messages while Bill was in the washroom at the hotel room before they left.

"You know," she said, "I hate talking about personal things when we're in such an interesting restaurant. Bill says that these antiques date to the conquistadors. I'm amazed they're not in a museum."

Bill said, "You know, the sixteenth century might have been the greatest century of recorded history, in many ways. The new world was discovered then, and they crossed a very large body of water to get here. The conquistadors not only found the Americas but they proved that the earth was not flat but round."

"They also managed to conquer a lot of people," Annie said. "Not just the Aztec and Mayan peoples but the Incas in Peru as well. If I remember my history correctly, there were some very bloody battles."

"There were. But then those people were also bloody, so it wasn't just the Spanish."

"We were in Chichén Itzá," Mercedez offered, "and saw the Choc Mool with the bowl for the sacrifices, and the well of virgins, and other things. It was a different time. You can't judge the past by present standards," she said, thinking that she was now quoting what people have been saying to her.

"Hell, look at all the foods they introduced to Europe," John added. "Pineapples, turkeys, chilies, chocolate. Potatoes even."

Annie laughed at him.

"Of course," Bill said, "the Europeans brought things too: smallpox, measles. . . . Millions died in pandemics. There's a lot that's sad about history. And then the Europeans also brought over Christianity."

"I guess," Mercedez said, "there's never change without risk. Never a chance for something new without the possibility that things can backfire on you."

"That's true. And a lot of the Spanish died on their way here. And other settlers, too. Some say more died than survived on the boats and on the treks overland. But we wouldn't be sitting here today if the conquistadors hadn't made those journeys. Well, maybe Mercedez would be. Not here, exactly, but in some part of the Yucatán. But then we don't know what wars between the Mayans and the Aztecs would have developed, who would have won, who lost, who would have lived and how they would have lived."

"Hindsight is best left behind," John said, and they all laughed.

After the meal, Bill and John smoked cigars and the four had snifters of brandy. The food had been excellent, the conversation easy, and now, with the fiery liquor sliding down her throat, Mercedez had turned very mellow indeed.

"Shall we go back to the hotel?" Bill asked.

Everyone agreed, so they did.

Up in the room, Mercedez and Bill played hostess and host and offered up drinks from the minibar to their guests.

They sat in easy companionship for close to an hour around the table. Mercedez went to the washroom and when she came back sat on the edge of the bed, just for a change of view. Suddenly, Annie went to the bed and sat next to Mercedez. The two women looked at one another, eyes sparkling, Annie's mischievous, Mercedez' full of humor.

Annie slipped her arm around Mercedez' waist. Mercedez did the same with her. Annie's sculpted features, her almost opaque skin, and that spiky sexy white-blond hair were a real turn-on.

Simultaneously they moved their faces closer together and kissed. The room became utterly silent; Mercedez knew they were a real show for the guys.

She slipped her hand down Annie's low-cut dress until she reached a nipple, then took it between her thumb and forefinger and squeezed. A gasp escaped Annie's mouth, still glued to Mercedez'.

Annie's hand eased down the red dress and liberated Mercedez' tit from the bodice. Then she tweaked the nipple until Mercedez felt it burn, and wetness slide down her thighs.

Soon the women were easing down the dresses of the other until the fine fabrics lay in a heap by the bed. They were both braless, just wearing panties, Mercedez one of her usual thongs in red tonight, and Annie crotchless black French panties.

They lay back on the bed, writhing together, pussy rubbing pussy, breasts pressed together, nipples touching, while their lips continued to interact and hands felt skin: backs, buttocks, waists.

Annie broke apart and grinned at Mercedez, then she crept down to the other end of the bed and as she did so, she slipped Mercedez' panties off. She thrust her crotch into Mercedez' face and put her lips to Mercedez' pussy.

Mercedez opened Annie's legs and found her pussy displayed between the swatches of frilly black lace. The pussy glistened with moisture, and the clit was already hard and inviting. She pressed her tongue to it, tasting the salty-sweet pussy juice, running her tongue all the way along the clit, making it harder, causing Annie's butt to quiver.

Whiles Mercedez did this, Annie sucked her clit, pulling

the sensitive nub with her teeth, chewing gently, making Mercedez moan and cry out. Annie spread her ass cheeks. She moistened a finger in her mouth then slid it around her anus. Mercedez decided to do the same. Together, at the same moment, they entered one another's asshole. The passion in both women escalated and they ate each other out with a hunger brought on by good food and drink and a sexy partner in bed.

Mercedez was aware that Annie was trying to time their orgasms and she thought this was a good plan, so she aligned herself, too. They licked and sucked and nipped and rubbed with their tongues and lips and fucked each other's behind in a rhythm that Mercedez knew only women could master. And then they came together, bodies convulsing, fingers fucking harder and deeper, clits being tormented further while the passion rippled through both of them and their pussies spasmed as they cried out, each in her own style.

Then they laughed and hugged and kissed freely. And Bill and John laughed too and were soon removing their clothing to join the girls.

They all moved from the bed to the couch. Mercedez lay over one end, her rump sticking up in the air, and Annie did the same at the other end. Bill took up a position behind Mercedez and John behind Annie. The two women were able to stretch forward enough that they could kiss and, while propping themselves up with one arm, fondle the tits of the other.

The guys slid their cocks in and at first began with a syncopated rhythm. Bill thrust forward as John pulled back. Then

Bill pulled nearly out of Mercedez and John shoved his cock deep into Annie.

This rhythm had the girls alternating moans as their tongues played together and their fingertips squeezed and twisted nipples.

Soon, though, the two males aligned so that both thrust in at the same time. Mercedez and Annie's lips broke apart but they were still able to toy with the other's titties, one at a time, by reaching under.

Mercedez looked up to see John behind Annie with his fists on his hips, trusting mightily, and she imagined Bill was a mirror image, and that stance turned her on. The cock in her pussy stroked deep and steady, in, almost out, in, almost out, the folds of her walls getting a good rubbing and starting to heat from the friction.

"Fuck us!" Annie yelled. "Fuck us hard!"

"Yeah, I'm fuckin' you, baby!" John yelled back.

"Oh, give it to me good," Mercedez joined in, getting more excited.

"I'm going to fuck you 'till you come," Bill said, "then I'll fuck you some more."

The "dirty talk" continued for a while, and Mercedez found it exciting to speak and to hear. She wasn't used to such verbal fucking. And when she heard John say to Annie, "I'm gonna make your pussy burn, bitch!" Mercedez felt the walls inside her contract and the cock poking her cunt thrust hard and deep and shot hot cum inside her while she cried out her orgasm.

Seconds later Annie screamed out, "I'm coming!" and John yelled "Yeah, baby, yeah!" and the two of them came.

The four started laughing. Bill fell on top of Mercedez and John draped himself over Annie's behind and they laughed and laughed at their antics.

Eventually, Bill pushed himself up. Mercedez started to as well but he kept a hand on her ass and said, "Stay there." She saw him motion to John and within seconds the guys had changed ends.

Annie gave Mercedez a raised eyebrow and a playful smile.

Mercedez had never been fucked by a guy as large as John. She hoped he wouldn't be too rough with her, his cock too big. But as he passed her, his stick dangling between his legs semi-hard, she realized just how big he was, and that the myth of big-guy, small-dick was not justified. John had a huge cock, at least twelve inches. It both excited her and caused her a bit of worry. And he wasn't just long, he was thick too. Big man, big cock. She'd have to remember that.

But now John was behind her. He placed his hands on her fleshy ass cheeks and spread them wide, opening her so she could feel the cool air-conditioning on her pussy lips and asshole. *Don't tell me he's going to fuck me there!* she thought.

But sure enough, his cock head poked at her asshole. She glanced up and saw Bill behind Annie, and from Annie's surprised face, it looked as if he had the same idea. Suddenly she felt a hand wipe over her pussy lips as if capturing all the juices there. Then, when the cock poked at her again, she realized that it was moist now.

The idea of that big fat cock stuffed into her tight hole sent shivers up her spine and made her hot. She wanted him to stick it in her, hard and deep. She wanted to feel him there. "Fuck my ass!" she whispered.

"What? Say again?"

"Fuck my ass," she said a little louder.

Suddenly he smacked her sharply on the ass. The big hand left a stinging behind. "Say again?"

"Fuck me in the ass!" she yelled.

"Yes, ma'am!" His huge cock pressed against her asshole and she opened to it, feeling the mass of it entering her oh-so-private place. "Give it to me!" she cried.

John moved slowly, but relentlessly, and Mercedez felt full to bursting with him, and now all she could do was moan. Every breath coming from between her lips was a sound of unbelievable pleasure as he moved in deeper and deeper. She began to feel delirious. How deep could he go? How fat was that cock? Could she really hold him there? But she could, and would, and did take him in, all the way in, feeling the full length and breadth of him as her body made way for the cock to impale.

Then he fucked her good and steady but not hard, not hurting her, not tearing her, just giving it to her as she wanted and needed it given. She lay sprawled over the end of the sofa being fucked, doing nothing but enjoying it, receiving it, and it took him a long time to come and she loved every minute of it.

Bill and Annie were through and they got off the couch, Annie getting behind her man, stooping down and licking between his legs, his asshole, his balls, the place between his balls and cock as he fucked Mercedez in the ass.

Bill positioned himself on the couch and lifted Mercedez' head. She opened her mouth and took his semi-hard cock between her lips and it hardened quickly. While he fucked her mouth, John kept fucking her ass. He held onto her ass cheeks, gripping them in a tight embrace while he stroked her. Then fingers that must be Annie's found her cunt and rubbed her clit and entered her at the same time.

Mercedez lay open, receiving, being fucked in every orifice. All of the fuckings managed to align and she became one big powder keg heating up, getting the fucking of her life. And when she came it was a huge explosion, in her ass, her cunt and all the hot cum firing into her mouth.

She remembered screaming out the pleasure she felt as her mind, body, and soul melded into one. *This is good*, she thought. *This is really good.* And as they all sat in the Jacuzzi afterward, she said, "Boy, I'm so glad I came to Mexico!"

CHAPTER *14.*

*M*ercedez and Bill were up early after very little sleep. Bill had done an automatic checkout so they could scoot to the airport in record time. Mercedez insisted they call Pedro, even though it was cramped in the little taxi with two of them in the back and three suitcases in the trunk at the front.

"I hope you both enjoyed your stay in Mexico City," Pedro said, grinning, more narco corrido blasting from the radio. "And in Mexico."

"Pedro, it was wonderful," Mercedez said, grinning herself. "I've had such an amazing time. I'll never forget this place."

"Then you must return. That is what we always say: your heart will bring you back to Mexico, your home."

"As long as it's not in the Choc Mool's bowl!" Bill said, and he and Mercedez laughed. Pedro didn't quite get it, so Mercedez translated into Spanish, and then he laughed, too.

"Good one, señor!"

At the airport, Bill found a handler to take their bags to the check-in while Mercedez gave Pedro a big tip, and a big hug. "You've been so good to me, taking care of me. I can't thank you enough."

He looked a little weepy, as if his daughter was going away, and not a stranger who had only been a passenger in his taxi many times. "Señorita, you are special. I hope you have a long and prosperous life, and that you return to Mexico soon. Please, when you come here, call me. I will come to get you, anytime."

Once she and Bill boarded the plane, they sat back and enjoyed breakfast on the short flight to Oaxaca. Mercedez was eager to see this place. Her mother had been born there, although she never talked about it. She had left as a young girl, and claimed she didn't remember much. But *her* mother, Mercedez' grandmother, had spoken of Oaxaca. Mercedez remembered the stories. The city was small now, a large town really, but it had been smaller back then. Her grandmother talked of the tribes that still dwelled in the mountains surrounding the city in the valley, and the banditos that extracted tolls when anyone wanted to go to another town. She also talked about el Día de los Muertos, of visiting the graves of her parents and later her brother's grave during the holiday. The two-day holiday started today, and Mercedez was eager to see how it was celebrated.

As they drove by taxi to their quaint hotel in the heart of the small city, Oaxaca proved to be a dusty town in a fertile valley surrounded by mountain peaks up to 10,000 feet high, some with snow at the top. The buildings here were low, one or two stories, the pastel colors faded. Tropical flowers bloomed everywhere, and tall palms did their best to offer shade. And everywhere she looked, Mercedez saw skeletons.

They checked in and immediately Bill was on his cell phone. Mercedez stood by the window and looked out at the part of the town she could see that had come alive with the morning and would close up again in about two hours. She wanted to be out there now, seeing, exploring.

When Bill got off the phone he started to say, "Honey, I—"

"I know. You have a meeting. I should go and enjoy myself."

He laughed and kissed her. "Need some money?"

"I have plenty, thanks."

They left the hotel together. He headed on foot to the tiny financial district while Mercedez made her way to the Plaza Central, or the Zócolo, the square. A small brochure she picked up at the tourist information said the cathedral there was built over the Aztec place for the dead. The opposite side housed elaborate buildings used as municipal offices. The Aztec had built here in the mid-1400s, and the Spanish took it over and revamped the architecture in the early 1500s. The city looked and felt old. It had history. Mercedez could feel that a lot of different cultures had overlapped in Oaxaca.

The square was full of vendors, and surrounding it were shops and cafés. She wandered by the various stalls and tables, listening to the conversations of the tourists and the locals—

far more of the latter than the former. Many Day of the Dead items were for sale, including sugar skulls. She picked one out with the name "Puch" on it, not knowing what it meant, but somehow attracted to the letters, as if she knew the name. The region was famous for black pottery, and she admired bowls, pipes, and a large black crucifix of clay.

Eventually she took herself to one of the small cafés and ordered a café de olla, coffee with cinnamon and cane sugar. She loved the sensual taste, and the aroma left her feeling stimulated. She wasn't hungry but decided to look over the menu, stopped dead by an appetizer of fried crickets! A man at the next table ordered them and a plate with a mound of small bits of red-coated food arrived, which he dug into, but which Mercedez knew she could live without ever tasting. Seeing her interest he asked, "Señorita, would you like to try some?"

And even though she had told herself *forget it!*, she heard herself say to this man, "Alright!" She handed over her small saucer and he piled it high with shake-and-bake crickets. She tried one. Crunchy. Otherwise, the taste was mostly the coating.

"They're different," she told the man.

"A specialty of the region!" he laughed, and spooned a mound of crickets into his mouth.

Another look at the tourist info and Mercedez was reading about the Oaxaca temples, which were the most lavish in southern Mexico. The patron saint of Oaxaca was María Santísima de la Soledad. At one time, it stated, her crown was made of pure gold and contained six hundred diamonds and other jewels. *That was then*, Mercedez thought. Times have changed. Not too many gold crowds studded with jewels out in public anymore.

Mercedez wandered the streets. On one she found children making sand paintings, mostly skeletal figures, with brilliantly colored sand. She used the throwaway camera she'd bought at the hotel to snap photos. Another street hosted a parade that she got caught up in. Again, more skeletons, this time people in costumes, stilt walkers, and two men holding a large wooden skeleton high in the air. The music was lively, the paraders having a great time, and Mercedez joined in the dancing for a few blocks.

More wandering brought her to an area that the brochure said housed the city hall, where she would find a competition.

Inside the building, the vast atrium was crowded around along all the walls with altars. She knew about these from her grandmother. Families built *ofrendas* for the holiday. As she wandered the room, what her grandmother had said began to come back to her. The altars were decorated with flowers, incense made from fragrant resin of the copal tree, and the little Day of the Dead figures, which represented the departed. There were fruits and bowls of favorite foods of the deceased family members, and something the person had enjoyed when they were alive, perhaps a cigar, some tequila, a favorite piece of embroidery. There might be a photograph of the loved one. And always a glass of water. "The dead get thirsty on their travels," her grandmother had said.

Every one of the fifty or so altars was different. Some were awash in candlelight, candles that formed circles around the altar itself, or a cross before it. Others were stacked with pan de muertos, bread of the dead, in which a small figure had been baked that represented the one who had gone before. One woman offered Mercedez a piece of the hard biscuitlike bread. She accepted and when she bit into it, instantly found that she had a small male figure in her hand.

She held it out to the woman, who closed Mercedez' hand around the token and said, "You must keep this with you. He will come for you. He will bring you luck."

She looked at the small image, a male with dark hair and eyes, just the head really. Everything in Mexico seemed to have symbolism attached to it.

This altar competition would be judged tomorrow, but she and Bill would be gone by then. At least she was here for one of the days of the holiday.

She headed back to the hotel, but Bill was still out. A dip in the pool was just what she needed, and it felt refreshing. She wished she could sunbathe nude, but that probably wasn't such a good idea; this was, after all, a public place. She contented herself with lying on a poolside chair under the late afternoon sun for an hour and napping, the back of her bikini bra undone. Napping. And dreaming.

The small figure of the man from the pan de muertos grew in her hand, then, before her eyes, it took the shape of a full-size man. His face looked just like the tiny effigy, but his body reminded her of someone. His arms were massive, and around his biceps were Mayan and Aztec images intertwined.

"Come to me," he said, opening his arms.

Mercedez walked into those arms, and instantly they folded around her, pulling her close. Hot, thick lips came down against hers and she smelled flowers, flowers she knew but couldn't place.

His cock grew against her leg. Suddenly he picked her up around the waist and lifted her into the air, plunging her down onto that hard-as-a-rock penis. "Who are you?" she gasped, passion surging through her.

"I am Puch. Are you alive?" he asked.

"Are you alive?" The voice caused her to open her eyes. Bill stood by the chair. "Honey, you were sleeping like the dead."

"Oh, I had such a nice day, but I guess it wiped me out. When did you get back?"

"Fifteen minutes ago. Listen, I thought we might catch an early dinner. I've got yet another meeting tonight, and then in the morning we fly out early. It's our last night here. We should at least have a meal together, under the palm trees."

She smiled and sat up. "Okay, let me freshen up and dress and we're off."

They dined outdoors at a lovely little restaurante that served local cuisine, which was a mix of many cultures from the area, drinking Mexican wine and chatting easily like old friends.

"Did you have a good time?" Bill asked, really wanting to know.

"Yes, I did. It's been the most amazing holiday. And I can't thank you enough for your generosity."

"Hell, it's all on the expense account. They budget me for twice what I've spent on both of us. It was nothing."

She reached out and put her hand over his. "It was a lot. Special to me. You're a special friend."

He smiled at her.

"And," she said, "I think the woman that you talk with all the time is special to you. Someone you should probably spend more time with."

For a moment he looked astonished. "How—how did you know?"

"Oh, we women have our ways. I saw your face when you were talking with her. And you never let anything or anyone come between you when she phoned. It just made sense. She's someone you care deeply about. More than a fuck friend. Someone you need to be with."

He colored slightly. "You're pretty understanding."

"I'm just in touch with reality. And my expectations have changed. Thanks to you and this opportunity, I think I'm getting a grip on what I really want."

"And what's that?"

Mercedez smiled slyly. "It's . . . just forming. I think I'll wait a bit before making it known."

"Fair enough." He picked up his wine glass. "To you. And your quest."

Mercedez clinked glasses with him. "I guess it has been a quest. And I didn't even know I was on one!"

Later, after Bill went to his meeting, Mercedez inquired at the hotel where she could go to see the Day of the Dead festivities in full swing.

"Why, the cemetery, señorita!"

She called a taxi and he took her to the large municipal Panteon. They drove along the wide main street, then turned left up a smaller street and drove for a fair distance. Suddenly the taxi was surrounded by traffic that grew thicker and thicker until the taxi could drive no more. "Señorita, you must walk from here."

"Okay," she said. "But how will I get back?"

"I will return for you." He looked at his watch. "It is nine o'clock. Shall I return at eleven?"

"Make it eleven-thirty. I'll meet you here, by this taco truck, by midnight at the latest."

"Sí, señorita. Enjoy the night of the dead. This is the first night, you know, for the children. Tomorrow is for the adult dead to return."

She walked up the crowded street full of men, women, and children, most carrying candles and enormous bouquets of flowers, yellow and orange marigolds, the fragrance that she now remembered from her daydream. The flowers of the dead.

Up ahead, around a curve in the road, she saw bright lights, and thought maybe she was not in the right place. Suddenly the street was not just filled with people but also with stalls selling goods, everything from carpets to clothing, carts with food—one specialty a cactus treat, another a square tortilla with a bright red coating—tables with games of chance, and, much to her amazement, neon-lit amusements. A Ferris wheel, a small roller coaster, a ride like the salt and pepper shakers of old. People were laughing, talking, dancing, music played loudly, and incense wafted through the air.

This carnival atmosphere was a celebration—but of what? Shouldn't they be sad in remembering their loved ones who had died? She wasn't sure. Maybe she would find out.

Finally she came to the huge gates of the cemetery, guarded

by police. Mourners were permitted in and somehow they admitted her. She wished she had flowers to place at a grave, but how would she find the graves of her ancestors? Were they even here? Was there another cemetery in Oaxaca?

Inside the gates it was dark. The grounds were crowded with graves, almost all of them lit by candles in niches at the grave heads. People prayed and read poems aloud. A trio of musicians sang songs and she realized the mariachis were going from grave to grave and family members were paying them to sing a favorite tune of the departed. It was all very sweet and sad and festive and at the same time the sense of another world hung heavy in the air.

Mercedez wandered to one end of the vast grounds, then turned and walked back toward where the entrance gates were. By the time she had reached them, the number of mourners had diminished considerably. She thought she should leave; maybe they would lock the gates. But something compelled her to stay. She wandered in the other direction and this area contained older graves, with more ornate stones, and small statues of saints and the Madonna guarding the final resting place.

She heard a sound behind her. Being alone here felt a bit intimidating and she turned rapidly in time to see one of the candles on a nearby grave go out.

"Do not be afraid," a male voice said. "It is just the wind. The wind of the dead."

The man speaking to her was tall and looked Indian, with the broad, earthy features of the Mayans. "Walk with me," he said.

Something compelled her and she joined him as they strolled through the grounds.

"There are many here, and many to come," he told her. "One day you too will come, but not today."

Despite listening to his voice, and looking at his face, she couldn't get a fix on his age. He seemed young and virile, yet spoke with an authority of a long life.

"Tell me about the Day of the Dead," she said.

"Today, the first day, the young dead return."

"Why?"

"They are called back by the living, who miss them, who have things that were not said which must be said. Longings that must be filled."

"But how do the dead return?"

"On the wind."

They rounded a corner to an even darker part of the cemetery. Here there were few graves with lighted candles, as if these people had been forgotten. "The dead travel from another land. It is a long journey, arduous. They have been making this journey for centuries, for millennia, and the dead will always come back, as long as the living need them. The dead are generous."

She thought about that. "I don't know why I'm here. I know it's been good for me, but I'm not sure what I'm doing, or what I want."

"You want the dead to return to you, like everyone."

She felt startled. "But I don't know any dead. Not really. I have my grandparents, but they're buried in Texas. My great-grandparents are here, and their parents, somewhere, but I don't know where. This might not even be the right cemetery."

The man stopped and faced her. In the darkness he looked even blacker than the night, as if he were living shadow, barely substance. "Come," he said, opening his arms.

Mercedez trembled. *What am I doing?* she thought, as she stepped into those arms. And as with her dream of the afternoon, the arms enfolding her were enormous. They seemed to wipe away her fears, leaving her body tingling. Lips pressed against hers and she grew hot and moist and hungry.

The man moved close to her and her back pressed against the bark of an ancient tree. In the distance she heard music and people chatter, but they were faint sounds, soon drowned out by breathing, hers, and his. And as in her dream, she felt his cock swell and pressing against her leg.

His hands grasped her waist and he lifted her into the air. She spread her legs and pulled the crotch of her panties aside and he plunged her cunt onto his hard cock.

"Who are you?" she gasped.

"I am Puch."

"Puch? What does that mean?"

"Are you alive?"

"Señorita? Señorita?" She saw a light flashing through the grounds. It was a guard.

The man lifted her again, this time off his body. He said in a quick whisper, "Tomorrow night you must go to the old cemetery. Wait there. At midnight, I will come."

"Señorita?"

The light flashed across her breasts and then up to her face.

"Yes. We're here. We were just—"

But when she turned, she found herself alone. She snapped

her head in every direction looking for the man she had just been with, but he had disappeared.

"Señorita, the cemetery is closed. You must leave."

She straightened her dress. "Yes. I'm sorry, I didn't know."

"Follow me. I will lead you to the gate."

She followed the light of his flashlight illuminating the path between the graves. At one point she thought they passed the grave where the candle had gone out, but she wasn't sure, because it was lit now. All the while she looked behind her, right and left, and thought she saw a pair of green eyes, jaguarlike, glowing in the darkness, but when she blinked they were gone.

At the exit, the guard escorted her out, then closed and locked the tall, wrought-iron gate behind her. The carnival was winding down, the amusements still running but with fewer customers. As she turned and walked back toward the taco truck she noticed fewer people at the stalls, and the food shops had sold most of their products.

She wandered in confusion, wondering why she had dreamed the man and then met him. And why in a cemetery? It should have been unnerving, but it was not, and that was even stranger.

When she reached the taco bus, the taxi was waiting for her.

"You are here, señorita. Good. I was about to leave."

"What time is it?"

"Midnight."

He drove her back, music playing on the radio but not the frantic, aggressive, angry music of Mexico City, or the same high volume. This piece talked of love and the return of it, like the dead returning, and she knew it was a song that was played once a year, during the Day of the Dead.

"Excuse me," she said to the driver, a taciturn man compared to Pedro. "I'm wondering if you know the name 'Puch.' Does it have a meaning?"

The driver pulled to the curb at the hotel. He turned in his seat to look her in the eye. "Señorita, you must visit the old woman in black by the old cemetery tomorrow. She will tell you everything."

"But we're leaving tomorrow!"

With that he held out a hand for payment and she gave him the requisite number of pesos. He turned away and there was nothing to do but get out of the taxi. Before she closed the door, she asked, "What's your name?"

"Pedro."

"Of course." She closed the door.

Mercedez climbed into bed, her mind filled with thoughts of everything that had occurred. She couldn't make sense of it, not at all. The sugar skull she had bought today, still in her purse, had the name Puch on it, and now she had met a man with that name. What did the name mean? She would have to find out, somehow, before she left. She sensed it was crucial that she know.

She was asleep when Bill climbed in, and he was obviously tired. He gathered her into his arms and she slept protected in the grasp of the living, drifting back to sleep wondering if there was much difference between the caress of the living, and of the dead.

CHAPTER 15.

*A*s they sat over breakfast in the hotel's dining room, Bill was saying, "So, we'll go back to the room and pack, then we'll check out, and head for the airport. The flight to Mexico City is at noon, then my flight to Chicago leaves at two-fifteen and yours to Los Angeles at three-fifteen. I'm sorry you have to wait at the airport alone. If I could have gotten a later flight I would have, but the next flight is at nine Do you feel alright about waiting alone?"

Mercedez had been sitting silently, listening to him. She'd been thinking about this last night in bed, before she fell asleep, and since she woke up this morning. "Bill, I want to stay in Oaxaca one more day."

He paused, fork partway to his mouth. "Honey, I have to get back today. Tomorrow morning I'm expected in a meeting and—"

"It's okay. You don't have to stay with me. I'll get a cheaper hotel for the night and fly myself back tomorrow."

He lay his fork down. "Well, if you really want to be here, that's fine. But you're staying in this hotel where it's safe and clean. I insist. And we'll get your ticket day and time changed. That shouldn't be a problem. But why do you want to stay here? I know it's a cute town, but I'm not sure there's that much more to see and do."

She had no idea how to explain to him everything she felt. "I can only tell you that somehow, I feel connected to this place. My roots are here. My mother was born in Oaxaca, and her mother and father. I have ancestors buried here. This is the Day of the Dead holiday and I'd like to stay here and—I know it sounds weird—but I guess I want to honor them in some way."

Bill looked at her for a long while, then reached across the table and took her hand. "Mercedez, you are one very special girl. I don't think I've met anyone like you before, and likely won't ever again. I know it's been a bit rough around the edges, this trip, me working so much and—"

She reached over and placed a finger against his lips to silence him, then kissed him gently but lingering. Then she said, "It's been amazing. You've given me a very special gift; the chance to explore parts of myself that I didn't even know existed. Thank you."

Once Bill had taken care of the room for another night, and changed her airline ticket for the following day, he picked up his two suitcases plus his laptop case and headed for the door where Mercedez waited. He kissed her lips sweetly. "Take care of yourself, honey. And you've got my cell number, if you need me. And let's keep in touch, okay?"

She waved good-bye and said again, "Thank you, Bill, for everything. We'll keep in touch." At the same time she was laughing to herself, thinking, well, if I *did* try to phone him, would I be able to get through?

Being in Oaxaca alone felt liberating and a bit intimidating. Even when she had gone off by herself, she knew that Bill was still in the country and just a phone call away if she needed him. He was good at taking care of things, and that left her feeling protected, and that she had backup. Now she was truly on her own.

She thought about phoning Hugh but felt reluctant. In her gut she sensed there was something she needed to do first, some conclusion that should take place. Then, and only then, would she be free to proceed with her life. She knew it involved el Día de los Muertos, and that she must visit the old woman the taxi driver told her about before she did anything else. With that in mind, she dressed for the heat in a turquoise sundress, slipped on the espadrilles, grabbed her straw hat, her straw bag, and made sure she had everything in that bag she might need, which included the charm given to her in Corpus Christi; the muertos candle the vendor insisted she buy in Mexico City; and the sugar skull with "Puch" written across the top that she had bought yesterday at the Zócolo.

Mercedez caught a taxi and asked the driver in Spanish if there was an old cemetery in the city.

"Sí, señorita, there are two, one near the mercado, and a tiny one of three graves up in the mountain."

"Let's try the one by the mercado."

He drove across town and as they neared the market, traffic picked up. The roads soon became chaotic, cluttered with vehicles, horns blaring, animals for sale, and people loaded down with purchases. The driver turned off the main road to the right of the market and followed a small street, then turned onto another. Soon they were traveling on a rutted dirt road and Mercedez had to press her hand against the roof of the taxi's interior to keep from being thrown up into the air and banging her head.

Finally she saw whitewashed cement pillars ahead with a wrought iron arch connecting them. The driver stopped there. She paid him and got out.

The area was strictly residential in what might be the sub- urbs. Short, broad women carrying baskets and fabric-covered bundles and only slightly taller men in straw hats walked through the gates, copper-skinned children of all ages running ahead of or behind them.

Mercedez drew a few looks from the locals, but not as much as she would have thought a stranger would garner.

Inside the gates she found a small well-kept cemetery, no more than an acre square, but crowded with graves and people. The graves were aligned in neat rows and every one was alive with brilliantly colored flowers, bouquets in vases, or plants in the ground that formed patterns. Most of the flowers were the familiar rusty-looking marigolds, in yellow, orange, but also in dusky red.

Everywhere people were busy taking care of the graves. Women swept the debris, planted flowers, and cooked meals on small oil-heated burners beside the grave for their families which, it seemed, would spend the day here. Men white-washed the graves, refreshing them, and a few old men slept curled next to the flowers. Older children helped their parents and the younger ones ran around singing and eating sugar skulls. Mariachis played cheerful music through the small graveyard, and the feeling was one of festivity, life, not death, leaving Mercedez both enchanted and thoroughly confused.

As she walked the narrow cement rows between graves, people nodded and smiled at her. She wondered how old this cemetery was, and if her ancestors were buried here. They could be in any or all of the three cemeteries. She had no names, no way to find out.

If this was the cemetery the newest Pedro had meant, she did not see an old woman in black. There were many old women, crinkled sun-darkened faces, stooped shoulders, but none fully in black.

She wandered for a while, enjoying the ambiance, chatting with a few people here and there, discretely asking about the old woman in black, but everyone shook their head or lifted their shoulders.

Finally she headed for the exit, thinking she'd try to find another taxi and perhaps go to the third cemetery in the mountains. Just as she was exiting the gates she saw her.

The hunched figure moved slowly down the dusty road,

which was suddenly empty, her movements a bit jerky, and Mercedez was reminded of a crow.

Mercedez followed, her pace faster, and she caught up quickly. When she reached the old woman, covered head to toe in black, she gasped at the face. The lines were etched deeper and there were far more of them than in any face she had ever seen, like pottery that had fallen and now contained a million cracks. The tawny skin was accented by tufts of brilliant white hair peeking out from under the black headscarf that gnarled hands held close to her neck. This woman could be a hundred years old, or older, Mercedez thought, and was decrepit in every way but one—her eyes. They gleamed like brilliant blue-white stars, and both the luster and the color were startling.

"Excuse me, abuela; I think it's you I'm to see. Pedro, the taxi driver, sent me."

The old woman nodded once, and then started up the road again, Mercedez following at an excruciating pace. They walked for perhaps ten minutes and then the woman left the dusty road for another smaller dusty road and soon entered the tiniest whitewashed dwelling Mercedez had ever seen. The door stayed open and she followed, forced to duck her head to enter.

The old woman sat in a wide rocking chair that took up most of the little room. The only other seat was a footstool and Mercedez perched on it. A little table sat next to the rocker. That was it. No bed. No cooking facilities. "I came to you because—"

"I know why you came." The voice was crackling paper, but

as solid as the mountains surrounding this valley. "Show me what you have brought."

Mercedez thought for a minute then opened her bag. She pulled out the charm, the candle, and the sugar skull and handed them to the woman one at a time.

The crone examined each carefully then set them on a small table beside her. When she was done she folded her hands over her stomach and stared at Mercedez.

Seconds became minutes which soon closed on the hour. Mercedez wondered if the old woman had fallen asleep because progressively her lids had lowered. Her legs were beginning to cramp from sitting on this low stool and she was just about to get up and tiptoe out the door when the old lady said, "Tonight you will die."

Mercedez jumped to her feet, her body rigid.

The woman's eyes snapped open. "Your ancestors await you. Are you prepared to meet them?"

"I—I don't know. Why do you say I will die?"

"You have met him. He will come for you again. You cannot escape your fate."

Mercedez' body began to tremble. *Okay, she told herself, get a grip. Just get a grip!* To the woman she said, "What does the name 'Puch' mean?"

"Au Puch, from the world under this one. His body is all bones, even his adornments are bones. He has no eyes."

And suddenly Mercedez remembered where she had encountered the name before—in Chichén Itzá, the wall of skulls.

"Why—why has he come for me?"

"Because he desires you. He is attracted to your blood."

DAY OF THE DEAD

And that blood in Mercedez' veins turned to ice. She tried to remember what she had learned about Mayan myths, but nothing seemed to have prepared her for this.

"You have attracted death," the old lady said. "And now it is time to face your lover. Here!" She gathered up the three items Mercedez had handed over. "Wear the charm close to your body. Light the candle before midnight and eat the skull. Then he will come for you."

"But—but how can I avoid him?"

The old woman placed her hands on her stomach again and closed her eyes. "You cannot."

Mercedez had a million questions but she couldn't formulate any of them. All of her thoughts revolved around how to avoid this encounter that the old woman seemed convinced was her destiny.

She placed a few pesos on the table and then left with her three items, walking in a daze along the dusty, rutted road until she came to a street with traffic, where she hailed a taxi back to the hotel.

She spent the day fearful, staying in her room, skipping lunch, then dinner, drinking only water, torn between the desire to run fast and far to escape her fate, and the sense that she must face this, whatever would happen. Life could not be lived in fear. She must see it through. She had come here to find her roots, and this too was her past. If she could not deal with the past, it was very likely she could not deal with the future.

As 11:30 P.M. approached, Mercedez was walking stiffly through the fair grounds toward the large cemetery. Reluctantly she entered the gates which tonight were open and unguarded. Within, more graves glowed with candlelight that illuminated the fresh paint, and the flowers that had been placed so carefully, but fewer people wandered the grounds participating in the rituals. She heard music and laughter, but the sounds came from outside the cemetery.

She headed right to the corner where she had met him last night. On the way she passed the same grave, and again the candlelight flickered then went out as she looked at it, sending a shiver up her spine on this warm night.

Mercedez found the old tree and stopped. This area of the cemetery was utterly deserted. There were few graves with candles, and darkness prevailed. She removed from her bag the tall glass holding the muertos candle and a disposable lighter. She tilted the glass and lit the wick, then placed the candle on a nearby tombstone. She also took the sugar skull from her bag and sat it next to the candle. Earlier in the day she had tied the charm to the silver chain that held the black pearl and now both pendants hung around her neck, nestled between her breasts.

Then she stood, quietly waiting. It wasn't long. The air around her began to change in texture, more dense with moisture, and yet it seemed to crackle as if electrical currents were passing; she wondered if a storm was approaching. Suddenly the wind picked up, blowing her hair and her skirts around her. Tree branches swayed and leaves flapped loudly in the silence. Candles around the cemetery went out, increasing the darkness, but the candle Mercedez had lit was protected by glass and remained bright, although the flame flickered. The sky was overcast, obscuring the stars, and if there was a moon she hadn't noticed it before and could not see it now.

"You have returned to me," a deep and familiar voice said. "A lover lost, a child forgotten."

Massive arms that reminded her of shadows surrounded her. She turned her head slightly and from the corner of her eye she could see that the man she had encountered last night was here again, but tonight he was different. Clearly, he was no mere man. Her surreptitious look took in the fact that he had no eyes, just spaces where they had been. She felt her heart race. The jewelry he wore at his wrists was made of bones, and she realized that although his arms felt muscular to her, they also felt bony, as did his chest as he pulled her back against him.

Her body trembled in terror. And yet some part of her knew that whatever the outcome, she wanted to meet this man, this creature, this deity as an equal, not sniveling, not pleading in terror for her life. A life which the old woman had said would end tonight. Regardless, Mercedez wanted to meet him with honor.

"I know who you are," she said, her voice not as frightened as she feared it would be, and that gave her courage. "You are Au Puch, the ruler of the underworld. Of death."

"Then you know why I have come," he said.

His hands slid down her body, pulling her dress down, and her panties, and then slid up her body, then down again. The shadowy bony hands felt cold then hot, making her body quiver as he stimulated her nipples and rubbed her clitoris.

His two hands became four, and the four eight and soon

every part of her torso was rubbed and caressed at the same time as the hands moved in different directions, surprising her, and she could not anticipate where they would roam next, what they would do. They became a continuously moving sheath of fingers tormenting her, entering her, stimulating all of her erogenous zones at once.

Mercedez' head fell back against his chest, and the hardness of his upper torso felt like a bony breast plate, but that did not trouble her. Heat built as she stood helplessly being stimulated, and her head snapped from side to side. She felt unsure if she could cope with this much stimulation all at once but it did not let up, and soon she found her passion building, higher and higher, headed into unknown territory.

More hands formed. They stroked her legs, caressed her arms and her neck, massaged her scalp and roved over her face. She kept her eyes closed tight; she did not want to see what touched her.

She felt herself lifted up into the air by all of these hands. Then her body was forced to bend forward. He pressed her over the tombstone that held the candle and she grabbed at the sugar skull and shoved it to her lips, biting into the hard sweetness. The sugar filled her mouth and coursed through her body as she swallowed.

He pulled her ass high into the air and spread her legs wide, all the while the thousands of bony fingers touching her, fondling her, bringing her to new heights.

She had no thoughts. No questions. No answers. The past was alive, the future did not exist, and the present was about to overtake her. Her ass stuck up into the night air inviting him to plunder her. He forced her legs wide and pushed her head down until her lips kissed the earth. But he was not just hands and soon she discovered what else he could be.

Three cocks found her orifices at the same moment, causing her to gasp. One hovered at the edge of her pussy lips, one positioned itself at the pucker of her anus, and the third met the lips of her mouth, demanding entry.

"Are you alive?" he asked her.

Terrified. Titillated. Overwhelmed with sensation she could say nothing, only tremble uncontrollably, her body throbbing in anticipation. She knew she was about to be fucked as she had never been fucked before, everywhere, all at once, by one being. A being that was as old as mankind and had the combined knowledge of every fuck that had ever taken place between all the life forms of this planet. It was a fuck that would likely kill her. She knew this. It was what the old woman had told her. She focused on her asshole and cunt, relaxing the muscles, and parted her lips.

Suddenly all three cocks entered her simultaneously. They plundered her deeply, and her eyes snapped open. A second later, other protuberances entered her nostrils, her ears, slid over her eyes to blind her, and panic seized her as everything from the outer world was suddenly cut off. The only world that existed was her body.

A moment of darkness gave way to a sensation. She felt her nipples. One was squeezed, then the other, then the first, back and forth, as she laid spread over the stone of this grave, impaled in every orifice, her tormented nipples began to throb. The squeezing turned to twisting and that became pinching that continued unabated, each nipple tortured over and over, alternating, driving her insane with lust, then the two nipples burst into flame, searing her, and forcing her to cry out around the cock stuffed deeply into her mouth. Then the fucking began.

She could not see, could not hear, could not breathe. But the three cocks fucked her in a syncopated rhythm. Her mind struggled to focus on one sensation but the next came quickly. Ass, cunt, mouth. Ass, cunt, mouth. His cocks seemed to grow in each orifice as he thrust into her, every stroke causing him to swell. Her cunt widened, her asshole expanded, the lips of her mouth parted wide and her throat opened to him. She did not know she could stretch so far, incorporate so much inside her, give and receive so much pleasure. Hot juices boiled in her cunt and her nerve endings screamed with delight. She loved the taste of his cock that seemed to come up from the ground and into her mouth, and she used her tongue to encourage him, making him larger still. Her asshole vibrated with life, demanding more, demanding all of him that he could give.

The fucking increased in pace and became so rapid that she could not keep up with the rhythm. All three cocks fell into alignment, expanded to their full capacity. Mercedez could only moan in ecstasy as she took all of him in.

Now he fucked her fast and hard. Any remaining thoughts she had shattered. Her body became pure fire, an eternal blaze ignited from the fire at the core of the earth. Heat incinerated every inch of her flesh, leaving only a fuckee, a pleasure machine, a woman whose desire to be fucked had, at last, been completely fulfilled.

"Are you alive?" he roared.

"Yes!" she screamed. "Yes, I am alive!"

She came in an explosion. Light burst inside her, shards like glass, a prism. Her body shook as if the earth were quaking. Pleasure and happiness rolled through her in volatile waves that she thought, hoped, would never end.

Instantly he was gone. Vanished. Her eyes snapped open. Her ears and nose and mouth were clear. No giant cocks plowed her ass and cunt, and her mouth was free but hot cum lingered that tasted like blood, or chocolate, she could not tell the difference now. She lay naked over the stone panting in exhaustion, the warm air floating over her naked body like silk, feeling the drizzle as the light rain descended onto her back and ass and pussy slit, the warm liquid dripping down her flesh. Suddenly, she started to laugh.

She pushed herself to her feet on wobbly legs. Her orifices felt raw, well used, but in a good way. She looked down and saw that her nipples were huge, blood red and sore, but she liked the feel of this, too.

The rain fell in earnest, sinking into the ground, soaking her, causing her long hair to flatten against her head and back, making her body tingle all over. She slipped her dress on, but couldn't find her panties anywhere. Maybe, she thought laughing, Au Puch took a souvenir!

She left the cemetery in the downpour, passing the same grave, the candle lit now, burning brightly, and exited the gates. Then she walked back to the hotel in the rain, letting it wash her over and over. Her hair and her dress clung to her body, sliding with it as she moved, so alive. She felt her ass muscles extend and contract with each step, felt her pussy lips rubbing together longing for kisses, her waist twisting, her arms swaying, her hard nipples brushing against the wet fabric of her dress as her breasts bounced slightly while she walked. She took off her shoes and went barefoot through the slippery mud squishing through her toes. Lightning crackled around her and thunder rumbled, rocking the earth, but she knew she had pleased Au Puch and was under his protection; nothing could harm her tonight.

She had come to Mexico and found her roots. She was the descendant of powerful civilizations, the Mayan, and probably the Aztec, too. And the conquistadors, who took and who gave at the same time. Mercedez was the product of all this. She had opened to her past, dying with it to be reborn in the present, bringing that history with her. She had faced both life and she faced death, with sensual bravery.

She walked for over an hour, and when the hotel came into view, she knew what she wanted. She would call Hugh. Tonight. No matter the time. And tomorrow, if he still felt the same way—and she knew in her bones that he would—she would fly to Toronto to be with him. Her pussy tingled at the thought. At the expectation. The hot juices like lava were already starting to flow.